CW00855551

Praise for Andrea Bougiouklis

"*The Art of Becoming a Traitor* is a military thriller set after a war into a dystopian society, discussing raw themes of ethics, military politics, the good, the bad, and of course, the ugly parts of war and delving into deep topics on who to trust when someone chooses to "fall out of line" as it were. **If you enjoy mystery intrigue with a nice casual military backdrop, you'll find much to latch on to. For me, it was an exciting thriller.**"

–Armanis Ar-Feinial, author of the *Holy Grail War*

"**Excellent work! I hope one day that it gets a well-earned award for its quality. I enjoyed reading it.**"

–Mark Runte, author of ARH, A Mythos Novel

"**Young adults who enjoy girls who kick ass and take no names will like this dystopian fantasy** as it resembles many of the same themes as action movies... I saw many parallels to this story to events happening to today. **What do you do when you discover you are fighting for the wrong side?**"   –Veronica Krug, author and educator

"**A science fiction military story with power and guts... The story keeps you on your toes with many twists and turns**, Eleri never really knowing who to trust. Eleri realises almost too late how much she and her generation have been lied to... **I enjoyed it.**"   –Maria P Frino, author

About Andrea Bougiouklis

Andrea Bougiouklis is a writer and a filmmaker from Toronto, Canada. She is currently a student at Ryerson University and is actively pursuing all opportunities in her respective industries.

Writing her debut novel, *The Art of Becoming a Traitor*, at 19 years old, Andrea is only at the beginning of what is sure to be a long and prosperous career in the creative industries.

Andrea loves sports and music and will name her top five films before you get the chance to ask for recommendations. She hopes to one day be able to direct blockbusters and write novels in tandem.

Keep up with Andrea on social media!
Twitter: @andiebou9
Instagram: @andreabougiouklis
-
Follow @5310publishing on Twitter and Instagram.

Every second counts, and their decision
will impact the lives of thousands.

THE ART OF
BECOMING A
TRAITOR

Andrea Bougiouklis

5310
PUBLISHING

THE ART OF BECOMING A TRAITOR

EVERY SECOND COUNTS, AND THEIR DECISION WILL IMPACT THE LIVES OF THOUSANDS.

ANDREA BOUGIOUKLIS

Published by
5310 Publishing Company
5310publishing.com

Our books may be purchased in bulk for promotional, educational, or business use. Please contact your local bookseller or 5310 Publishing at sales@5310publishing.com.

THE ART OF BECOMING A TRAITOR
Hardcover: 9781990158582 (this one)
Ebook / Kindle: 9781990158452 | Paperback: 9781990158445

Author: Andrea Bougiouklis
Editor: Alex Williams - 5310 Publishing
Cover design: Eric Williams - 5310 Publishing

First edition (paperback) released in February 2022.
Hardcover cover edition (this edition) released in April 2022.

YOUNG ADULT FICTION / Dystopian
YOUNG ADULT FICTION / War & Military
YOUNG ADULT FICTION / Action & Adventure / General
YOUNG ADULT FICTION / Science Fiction / Apocalyptic & Post-Apocalyptic

Themes explored: War, combat, and military adventure fiction; Science fiction: military; Alternative history fiction; Dystopian & utopian fiction; Narrative theme: Politics; Narrative theme: Identity / belonging.

For my family and those closest to me, for always encouraging and loving my unconventional way of being.

And for Chloe, who believed in me so much, that I learned to believe in myself, too.

Prologue.

Eleri Roman had long since understood the effects of the war, despite being unfamiliar with anyone who had actively been in combat. It began with the suicide of her father, and it evolved into her mother's descent into madness. It planted a seed in her - one that was born of a thought and would grow into a mantra - that the only way to live was to have worth, and the only way to have worth was to fight.

She had first heard the stories of the kids who were selected to join the fight years before their set draft dates when she was eleven years old. There were only a handful of them, but they often became some of the most powerful, most influential, *most important*, most worthy people in their respective sectors. She was told a story by one of the boys in her writing class about someone who'd been selected to go up the ranks at fourteen years old, who had become legendary. He said he had heard about it because his older brother had just come back from his mandatory service. He said that he wanted to be selected early. He said that he wanted to be brought up at thirteen.

Eleri only nodded in response. She knew thirteen was unrealistic. She knew that even if it was true, being selected at fourteen had to be incredibly difficult, as well.

She set her sights on fifteen. That would give her four years to prove herself enough to be selected, and three years after joining the fight to make her way up before her peers became a part of it.

Six days after her fifteenth birthday, Eleri received a letter. The next afternoon, during her reading class, four men in black military suits entered, called for her, and ushered her out.

She was the only early selection made that year.

The war between Aloneia and Voskivy had been grueling. Despite the abundance of lives being lost, the superiors had elected to tighten the reins and only take people who were up to par with their standards. In some cases, that meant skipping a year entirely, selecting nobody, ignoring the group all together. In others, it meant taking upwards of fifty kids at once.

The initiation was fine for the most part - numbers were taken, she was put into databases - but having to assist in writing a report about herself was a horribly painful experience. The man sitting across the desk from her was staring her down from the moment she had stepped foot in the room, his eyes leaving her only to take notes, his voice monotonous and commanding as he pushed through the list of required prompts, only slightly muffled by the mask covering the lower half of his face.

"Full name?"

"Eleri Vera Roman."

"Date of birth?"

"June 1st, 2222."

"I didn't realize you were a Kind baby,"

She nodded. "Yes, sir."

He let out a breath - she wasn't sure if it was a laugh, a scoff, a cough, or some hybrid. A Kind baby being selected was a rarity. There was some old legend, dating back centuries, stating that children born in a year with four of the same numbers, such as 2222, had the potential to become great. Folklore was folklore, but Eleri had heard that Kind babies could become much smarter, stronger, and much braver than normal children. She wasn't too sure how much she believed it, and evidently neither did the man, as he blinked slowly, once, and he continued his formal questioning. "Present us with your documents, please,"

She handed the folder to the man at the computer, her hands clasped together in her lap. Her thick, dark hair was tied tightly behind her head, as per request. She wore a black uniform that matched that of the man in front of her. Her boots were laced, her face clean of all makeup and body of all jewelry.

He scanned through her papers quickly, and then without looking up, he spoke. "These are old, no?"

She bit her lower lip, her dark eyes searching for any emotion in his light ones, any indicator of the implications of the potentially old documents. "Sir," his eyes met hers, "since I am still a minor, my parents are responsible for my documents. I'm not too sure."

He narrowed his eyes at her. "So why haven't they been updating your things?"

The laugh that escaped her was bitter. It was inappropriate for the setting. The man took note of this. "My father shot himself. My mother lost her mind."

The man looked her up and down once, bullet grey eyes memorizing her features, before closing the folder and sliding it back across the table to her, clearly dissatisfied with her response. He began to type as he spoke. "I will let it go just this once, on the grounds that your scores and performance are much too high to ignore. Just know, though, that as you progress, anything not up to date is unacceptable."

She nodded. "Yes, Sir."

He continued. "You have the highest technical scores of anyone born in your year and the second-highest physical. We do not want to let a talent like yours go to waste. However, we will not hesitate to do so if you can't get yourself together."

She was thrown into the mix the next day. There was a briefing for all of the new recruits - she was the only child in a room of adults - as a woman explained what this war was for and why they were fighting. She told them the same thing that Eleri had heard in school every day for the past five years - that this was a war started on the premise of revenge, that they would never have initiated this conflict had they not been invaded first, that they were going to fight until there was a surrender, not until there was a negotiation. They were to win or die trying.

She shadowed an Intelligence Officer for her first three years. On her eighteenth birthday, she was promoted and was given a legion of her own to control.

She was moved up the ranks the same day her year was brought to their mandatory draft. She could've sworn she saw the boy who had told her the story of the fourteen year old all those years ago scowling at her in the crowd.

She hadn't done this out of spite - or maybe she had - but she did feel good about seeing him seething at her.

Her first year had been difficult. She continuously threw herself into combat, whether it was approved or not, and she worked quickly regardless of task. The superiors noticed her almost immediately; her quick thinking, her confidence, her ability to shoot without remorse. If they wanted to win this war, she was going to have them win this war. That was it. That was all.

At twenty years old, she was moved from her position as an active I.O. to a slot that was far more dangerous, but that would be far more rewarding for someone with her skill set. She was put into a group of six highly skilled soldiers who would be sent into areas that the superiors felt others could not handle. Over the next five years, that group of six would stay together. They would complete more missions than any other squad. They would have more kills - non confirmed, especially - between them than the rest of the army combined. They were lethal, and they were scary.

It was during these years where Eleri picked up the nickname Reaper. She wasn't sure who had bestowed it upon her, but she did notice that as she walked, people moved out of the way, their eyes trained on the rifle across her back or the knives strapped to her legs. She loved the attention. She loved the power.

Two weeks before the enemy surrender, the six were cut down to two; five years and only a handful of injuries, no casualties, only for everything to fall apart. She remembered seeing the trap just before it was stepped on. She remembered holding her arm out to stop whoever was behind her from moving forward. She remembered screaming out just as the damage was done.

Kassander Strome, Sevyn Ingrid, Elijah Newsom, and Yves D'Arsie all died in the blink of an eye. It was as if they had disintegrated. Their bodies were unrecognizable. Their skin mangled, their bones exposed, their blood already dry.

Eleri Roman and Fyodor Kacer were alive.

Eleri had knelt down, collecting whatever materials hadn't been blown to bits. Fyodor had been hit, the deep, dark cut that had etched itself into the skin around his eye a permanent souvenir of the experience. Neither she nor Fyodor spoke of the incident unless they were asked to help with reports. Neither of them dared to remember it.

She and Fyo were together when the message of surrender began to spread. She remembered that she wanted to be relieved, but all she could feel was regret.

She looked over at Fyodor and knew he felt the same.

This had taken everything from them, and they had no plans of sparing their future. The war was over, but it would never truly end. Not for them.

PART ONE

JANUARY 13TH, 2248
18:00
94 DAYS POST-WAR

One.

The lie they sold me was compelling, and it was convincing, and it was laced with a fusion of fear and hope and the promise of a better future. I wish I had known, at the young age of ten, or eleven, or fifteen, how little they truly meant what they said. I wish I had known not to put my trust in them. They told me that they'd had their eyes on me for a while, that I was far beyond anything they'd ever seen, both mentally and physically. A compliment like that, from superiors like them, at such a young age… it was unheard of. They knew I would be putty in their hands. They knew we all wanted to be selected before the draft. They knew we wanted to be bathed in pride and respect. We all wanted to be important, and they controlled what constituted as such. I think, even worse than how eager I was to please, was how much I'd enjoyed it. A little girl with no family or friends suddenly being hailed from all around. I was not Eleri, I was not a burden, I was not some kid in class, I was The Reaper. I was someone feared by men bigger and stronger than I was. I was merciless and scary, and the power trip I was on from knowing that I could do as I pleased without consequence felt so right to me. I went from invisible to one of the most important people in the force in the blink of an eye. I wish there was someone there to tell me to slow down. I wish I'd had the wherewithal to realize what I was doing.

- The Found Diary of Eleri Roman, p. 11

———

She marched to her Commanding Officer's building with determination and grit - the same kind that got her this far. Her hands were shoved deep into her pockets, her chin tucked to her chest to keep the collar of her jacket as high up her face as possible. Who the hell knew where her scarf was? She didn't, and she had no time or patience to find it, either. She'd steal the first one she saw, anyways. A replacement wasn't too far out.

The crunch of her black boots against the fresh white snow was a stark contrast to the harsh sound of her teeth chattering in her mouth. Her eyes were watering, and if she were any colder, she'd swear they were freezing as she walked. She was one of the only idiots out in this weather, but she had to be. There was almost never an opening to talk with her C.O., and if she had to brave the elements and face hypothermia to do so, she would gladly take the chance.

Milton Haas was well respected by those above him, barely tolerated by those below. He, on paper, was an incredible officer. He had fought, he had led, and he had saved lives. What the papers didn't talk about, though, was his attitude or the fact that the only reason he was able to do those things was because of those he had the honor of serving with. He was one of the luckiest sons-of-bitches Eleri had ever met. He didn't deserve any of his medals or qualifications, and if it were her decision, she'd be taking them away.

The door to the Administrative building swung open as she walked up the steps, a soldier holding it open and saluting her, to which she only smiled: not because she didn't appreciate the gesture, but because her hands were too frozen to bring them up and properly salute back. She walked through, the door closing behind her, and she sighed.

She made her way through the foyer and pretended not to notice the hushed whispers of those whose eyes landed on her. She trudged up the stairs, avoiding all communication with those she passed, her head down until she finally reached his floor.

Eleri took one deep breath, shaking her hair out, unbuttoning her coat, and stepping into his office.

She took a seat, standing back up almost immediately as his eyebrows raised. The form of acknowledgment that had long since been abandoned by most of the superiors - standing until being offered a seat - was one that Milton Haas was adamant on continuing to practice. "Roman?"

"Sorry," she mumbled, remaining upright, hoping she appeared as disinterested in his dedication to respecting the rules as she felt.

"Alright, alright, have a seat, Christ."

Since the war had ended, there had been a lot of movement within the ranks. The C.O. that she had reported to throughout the war - Xavier Talon - had retired once it had finished, leaving her and the rest of her equals with some new guy with an attitude problem and a God complex. She often tried to convince herself that it was not all that bad, that this new guy just needed to warm up, but it had been three insufferable months, and she decided that she unequivocally *hated* Milton Haas.

She did as she was told, crossing one leg over the other, waiting for him to finish writing so she could begin.

"I'm listening," he said.

"I want your eyes on me when I speak, Sir."

He paused mid-phrase, the pen hovering above the paper before he exhaled every ounce of air in his lungs and threw the utensil down onto the wooden desk. "What is it then?"

"It has come to my attention," she said, confidence and indifference working their way into her voice simultaneously. "That there are still troops in Voskivy."

He nodded, his eyes blank. "That is correct."

She shrugged. "Why?"

"It's a necessary evil, I'm afraid."

She scoffed. "You have thousands of troops in a region we've already defeated."

"And those troops are doing a great job."

She narrowed her eyes at him. "Sir, with all due respect, Voskivy is no longer militarized. They don't even have an army anymore. I don't understand why we're wasting our time and resources like this. We may actually need them one day, and then what?"

"Then we take them back." He adjusted his glasses. "You have to trust that as your superior, I am making the right decisions. We have thousands of troops there because we need thousands of troops there. End of story."

"They have no army. You're running a military state out of your district. That's borderline terrorism."

He scoffed, fully paying attention now, his eyes locking onto hers. He was challenging her, and he wanted her to know that.

"Eleri? You have no right to tell me about terrorism, at all."

If his comment impacted her at all, she didn't show it. Her arms remained folded, her eyes unblinking, her face stoic.

"I am one person. You are effectively an entire army." She said, tone even.

The laugh that escaped him was no doubt unintentional, but it was honest. "Your confirmed kills are well over seventy-five." He paused, tilting his head to the side, smiling widely, the gaps between his crooked teeth seeming to grow further apart by the day. "In truth, though, it should be well over one hundred, maybe two, right? You did that, Roman? You killed two hundred people?"

Challenging her. Again. She was smarter than to take the bait.

She leveled him on all fields - voice, expression - as she spoke. "I'm not here to talk about myself. Pull them out."

"How can you, of all people, come to me to lecture me on *terror*? You are the embodiment of it!"

She smiled lightly. "If I am the embodiment of terror, Sir, then I am the most qualified to lecture you on it. Everything I did was in a time of war. I stopped when they surrendered. You didn't."

There was an uncomfortable silence that followed. Eleri had more to say, but she was aware that she had to measure her words carefully. Milton Haas was the type of man to forcibly remove her from his office if he saw fit, and to him, even the slightest influx of a voice was reason enough.

He ran his hands through his thick grey hair, his light eyes watching her every move. He was waiting for her to tilt her head the wrong way, or for her mouth to twitch, or for her to raise an eyebrow. Unfortunately for him, she had control like no other.

"I don't take orders from you," he said, adjusting the collar of his shirt.

"Xavier wouldn't have put an army in a place we had already defeated."

"Good thing Talon no longer works here, eh?"

She clenched and unclenched her jaw. "The war is over."

"Don't you see?" He laughed, this time on purpose, his eyes full of fury and rage that was all too familiar to her. "War is the only way we keep control. War is the only way these people still listen to us. You should know all of this by now."

He stood, brushing his hands against his pants, slicking his hair back, clicking his tongue. "I am going to have to ask you to leave my office, dearest Roman, before this conversation becomes an altercation. Thank you."

He walked past her, opening the door, motioning for her to step out. After a brief moment of hesitation, she did as she was told, brushing past him in the process, making sure that she *touched* him.

If he was going to challenge her, she was going to challenge back.

She made her way back down the stairs, pushed back through the doors, and stepped out into the snow. Was this a wasted effort? Maybe, but she got in his face, and that was good enough for her. This man did not take her seriously - be it because she was much younger than him or because she was a woman, she'd never know - and her goal had shifted from trying to overtake him to simply trying to let him know she meant business.

She didn't care to be respected by Milton Haas. She only cared to be a force that he would have to *struggle* to deal with.

She made it back to her building faster than she had anticipated - the snow had stopped falling, and all that was left to deal with was whatever was on the ground. Eleri stomped up to her floor, stood in front of the entrance to her room for a moment, and proceeded to dramatically throw the door open with a sigh.

"Look who made it back,"

She rolled her eyes at the unexpected voice, slamming the door shut behind her, resting her hand on the knife she kept against her hip at all times. It took her a moment to peer around the corner and process the fact that it was only Fyodor, sitting on her bed, laughing at her reaction to a familiar interaction.

"Killer instinct, huh?"

Her face scrunched, and she ran over to him, tackling him back onto the bed. "What the fuck is wrong with you?" she laughed, smacking him on the back of the head. Then, her hand rested in his hair. "You need a haircut."

He shook his head, effectively removing her touch. "I do not."

Her eyes trailed from his blond hair to his blue eyes, finally landing on the scar that ran from above his eyebrow to just below his lower lashes. The jagged line was a constant reminder of one of the worst days of their lives. It was red, still, after all these months; the marks from both the initial impact and the haphazard stitching that she'd done on it in an attempt to help the healing process equally contributing to its unevenness. She sighed. She wanted to ask him if it hurt, if they should try to get something to get rid of it, if he felt that it may be infected, but she knew better.

The understanding was mutual. They were not going to relive the moment in which they'd lost four of their best friends. That meant discussing none of it, not even the related events.

"Did you get what you needed from Mister Haas?" He asked, watching her hand fall from his face onto the mattress.

She stood, shaking her head. "No, of course not. Did you think I would? That stupid bitch couldn't even pull his own head out of his ass if his life depended -"

"Hey, hey," he said, standing, his arms out, "take a breath, Jesus."

"He is such a *loser*," she said, turning away from Fyo, looking for a more comfortable shirt to change into. "I can't stand him. Oh, I know all this, I know all that. Bullshit, you don't know *anything*. If your -"

"Eleri," he said, raising his eyebrows. "You complain a lot for someone who doesn't even know why they're complaining."

She groaned, stepping into her closet, quickly pulling a sweater over her head. "I'm just mad, and you know that. I don't know why he doesn't listen to me. I've been doing this longer than he has."

"He's still your superior," Fyo reasoned, leaning on the doorframe of her washroom as she removed the makeup from her face. "He couldn't care less if you'd been born and bred in this army. He's above you, and he's going to make sure you know that."

"Do you think he's doing this out of spite?" Eleri asked suddenly.

Fyodor furrowed his brows. "Like, keeping the troops there?"

Eleri nodded into the mirror.

"No," Fyo said. "At least, that's not why he started. That may be why he's keeping them there, but that couldn't have been why he sent them there to begin with."

She sighed, throwing her dirty towel into the basket. "What do I do, then? Should I request a transfer?"

Fyo laughed. "You're kidding,"

Eleri walked past him into her kitchen, pulling out whatever leftover meal she had, sticking it into her microwave, leaning against the counter.

"Not really," she began, looking at him. "I'm sure if I speak to the right people, they'd put a good word in for me anywhere else. Plus, at this point, I'd take a demotion to be away from that weirdo."

Fyo rolled his eyes. "Right. And you'd just leave me here?"

"You wouldn't move with me?"

"Who says they'd let me?"

Eleri bit her lip. Fyodor had a point, as much as she hated to admit or face it. Despite his efforts and sacrifices in the war, he not only had fewer medals and a lower score but had also run into some problems with other - now discharged -

superiors. He ended up winning his case, but it still meant that he was going to be on high alert for at least the rest of his career, most likely the rest of his life. Eleri hated it. He had caught a double agent, but because it was a Major, he was punished for not respecting boundaries and regulations. It made no sense to her. She wanted to have a less than civilized conversation with anybody who had a hand in writing or enforcing these rules.

"I could work it into my contract," she said, pulling her plate out of the microwave.

"Okay, and you think that they would just let you do that?"

She huffed out in frustration, taking a bite. "Fine," she walked past him, onto her balcony, "but I still might try."

Fyo followed her out, sitting beside her on one of the two folding chairs they were able to squeeze onto the small space. He lit a cigarette and took a drag, handing it to her, before lighting one of his own. They'd done this for the better part of their relationship. It was some sort of pact — a promise. He'd light the smoke, and he'd give it to her. He didn't know what it meant or symbolized, exactly. He only knew that it mattered. He inhaled, content, wrapping a blanket around his legs, watching as the sun began to set over the city. "Oh," he said suddenly, pulling a paper from his pocket. "This is for you, apparently. Someone stopped by before you got back and I just said I'd give it to you."

She groaned, throwing her head back, but snapping forward again and taking the envelope from his hand. She shoved it into her pocket. "I do not want to look at another form ever again. Holy shit."

Fyo patted her hand gently, turning his attention back to the sky.

He and Eleri would sit in silence while she ate. The cold seemed irrelevant. They had decided some time ago that this tradition would stand, rain or snow or shine. For him, these were the most therapeutic moments, the calmest he would ever be. For a few brief minutes, as the sun would begin to set, as the winds would calm down, as the day would draw to a close, the anxieties that fluttered in the back of his mind would rest. On this balcony, he would feel safe. The cigarette would hang between his lips, like an extension of his body, filling his lungs with a warmth he craved so desperately but could never reach. His eyes would not see death, or violence, or chaos. They would only memorize the watercolors that the sun would paint into the sky, over and over and over again, until they were replaced by the stars. And as he sat, beside his best friend, beside the only person he trusted, beside the one soul he could say had been through exactly what he'd experienced, had seen what he'd seen, had lived what he'd lived, he would breathe a little deeper, his body feeling more alive than ever before.

He would never tell her this. He wasn't sure how to articulate it to her. In the years that they'd known each other, she had never been open with her emotions or sentiments, and she sure as hell had never wanted to have conversations regarding the nonphysical side of wellbeing. He had never seen her cry, never even seen her flinch, and had reluctantly come to terms with the fact that all he would get from her was anger, joy, or complete seriousness. He wasn't sure how to evoke anything else. He wasn't sure if she was capable of it.

The sun had set much quicker than he'd expected it to, and before he knew it, Fyo was standing, saying goodbye, and stepping out of her apartment.

Eleri watched him go, watched him walk across the street from her balcony, and made sure he got into his building safely before she closed her door fully and drew her curtains. She took the envelope from her pocket and tore it open, a single, thin paper inside. Cautiously, she took it out, eyeing it carefully.

A phone number.

With a clenched jaw, she made her way to the phone that hung on her wall, pressing the numbers as they appeared on the paper, holding the headset to her ear.

Two rings and a voice was heard: "Eleri Roman,"

"This is she,"

"Good. I've been waiting to hear from you. This is Ruben Yorke. I wanted to arrange a meeting with you."

Her breath caught in her throat. Ruben Yorke was the second-highest in command in all of Aloneia. He was a ghost by all means - no one ever seemed to know anything about him, about his past or present, about what he'd done in the war. All everyone was very aware of was that he was a very, very powerful man and that he was almost never available to speak to. Whether he was busy, or he just didn't want to deal with people, she didn't know, but she was certain that if he wanted to talk to her, something big was going on.

"Of course," she said, her voice steady. "When works best?"

"Are you busy tomorrow? Around 13:00?"

She shook her head, then, remembering he couldn't see her, "No, that works for me. Did you have anywhere in mind?"

"I'll come to you."

And the line went dead. She pulled the phone away from her ear slowly, staring down at it for a moment as if she were waiting for it to ring again, before hesitantly placing it back up on the wall.

As the darkness came over her like a blanket, all she could hear was screaming. All she could see, playing through her mind like a film, were moments that she had tried so hard to forget about. All she could feel was her uniform and her heavy rifles and the blood trickling down her forehead.

As the darkness came over her like a blanket, all she felt was pain.

Two.

I was angry growing up. My father beat my mother nearly every day, and all I could do was watch from behind the wall. If he caught me looking, I was in for it worse than she was. If he didn't, I'd feel bad that I wasn't doing anything to stop him. It was a torturous cycle. One that I'd never escape. I used to go to sleep, begging for him to die, hoping that one day, I'd never have to worry about seeing him again. My father, who drank more than we could afford. Who forced me to go to school with scars and bruises on my face. Who would pour alcohol and oil down my throat if he heard me scream. I didn't understand the concept of death. All I knew was I wanted him to experience it.

I remember the night he blew his brains out.

The war had just begun. Conscription had only just been put in place. Within a week, he was to enlist or be arrested. He was set to go to war but couldn't last a day without two full bottles of liquor. He was set to go to war, but he could barely string together a coherent sentence. He was set to go to war, but the only war he wished to wage was that in our own home.

The day he blew his brains out, he broke my wrist.

In a fit of rage, he had thrown me down the stairs, pulling me from my hair and launching me as if I were a ragdoll. I would later learn that other than my wrist, I'd broken my ribs and I had a concussion from the fall. At that moment, though, as I laid at the bottom of the stairs, I watched him raise a gun at my mother before he turned it onto himself. The last thing I saw before I lost consciousness was the color red spread across our clean, white walls. When I woke up, I was in the hospital. Past all the rage I felt, the only emotion I could pin was peace. I'd never have to see him again. I'd never hear his rage or feel his wrath. It was a gift.

On the draft of my peers, I was being promoted to head Intelligence Officer. I was eighteen years old with so much power - and I knew I could handle it. I put myself in almost every mission, and the senior advisors noticed. They noticed how merciless I was. They noticed how I moved through combat with no remorse, no second-guessing. I trusted my instincts, almost to a fault, but was never quite stupid enough to have my recklessness deemed inappropriate. I was a natural-born killer, they said. I took it as a compliment.

I wish I hadn't. It only meant that I had turned into my father.

- The Found Diary of Eleri Roman, p. 23

—

In her time with Ruben Yorke, she had learned two things. The first: he was much less intimidating than she'd anticipated. He was all soft smiles and high compliments, giving credit where it was due but never overstepping any boundaries. They'd gone to some restaurant, sat down in a private room in the basement, and had a conversation that flowed as if the pair had worked with each other for years. He knew about her, through and through, but never seemed overbearing nor upset. He congratulated her on the work she had done. He never mentioned anything sensitive.

She didn't know how he knew where to draw the line, but she was glad that he did.

The second thing she learned was much more important and much more disheartening. The troops in Voskivy were abducting, confining, and removing hundreds of people every day and killing unknown numbers per week. She was told that this information was top secret and that the only reason he was telling her was because he knew that she was heading operations to monitor resistance forces in the area.

"I want you to drop that project," He said sternly. "I want you to leave their resistance alone."

His thought was that they were dealing with enough, and if the troops kept up their work, the entire civilization would be - as he put it- dealt with too soon for them to mobilize any sort of revolution. Ruben Yorke's notion was that their resistance was not worth monitoring because soon enough, they'd be dead.

"That wasn't our goal, though," Eleri said carefully. "At least, that wasn't what we were told when we signed up. When I was briefed, we were told that when we won, it would be over. There would be none of this."

"Plans change in time."

"But if this was truly a revenge war, we wouldn't have to do more. We would've made our point and gone, no?"

She didn't mean to start an argument, especially not with someone who had so much power, but she had never been one to hide behind a smile or stay silent if there were things that needed to be said.

"I appreciate all that you've done, and I know you've been here quite a while, but there is so much that you don't know. Not every decision that is made has to be made public, and not every decision has to be explained to those not involved."

"It just doesn't make much sense to me," she said, eyeing him. "Sir, we're wasting money, we're wasting resources, and we are essentially committing a genocide. Someone's going to find out sooner -"

"No one is going to find out." He snapped, then took a breath. "Some things are out of your control. Maybe, one day, if you stay on the path you're on, you'll be able to make the decisions that I'm making, but as of right now, it is your job to sit back and listen to what I'm saying and what I'm saying is that you need to stop working on their resistance."

She pursed her lips. "And you'd like me to do what instead?"

"Nothing."

"Nothing?"

He shook his head. "No. Nothing. If people find out you've stopped working on them, we're gonna get a lot of questions that we can't answer."

"So you want me to pretend,"

The question hung in the air. "Yes. For now."

"For now?"

"I'll more than likely have a new job for you in the near future. Don't worry too much about it."

She contemplated telling Fyodor that her project was being dropped. She didn't want to start keeping secrets - not now, after everything - but she couldn't bring herself to justify letting him know. If he knew, he would tell someone, it was almost certain, or he would pry for answers, or she would have to tell him about what she had spoken about with Ruben. The thought was not overwhelming to her - she'd explain, sure, and he would listen - but the knowledge that if it left her lips it was out of her control that led her to a plethora of outcomes she did not, under any circumstances, want to see come to fruition.

She took a detour on the way home. She walked all the way to the pier, hands in her pockets, nose red from the cold. It wasn't nearly as bad as the day before, but the winter was still incredibly overwhelming, and the subzero temperatures were kicking her ass.

As she stepped to the railing, she noted that the water on the lake was not frozen, but there was a layer of ice forming across the top. She planted herself at the edge, peering over the side, to be met with clear blue waters and a cold reflective glass.

For a moment, she stared, and somehow, in the distorted reflection of the water and the ice, she could see the girl she was ten years ago. So young, so naive, so eager to make a change. That girl died when she first stepped into her training. Eleri wondered, for a brief second, if there was any way that she could get her back.

She could see her breath in the air as she leaned back from the water, looking out into the vast nothingness, to the line where the sea met the sky. She imagined stitching it together, tying two imperceivable elements to each other, rendering them either useless or unstoppable. Her eyes followed down the line, taking in the sight, thinking long and hard about the conversation she had just had with Ruben.

For the first time in her entire life, she felt the need to doubt those in power.

The phone in her pocket began to ring. She put it to her ear, closing her eyes, feeling the cold air nip at her exposed fingers.

"Hello?"

"Eleri," it was Fyo, "You need to come over. You need to see something."

She turned her back to the lake, stuffing her free hand further into her pocket, pushing her head down into her collar. "Why?"

"I... I don't know how to explain it. I just have something that you need to see. Please."

She sighed into the phone, making sure he could hear her irritation. If this call had come from anyone else, she'd be running. With Fyodor, it was hard to tell. He blew things out of proportion often, and more times than she could remember, she had found herself breaking her back to get somewhere, only to find that it was for something insignificant. She loved him, and she trusted him, but he had a talent for getting on her nerves.

"Is it that *important*?"

"Would I call you if it wasn't?"

"You would,"

He paused. "Fine. But I mean it this time. Just... come as soon as you can, okay?"

"Yeah. Sure. I'll be there soon."

She slid the phone back into her pocket before he was able to get another word in, and reluctantly, she began to walk away from the pier. She pulled her jacket tighter around her body, doing anything she could to keep out the cold.

The howl of the wind in the late afternoon reminded her of the nights they'd spent hidden away in broken buildings or underneath bridges or in dug-out holes in the ground during their time in combat. The middle to end of January always seemed to produce different winds than usual. She'd only noticed this because of how observant she'd learned to become. She could recognize the slight difference in the way it sounded or in the patterns it took and how it moved. Of course, this would sound ridiculous to anyone else - wind is wind - but she was certain there was something different about it for these few weeks.

So, each time she experienced it, she would once again live the moments of hunger and fatigue and pain. The wind carried many things, most of all, memories she wished she'd forget.

She pushed through Fyo's front door with ease - he had left it unlocked for her, as he always did - and she kicked her boots to the side. "Where are you?"

He ran around the corner to greet her, a binder in his hand, an expression written across his face that she could not quite put her finger on. He'd not slept, she noticed, as she walked closer to him. "You are not going to believe this," he said, waving the binder at her, leading her into his living room.

Fyo's apartment was worlds different than Eleri's. Hers barely had anything in it in terms of furniture, but the walls were lined with art and the shelves full of things she'd 'taken without permission' from places she'd been over the past decade. Fyo had nothing on the walls, almost no shelves or cases at all, but the space was full of carpets and couches and pillows. She knew that his place was so much warmer and more inviting, and she often thought about moving her things around to make her space feel just as welcoming. Then, she'd remember how much she disliked the idea of having close-knit relationships with people, and for that reason, she couldn't care less about how many people wanted to visit. She'd prefer if they didn't anyway.

She took a seat on the soft white couch, and he sat beside her, thrusting the binder into her hands, looking at her expectantly.

It often slipped her mind that he was slightly older than she was. He had somehow retained his youthful outlook on life. She was very, very jealous.

"What is this?"

"I don't know."

She looked at him, frowning. "You don't know?"

He shook his head, flipping the binder open so she was forced to look at the papers inside. "No. But I found a drive on the ground today, so of course, I wanted to see what was on it, and when I plugged it in, this huge document came up."

"So you printed it?"

"I printed it, cleaned the drive, and threw it …. who knows where." He took a breath. "I just… I don't really know what it is that I'm seeing, but I know I shouldn't have access to it."

"And so you want me to see it…"

"You're smart enough, right? You have more clearances than I do. I think you'll be able to figure it out."

This admission piqued her interest, and she turned her attention to the pages in front of her. She ran her hand down the blank first page before turning it, immediately intrigued by what she saw.

2249 PROPOSED CURRICULUM
VOL. III
D. ARMS, K. FITZGERALD, M. HAAS, S. CAMPBELL.

"Haas? Our Milton Haas?" she asked, turning the page gently.

Fyo could only offer a shrug and a sigh in return. "I don't know of anyone else named *M. Haas*, but I can't be sure."

She was met with a table of contents. Her eyes trailed down the page until she saw a heading that interested her.

THE FIFTEEN YEAR WAR (2232-2247): P. 198

She took a section of pages in her hand, going through until she found what she was looking for. Even before she had begun to read and absorb the content, something felt wrong. She looked up at Fyo for a brief moment.

"Have you read through this yet?"

"Only a bit of it," he said, "before I printed it. I got to page twenty, I think, but I was going in order. I wasn't going through headings. Either way, no, I haven't read this part yet."

"Hm," she managed.

She skimmed through the first two pages of the section. Nothing interesting, only a brief overview of why there was a war and when it began. She wasn't sure what this document was, exactly, but she knew she was going to become bored of it very soon.

"I know all of this," she muttered, her eyes not leaving the paper.

Fyo moved to look over her shoulder. He reached to the papers, flipping them, scanning over each one for only a second before turning to the next.

"What are you doing?" She snapped, smacking his hand. "You said you wanted me to see this."

"Wait," he mumbled, "I'm looking for pictures."

Then, before she had the chance to comment on his immaturity, his finger landed on the middle of a page. "Here."

She looked him over once before dragging her eyes to the page.

Her heart nearly stopped.

Staring back at her was an image of her and the five others she had been grouped with, a smile gracing her features that she had lost long ago. She was standing between Fyo and Kassander Strome. Her heart grew heavy. Kass had become one of her closest friends - her biggest support system, her biggest advocate, and hands down the smartest person he had ever met. Sevyn Ingrid was sitting cross-legged on the ground in front of them, her hands mid-action, hovering over her rifle. Elijah Newsom stood beside Kassander, his arms folded across his chest, a bashful smile gracing his features. And she could barely make out Yves D'Arsie, whose head was turning as the photo was captured, leaving his features blurry and his face almost unrecognizable.

She felt a lump in her throat. She wanted to scream.

She directed her attention to the words underneath the picture, and she froze.

Above. (left to right, top to bottom): The Company of Six – Landon Daniels, Fyodor Kacer, Eleri Roman, Marco Altonetti, Nathaniel Eriksson, and Jasmine Ingrid.

"What names are these?" Her voice was barely above a whisper. Despite how quiet she was, her rage was unmistakable. Fyo was almost scared.

"Well, that's -" he paused, getting a good look at the page. "No. What the fuck?"

She slammed the binder shut, suddenly rising to her feet, slipping her boots back on, grabbing her jacket.

"What are you doing?" He asked, following her hurriedly.

"I am going to sleep, and then I am going to talk to my dear Milton Haas."

"Eleri -"

"His name is on this document. He has to know what it is. Otherwise, he's more of an idiot than I thought he was."

"And if he asks you where you found it?"

Fyo's eyes were swimming with anxiety. He, of course, was always on thin ice, and if anyone found out that he was the source of this classified document, he would be dead. She knew this, and though she would never expose him, she was thankful for the opportunity to confirm.

"I'll just tell him to watch where he puts his shit."

Three.

The rumors that surrounded me were my greatest weapon for a long time. In an army that was predominantly male, it was hard to get people to take my word or to believe that I was capable, and because I had nothing to back myself up with, my first few years were absolute Hell. I think that may have been why I was so aggressive when I became active in combat. I think I felt that I had something to prove to everyone.

I regret a lot of what I did, but at the time, the only way to make sure that these men would listen to me was to make sure they were scared of me. If I had a reputation that was tied to stories of me killing one of my Superiors because he looked at me the wrong way, or that I would brutally slit the throats of anyone who came too close to me, or that my number of confirmed kills was less than one-tenth of the truth, then I had *a reputation that made me bigger than I was. Larger than life. I was seen as someone so unhinged that it forced people to listen. They thought their lives were at stake talking to me, and I loved every second of it.*

Keeping up that reputation was exhausting, though. I think it was a large part of why I taught myself not to become close to people... Why I have convinced myself that everybody is disposable, and nobody matters enough for me to care about with my entire being. It is so, very lonely, but as I've heard many times before, it is lonely at the top.

While it certainly helped me at the time, I regret the reputation entirely. I wish I could go back. I would take no power over this isolated, cold reality I've built for myself. I would take being loved over being feared.

I will never know what it is like any other way. This is who I am. This is who I've become. This is who I'm meant to be.

- The Found Diary of Eleri Roman, p. 30

———

"What is this?" She asked sternly, all but throwing the binder onto Milton Haas' desk. "What are these?"

"You can't be in here without an appointment," Milton said, not bothering to look up at her.

The sun had barely risen, and the day had barely begun, but Eleri was much too antsy to wait for a reasonable hour to roll about. When she'd gone to sleep, she had planned on getting him a coffee, maybe something to eat, in hopes of him becoming more receptive. But as she woke, the feeling of disgust and anger nestled itself back into her chest, and she was out the door before she could even consider getting him something.

The man in the foyer had told her not to go up, that it was appointment only, that she would be reprimanded, and in her rage, she couldn't quite remember, but she was fairly certain she'd threatened his life if he didn't move out of her way. She'd stormed through the door, she'd made it clear she was not leaving, and she finally found her way into his office.

"This is important."

He lowered his gaze for a split second before returning his attention to his work. "Drafts."

She shook her head. "For what, exactly?"

He turned then, irritated, looking at her fully. "History textbooks. For the kids. For when they start going back to school next year."

She briefly doubted herself. Had she seen the wrong names? Had she misread? But the doubt subsided fairly quickly. She was never one to second guess herself. She knew what she was doing, and she knew what she had read.

"None of this stuff is true, though," she said finally, folding her arms over her chest.

"Correct," he said, completely unphased by her comment.

"These people…" she opened the binder to the marked page of the photo that had made her so angry the night before. She traced her fingers over the group, chills running down her spine. "… they did not exist in the way you're claiming they did. And everyone who died…" she paused. "You gave them different names. You erased them."

He ran a hand over his face, taking his glasses off. "Have a seat."

She did as she was told, present in body but barely in mind, her eyes never leaving the image.

She remembered the day that photograph was taken vividly. It was two months after their formation as a group, and by the looks of the photo - wide smiles, sunny skies - one would assume that the war had just ended. That was far from the case, as the day the image was taken, they were getting ready to go on one of the most dangerous missions of their lives, one where they knew they'd be greatly outnumbered. It didn't matter to any of them, though, as they laughed and got their gear ready. A young boy - no older than thirteen - walked by with a camera and politely asked them if they'd pose for a photograph for the news. They did as they were told, arms around each other, posing as best they could in the midst of the rubble and the chaos, and the photograph was taken. As far as Eleri knew, it was the only image that the entire group had together.

"Do you realize how important the work we are doing here is?" Milton said, tearing her from her thoughts.

"I'm just… having a problem understanding." She furrowed her brows. "This isn't history. This isn't how anything happened. None of this is true. And… it's not that you have to fill in gaps. You people should have an entire registry of all of our reports... of which we did after every single mission. There are reports documenting every single day of this war, and you just... you made everything up? For a *history textbook*?"

"Do you think, Miss Roman, that it is very appropriate for a child to learn about how you and your comrades brutally murdered people? Do you think we should be detailing how to set up bombs?"

"Sir, no, but I-"

"I am going to be honest with you, and I am only going to tell you this once. If we tell it as it is, people will not only question you or question me, but they will question *us*. They will question our decision-making, our ability to lead, our legitimacy in the war... if we want a functioning society, we have to tell them the stories that they want to hear. We have to convince them that our leadership is the only answer. And, yes, to do that, we have to change history. But at the end of the day," Milton scoffed, "it won't matter. They won't know."

"So, what then?" She said as the rage she had been containing so well bubbling to the surface. "Nothing that actually happened meant anything? They died... Fyodor and I did everything that we did... for nothing?"

"Don't look at it that way. Look at the bigger picture. What you did as individuals never mattered, and I'm surprised you haven't clued into that yet, as smart as you are." There was an unfamiliar venom in his tone. "One day, you will die, and Fyodor Kacer will die, and once that happens, your names in this textbook will be changed, too. That way, your history… your life… is only a symbol. We can manipulate whatever we need to without compromising a real person."

"So, you plan to erase me, too. After all these years… what, so it'll be a reminder in the agenda? *Oh, by the way, when Eleri Roman dies, find a new name for her in the textbooks.* Isn't that -"

"Please, please stop trying to twist my words into something more complicated than they are." he shook his head. "All that matters is the future, and we will do anything we can to ensure that it goes according to plan. If that means removing you, then so be it."

She took the binder in her hands, standing, turning on her heels, and walking out of the room. She was certain that Milton had called for her to leave the binder on his desk, but she didn't care.

What was he going to do? Demote her?

She scoffed. As much as the pair disliked each other, Milton Haas knew he needed her more than she needed him.

Her walk home was one that was full of thinking. Over the past twenty-four hours, she had gone from having complete confidence in what she was doing to having none at all. Ten years of her life were dedicated to this group that did nothing in line with what they claimed to have stood for. She was giving everything she had for a machine that would not even give her the respect she deserved.

The idea came to her all at once.

She made her way to her office - the one Ruben had told her to abandon - and with the binder tucked under her arm, she found a new inspiration.

If her side was lying about the history, then was her side all that it made itself out to be?

She was always one to make decisions of her own accord. She was not loyal, almost to a fault. She, despite everything she did, had learned to move around, never staying in the same place for too long. Movement would create static, and the static would create a spark. She would only hope that the spark would create a fire. It did, more often than not. While she had been loyal to Aloneia for her entire life, it came second to what she felt she owed herself. She would put herself above her state, always. And if that meant she had to cut ties with the place that made her, then she would do it.

It was a dangerous combination of rage and of skepticism that coursed through her veins as she opened her computer and began to collect all the information she had about each individual member of the resistance in Voskivy that she had been keeping track of.

Bullshit. Putting them in confinement. Killing them off. The war was over, but the fight was not. It never would be.

Her moves were measured. She was not going to print any copies of their files. This would leave a trace back to her computer and her documents that she could not risk being seen by others. She'd been watching these people for the sake of watching them. Most other officers would be watching them for the sake of exterminating them.

She began to copy all of their information by hand. The light that hung above her desk was buzzing - she would have to change it, soon - and she had run through three pens by the time she was finished.

She put the papers into the binder, and after rummaging around in her desk for a moment, she found a bag, sliding everything inside. She logged off and left the building, hoping to whoever ran the universe that nobody saw her, and if they did, they didn't find her actions suspicious.

She moved out of the area with a newfound grace, walking into the nearest cafe and ordering a coffee for herself.

Her hand went to her throat on the way out. Right. She needed a scarf.

She would deal with that later.

She got home much later than she hoped she would, but just as she did every evening, she found Fyo standing in her apartment, looking through one of her bookshelves. "Look who's here," he said, smiling up at her.

"Hi," she breathed, throwing her things to the side, bringing her bag over to her living room table. As if on command, Fyo opened the door to her balcony, and she stepped through it, binder in hand. He closed it behind them, wrapping a blanket over her shoulders, taking one for himself. He lit one cigarette, then lit his own, and he watched her with a cautious curiosity as she fussed with the papers and began to read through them. The cigarette was barely hanging from her lips, a thin line of smoke finding its way up above her head.

He turned once, the sun had begun to set, and focused his attention back on her back to her.

"You okay?"

She nodded. "Yeah. Don't worry."

"What's all this? What did you and Haas talk about?"

"He's a piece of shit, is what we talked about. He says he's renaming people on purpose. Said he'll rename us once we die, too."

"Yeah?" Fyo leaned back into the chair. "No shit,"

"Mhm,"

He took a drag and looked back to the sky. "And so… what is it you're doing? Planning his sudden and mysterious death?"

She let out a breathy laugh. "Not yet. Maybe I'll do that next."

He cracked his neck, side to side, thinking about what he could say to her at this moment. Her brows were knotted together in the middle as she scanned through papers and sorted them into piles, she was all but chewing on the end of the cigarette, and he was certain she hadn't eaten anything all day. She was very difficult to deal with if she had something she had her sights set on, though, and judging by how she had barely spoken a word to him, he could only assume she had some goal in mind that she had to reach soon.

"You aren't going to tell me what this is, then?"

"Don't you want to... not be involved in my work? Something about you not wanting to accidentally talk about top secret information?"

"That was so long ago. I've changed."

"That was two weeks ago."

"And? I've changed."

She set the papers down, closing the binder, facing him. "You're going to think that I'm crazy."

"I already do,"

She smiled. "You know what I mean."

"Okay, because anything could make me think you're crazier. As I haven't found you crazy since -"

"Okay, okay, I get it. I'm crazy. I'm so crazy that... I want to talk to the resistance. In Voskivy."

There was silence, and she went back to opening the binder. "Wait," he said, shaking his head. "You're serious?"

She nodded. "Yeah. I am."

"Why would you do that? Is that not illegal?"

"So is keeping thousands of troops in a region you've already defeated and demilitarized."

He paused. "We have troops in Voskivy?"

"Oh, it gets worse," she scoffed. "We have troops in Voskivy who are kidnapping and murdering innocent people. Not soldiers. Not criminals. Just whoever they find on the street."

He put his cigarette out, leaning towards her, trying to get a look at her papers. "No, they're not."

"The phone number you gave me was Ruben Yorke's."

His eyes went wide. "No, it wasn't."

"It was, and I met with him, and he told me a lot of things, Fyo."

Fyodor shook his head. "Why would he... why would he just admit that? To you?" then, quickly, "No offense, of course."

She ignored the off-hand comment. "He said something about how he wanted me to stop keeping tabs on their resistance because they'll probably all be dead soon, anyway. He's not going to stop. I think they're literally trying to kill every single person there and then take over the land. Probably planning to write them out entirely eventually, too."

Fyodor sat up slowly, thinking. "So that's why they're doctoring the history books, right? Because you can't go around telling people that you killed an entire population for no reason. You have to make something up."

"That's what I'm thinking. Haas told me that they were trying to tell people what they needed to hear in order to trust everyone in power or something. I just... I'm not understanding where we draw the line. We change history, we kill an entire population, we take over. But we aren't the only ones in the world. Someone else is bound to find out eventually, and then what?"

"I don't believe anyone would do anything," Fyo said. "I think they're all too wrapped up in themselves. They have no obligation to us, right? So why would they give a fuck what we did over here? If anything, they'll maybe make sure we're put on a high alert list or something. But we didn't go for them, so they won't come for us. And that's only on the off chance that they do find out, which, by the way, I doubt."

She nodded. "Yeah, probably. But... I don't know. This seems really, really wrong to me." She paused her movement, thinking for a moment. "Do you remember why we started the war, Fyo?"

"We were invaded, it was a retaliation, we'd have never done it on our own -"

"Yeah, but *when*? When were we invaded? I was young, sure, but I don't remember that at all. What... what happened? Do we even know?"

Fyo took a minute to respond. His eyes locked onto the railing at the end of the balcony, his mind trying to paint a picture of his childhood. He couldn't remember much outside of his father going off to war, his mother following suit, and the day he dropped out of school to find work to raise his younger brother, who ended up dying only weeks after his draft, anyways. He tried to think, he really did, but there was nothing. He wondered if it was because he wasn't paying enough attention to the world around him or if it was because he was too young to understand, but whatever the reason, he had absolutely no recollection of any events leading up to the war. And now, knowing what was being done to the history books, he doubted they'd have anywhere to look, anyways.

"When did they start re-writing history?" He asked then, looking back over to Eleri.

She sat back, momentarily, before leaning forwards again. "Fuck if I know. This can't be the first time, right?"

"Do you think if we ask younger kids why the war started, they'll have an answer ready?"

She looked down at the notes in her lap. "Probably. Do you think if we ask someone older than us, they'll tell us the truth?"

"No," Fyo said, with full confidence. "Not a chance."

There was another comfortable silence. Fyo wandered into her apartment - the sun had set - and she called out after him.

"Are you going home?"

"No," he called back, "I'll be back in a second."

He returned with a plate of fruit, placing it onto her lap, on top of the notes. "Eat something, man."

He sat back down, crossing one leg over the other. "I was thinking -"

"Did it hurt?"

He leaned over, smacking her on the back of the head. "Asshole. No, it didn't hurt, thank you. I thought that Xavier may be willing to help us."

She pondered this proposition. Xavier was incredible, and he always respected both of them more than he did any other units. She rubbed her forehead, leaning forward onto her hand, considering him. She hadn't spoken to him in months, but he would definitely be more than willing to have a coffee with her or Fyo, more so if he didn't know what they wanted to discuss. Xavier Talon had always been there to answer her questions, or to give her intel, or to provide the fatherly advice she never had.

But with all that she'd learned over the past day, she wasn't sure how genuine he had been. She didn't want to admit it to herself, but the fact of the matter was that every single thing her greatest mentor had ever said to her was more than likely a lie.

"I could try it." She said finally.

"You don't sound convinced."

"Can we trust him?"

"Does it hurt to ask?"

"No. I guess not. I just wish we had a starting point, that's all."

There was another blanket of silence. He watched her work and eat, and suddenly, he spoke. "I have something that might help."

She raised an eyebrow. "Yeah?"

"I may have some of my old notebooks somewhere in my apartment. From school. I can look for them for you."

"My knight in shining armor," she said, sarcasm laced in her voice, but there was truth in her statement. "Sure. If you can find them, yeah, that'd be great."

He could hear the distance in her, and he knew it was his sign to leave. With a quick pat to her knee, he said goodbye and told her he'd be back in the morning. She only smiled at him, and he understood that she was too deep in thought to process what he'd said.

With a slight smile playing on his lips, he zipped his jacket, pushed his hands into his pockets, and set off across the street.

The snow began to fall again. The moon and the stars gave the snowflakes a newfound beauty as if gems were being dropped from the sky. He wiped his runny nose with the back of his sleeve, taking one good look at the city and sighing to himself.

The winter used to be his favorite time of year. Before things had all gone wrong, he and his brother would play in the snow for hours. They'd build forts and dig holes and lay down until the snow had buried them. His birthday was in the winter - his family used to throw huge parties for him and his friends to celebrate - and he was always so excited for the time of year to come along.

Fyo took one last look at the street - the concrete buildings, the overhead wires, the fenced-off courtyards between the structures. He knew that if he traveled even three blocks East, things would seem even less cared for. In fact, any section of the housing district outside of his own looked almost uninhabitable; the windows were broken, doors off their hinges, walls falling apart, roofs sagging in...

Twenty years ago, everything looked much different. The apartments were painted beautiful colors, there were flags and lights hanging over the streets, and if Fyo's memory served, there were vendors lining the sidewalks with food and candy and toys.

War took everything, he supposed. It took all he was, and it would take all he had, too.

He would consider himself lucky. There were people who didn't serve anymore, and there were people who were either too young or too old to make the cut at all. They were the ones who were struggling. They were the ones a few blocks away, with houses that barely supported them, with ten people sharing one bedroom.

He remembered Voskivy vividly in his mind despite the months that had passed since he had been there last, and he was infinitely grateful that he'd never lived there. He had visited once as a child with his family, but he barely remembered it. There was nothing special - it was much less colorful, but much cleaner than where he'd grown up - overall just another place. During the war, though, he'd watched it fall apart. Hell, he'd made it fall apart.

He knew he was only the ghost of the man he'd been when he first joined the fight, and the guilt he felt for what he'd done was eating away at him. It was something he would never admit, but he had been blinded by the adrenaline and the feeling of importance that came from being on that team and completing missions. The acknowledgment for his actions and the understanding that he was one of the most powerful people alive was too much for him, but he'd only realized it after things were done. He didn't even know what ideology he was subscribed to when he was planting bombs in buildings or killing people during combat. And now, with everything

Eleri had told him, it only further expanded the monster that had been born in the back of his mind the first night he'd come home.

That monster was his own reflection. Fyo, Eleri, and the other four had been on the front every single day since the group was formed. Being away from it for even one night put things into perspective for him, and he didn't like what he saw. He didn't like who he'd become.

He hadn't slept more than an hour on any given night since returning. He was broken, and he had done it to himself.

He wished he could go back and stay away from it all. He had made a promise to himself that he would never pick up another weapon.

He was never good at keeping promises.

Four.

We planted explosives in a building and were set to return later in the day to look through it and salvage anything we could. It was routine. We were told that every assignment we were given was necessary, even the ones that seemed pointless, and though we argued time and time again that demolishing random structures seemed almost counter-productive, our arguments fell on deaf ears. The goal, apparently, was to get rid of high-risk areas. We were told that Intelligence Officers would find buildings where the Voskivian forces would send snipers, or set up safe bases, or store materials, and it was up to us to go in and destroy them. That was what made it so dangerous, I guess; the idea that we were going in, not knowing if we'd be met with four walls or with forty soldiers.

We would send four in the mornings to plant and the other two in the evenings to retrieve. We'd never all be caught dead in one place. Most times, I was sent to plant in the mornings - something about having the quietest footsteps and the quickest hands - but every so often, I'd become preoccupied with something else, and I would only be available to go at night to collect. This one particular summer night, I had to collect at the end of the day. I'd gone with Kassander, and we split the rubble down the middle to cover more ground in less time. I remember seeing something glimmering underneath the dust, and with wide eyes and a smile on my face, I knelt down to push rocks and dirt aside to see what it was. It took some time, but eventually, I was able to lift the heavy bits and move them away enough for me to have a clear view of whatever had been trapped underneath in the explosion. I'd seen and dug through piles just like these hundreds of times, but nothing I'd ever found could've prepared me for the feeling I would have when I pulled back a stone and was greeted with a crushed skull of a girl who could not have been older than eight years old. Nothing I had ever seen, nothing I had ever done, had prepared me for the sick feeling that would find itself in the pit of my heart, or nausea I'd feel building in my stomach, or the tears that built behind my eyes when I saw the blood and the bruising and the fact that what I had seen from above - the thing I was looking to take - was a golden cross that hung on her neck. She wasn't supposed to be there, right? They'd never have us purposely kill innocent people.

Especially not children.
Right?

- The Found Diary of Eleri Roman, p. 44

—

Eleri woke suddenly, the knock at the door tearing her out of the light sleep she had fallen into. Her neck hurt something fierce - she'd fallen asleep slumped over her papers, and she would definitely be stiff for the next few days - and she tried desperately to roll it as she made her way to the door.

Fyo walked right in as she opened it, and she rolled her eyes, closing the door gently behind her. She caught a glimpse of the clock: 05:00.

"What the fuck, Fyodor?" She hissed, following him into her kitchen. "It's so early."

"Yeah, okay, but I found one of my grade school notebooks."

She closed her eyes for a moment as she shuffled towards her coffee machine, turning it on and retrieving two mugs from the cupboard.

"It's not going anywhere. Could this not have happened at a reasonable hour?"

Fyodor looked up at her, a playful smirk etched across his features. "Yeah, but I was up."

"Yeah, but I was up," she mimicked under her breath, pouring coffee into the mugs, setting one down in front of Fyo. She took her place across from him, taking a sip of the scalding drink, trying to ignore how it burnt her tongue.

"Here," he said, sliding a notebook across the table. "Look."

She rubbed her eyes once before opening the old red notebook. The paper had been water damaged, the cover was creased and torn, but when she looked down at the pages, all she saw was real, authentic handwriting from years long since forgotten.

"Your handwriting was atrocious," she mumbled, flipping through the sections, trying to find something of use.

"Still is," he responded with a smile, raising the mug to his lips.

She looked up at him, only for a split second, before turning her attention back to the notebook.

"Oh," she said, "here. This sounds good."

He dragged his chair across the floor, the screeching sound enough to make her reach out and slap him against the arm. He bumped her back, leaning over her shoulder, looking at something he had written years ago. The title, in sloppy, capital letters, read *MAJOR CONTRIBUTING FACTORS*.

"March 4, 2233…" she read, the writing on the top of the page indicative of the year. "They had you date your work?"

He scratched his head. "No… I don't think they told us to. I think it was just a habit I had. My mother always dated anything she wrote. I think I just did the same."

She bit her lower lip. "I don't ever remember dating anything I did in school. Do you think they did that on purpose?"

Fyo nodded. "If we don't know when we wrote things down, there's nothing to go off of. I mean, if there's no documentation, it might as well just be a high tale."

She took a deep breath, knowing he was right. How much easier was it to manipulate the masses if nobody knew when anything happened? Every distant memory felt simultaneous, as if it was only a day old but also like it happened lifetimes ago. The mind could never be trusted, and it seemed that they all knew that already.

"So this was... what? One year after the war started?"

He took a breath. "Yeah, I think so. So I was... twelve, maybe thirteen years old, I think."

There was a certain sorrow that seemed to overtake her as she began to read what he had written in his notebook. She couldn't place her finger on the source or the reason (she never could, when it came to sadness), but she knew that the tingling in her chest and the weight in her lungs was something she would never get used to.

"Do you want me to read it?" She said, taking another sip of coffee. "Out loud?"

He nodded. "That's so cute of you to offer,"

She rolled her eyes. "Shut up. I'm taking that as a yes?"

Fyodor tucked one leg under the other on the chair he was perched on, leaning forward on his elbows. He eyed her with anticipation, nodding once, a silent prompt.

"You wrote it in... oh," she said, her eyes wide. "You wrote a timeline. This..." she slammed her hand against the table in an incredibly rare moment of excitement, "It's what they were teaching us in school, right? This is the sequence of events they want us to believe."

He untucked his leg and shifted forwards. "Shit, I guess you're right! Does this help -"

"This helps. So much. Here, look: 'November 2229 - Voskivian governments militarize their forces, near Aloneian borders. January 2230 - summit between world leaders, Voskivian President Jia is notably absent. February 2230 - informal request for forces to step away from borders is denied. May 2230 - formal request for forces to step away from borders is denied. June 2230 - Voskivian forces cross Aloneian borders.'"

She trailed off before pausing completely. Fyo noticed.

"What is it?"

"I would've been eight years old here. I don't remember hearing anything about anyone crossing our borders."

Fyo rubbed the back of his neck, an exasperated sigh escaping him. He looked down at the page, then back up at Eleri. "I don't think I remember it either, besides these notes. It's like... I've written this all down, but it feels so distant from me. I know I'd never remember every single moment of my life, but at... what... nine... ten years old, you'd think I'd remember an *invasion*, no?"

She nodded in agreement. "That's exactly what I mean. My house was hectic, but I feel like things would have broken up enough to address an entire army coming into the country, right? Especially considering I used to live right on the border."

"No shit, you were a border town?"

She smiled sadly. "Yeah, and it was so nice there, you know? Every day when I walked to school, I'd literally walk right along the fence. Sometimes, I'd talk to kids on the other side." Eleri paused in thought. "It seems like a whole other world now, doesn't it?"

The dejected look on Fyo's face did not escape Eleri, but she thought it best to leave it alone. Not only did they have more things to get through, but she was also not awake enough to have this emotional conversation with him. Did she feel bad? Maybe a little bit, but not enough to make her change her mind.

She turned back to the paper, skipping a few dates, not seeing the importance. "Okay, someone was assassinated, someone was kidnapped but later released... here, look," she turned the book to him, "just after the kidnapping. August 2231, apparently Voskivy attacked our government quarters?"

Her head was hurting, and she felt as though she were trying to create a memory for herself. She had nothing to grab onto. She had no rational explanation for why none of this made sense to her *other* than the thought that she'd been taught information that she hadn't lived, despite having been alive during its alleged occurrence, and even this proposal seemed incredibly far-fetched. The thought that she had been feeding into these false narratives for her entire life was absolutely sickening to her. The illusion of free will was suddenly all too real, and she hated that she was unable to pick up on this sooner.

"I don't remember that on the news or anything," Fyo said. "I don't even remember anyone talking about it. My mom always made sure I was up to date with anything going on. It was one of the biggest things for her, from as far back as I can remember. She always talked about how she wanted me to be *informed* and how she didn't want me to look stupid in front of my classmates."

Eleri laughed at that. "So she did it to save you from embarrassment, not because she thought that it would be good for you to be smart?"

Fyo shrugged, finishing the coffee in his mug. "Look, I have about as much of a clue as you do. That's what she said, but I never knew with her." Then, after a brief moment, "Keep going with the book. I want to know what else I'm supposed to be aware of."

Eleri turned her attention back to the tattered pages, smirking at his quip. "Okay. Most of this seems irrelevant. Stemming from that apparent attack, there is literally nothing about any invasions or violence. In this timeline, they mobilized their army for no reason, they skipped a summit, they attacked our government, had their troops all around Aloneia for a bit, and then they just… left, I guess. So I think, according to your notes, we attacked them because they attacked our headquarters."

"That's the thing, though," Fyo said, "I didn't want to believe you when you said that they were lying in the history books because we're part of that history, and I didn't... I don't know, I didn't think they'd actually do that, I guess, but God, El, maybe I forgot the invasion, and maybe I forgot the attack on the government, but there is *no way* that I'd forget there being troops in the streets. No fucking way."

She closed his notebook gently. He was right. Maybe they had been too young to remember and keep track of current events. Maybe they were at an age where, frankly, world summits meant nothing to them. But seeing troops in the streets every day would have become a core memory. They didn't forget it. It never happened.

"I have to get a hold of Xavier, and Fyo, frankly, I have to get a hold of someone in the resistance, too."

Fyo stared at her. "Is that a good idea?"

"What choice do we have, really? I want to hear their side. We owe it to them, I think."

"Well, what if they're lying to you?"

She scoffed. "At this point, their lie is probably closer to the truth than this notebook is."

He leaned back in the chair. "And you're... planning on going alone?"

The question hung in the air. She hadn't thought about any logistics, including the hypothetical possibility of bringing Fyodor with her anywhere. She had only just begun to consider the prospect of crossing borders, and she knew that Fyodor would have a strong opinion on it regardless, but she had inserted him into the narrative in her head automatically. They did everything together, and she had no reason to assume that this would be any different.

"Are you opposed to coming with me?"

Fyo looked down. "I think you should go by yourself to talk to Xavier," he said, his voice quiet and soft. "But, if you step one foot outside of our borders, you promise me that you'll bring me with you."

He wouldn't look at her as he waited for her response. He was desperate, and he was tired, and his voice was raw with emotion. She'd never heard him so helpless, so *worried* before. In all they'd done and all they'd seen, Fyo always had a light air about him, one that comforted others. She would never guess that his wavering emotion would've met her as the sun rose, in the comfort of her own apartment.

For Fyo, this was life or death. He knew that there was a relatively good chance of Eleri doing something spontaneous or reckless, most likely venturing out of their borders and into Voskivy. It was in her nature to do so, and it always had been. That was what made her such a good soldier, so skilled in combat… but Fyo knew, because he'd heard stories and he'd seen it countless times, that if she was not careful, it would be the root of her downfall, as well. Neither of them had been back in Voskivy since the surrender. The last memories they had of the place were less than joyous, and Fyo hadn't considered going back so soon, if at all. He wasn't sure what being back in that environment would do to Eleri, and he *certainly* had no clue what it would do to him, but he would be damned if he let her go alone only for something to go wrong. He didn't want her there, and she knew it, but his word meant nothing against the determination of a woman who had seen too much.

She reached over, placing her hand on the side of his face, gently anchoring her fingers in his scalp. She moved, tilting his head, forcing him to look at her. "Fyodor," she said, her voice calm and gentle. It reminded him of the nights they would spend talking as they kept watch on missions. It reminded him of how she would speak to any children they came across on their journeys. The sound of her voice, like this, reminded him of the sunset. It was a blanket of warmth, and it was the feeling of home.

His eyes met hers, finally, the piercing, transparent blue getting lost in the depths of mystery hidden in the brown. Oil on water, but oh so beautiful.

"If I do *anything*, you'll be the first to know." she paused, moving her hand, resting it on top of his. "And when I go into Voskivy, you'll be the only one I want with me."

Five.

The day Fyodor and I met, I thought he was arrogant and stupid and, frankly, unprofessional. I thought that I'd have to avoid him, that he and I would be at opposite ends at all times, that we would never get along in a way that would allow our group to work. I thought that I'd have to move or have to go back to being an Intelligence Officer or even quit entirely. I was ready to give up everything to get away from him.

What I didn't realize, stupid as I was at the time, was that the only reason I felt such a strong negative sentiment towards him was that he was so different from me. I had only ever been told that my work ethic was what made me successful, and in hand, I had learned that the only way to be successful was to have my work ethic. So, when Fyodor Kacer arrived with his big personality and his disregard for convention, I thought he would drag us down. I was sure that he would be our dead weight.

I learn more and more from Fyodor every day. He never fails to teach me and to guide me, and without even realizing it, to take care of me. So I listen, and I watch, and I learn something new. But the first lesson I was ever given, and probably the most important I'd ever receive, was that it was okay to fear change, but it was never okay to reject it.

Fyo and I saw a lot of change in our day. But we embraced it, and if we didn't like where it took us, then fuck it, we'd just change again.

- The Found Diary of Eleri Roman, p. 52

———

Xavier Talon had moved away from the housing district in which he'd resided during the war long ago - not only out of necessity but out of a pure desire to be anywhere else. He hadn't hated the war, and he didn't hate it even now, but he supposed a lot of that had to do with the fact that he hadn't ever seen combat. Sure, he was responsible for a mass of attacks and plans, and yes, he oversaw almost everything that had transpired over fifteen incredible years, but he himself had never been on the front. He was somehow both overly involved and incredibly removed from it all, despite having one of the longest military careers in Aloneian history.

Xavier had joined the army long before there was a war. He'd never been particularly interested in any field of work, and being part of the military not only offered financial security but a strong sense of respect from those around him. There was no tension when he first joined at the age of twenty-one, and it remained that way for most of the fifty-four years he'd spend serving. He thought he had hit the jackpot before the war broke out - a steady career where he'd made his way to a powerful position with no immediate threats, but he, of course, would eventually have to adjust, as did everyone else.

He had always found it odd that, despite his influence and his status, he was not part of the decision to invade Voskivy. The news had reached him by virtue of someone below him, and he eventually learned that he had been excluded because everyone was sure he'd oppose the invasion.

They'd be right.

Xavier never quite fully understood the prospect of war, despite his time in the army. He vaguely saw how it was sometimes a necessity - he'd realized that sometimes things happened that could only be met with a force such as death - but he thought it should be a last resort if an option at all. He would make his decisions, no matter how difficult, through the lens of a soldier, and he would execute plans only thinking of the immediate future. War was not something Xavier was particularly interested in, but if he was going to be involved, he was going to do it right. The thing itself, though, was a nightmare.

It was very romanticized, and he never understood why.

There was an image that people had painted for themselves that was so far from the truth, Xavier found it laughable. The way he saw it, as someone who'd spent more than half his life serving, war was not glamourous, nor was it beautiful. He had read about an art movement once, one that had taken place hundreds of years prior, some avant-garde disaster in which war was glorified, and it was said that beauty could only be found in pain. He'd outwardly scoffed in the library when he'd read about it - it sounded so ridiculous, and so *familiar*.

That book, in fact, was how he'd meet the woman who would become his wife.

Daria Petrovic was a historian and an artist and, according to Xavier, the smartest, most beautiful person he had ever had the honor and pleasure of meeting. She was a firm believer in understanding history to plan for the future, and she always joked that she would never marry a military man because they were *nothing more than a weapon of the state*, that their violence and aggression were inexcusable in every way.

Xavier hadn't realized how much he didn't know about the world until she had begun to talk about it. He had never heard about any of these empires and conquests and wars from a time so far away it was inconceivable, and he had certainly never heard of World War One through Four. It seemed like something he should've known. It seemed like information that should've been common knowledge. But they'd never been taught about it in school, and he never saw the point in learning about events that had already passed.

When rumblings of the war began, Daria was less than pleased. She tried to fight the proposal herself. When Xavier had said there was nothing he could do, she had booked appointments with his superiors to talk to them. They didn't listen to her, unsurprisingly, and her only plan was to document what was happening. She took it upon herself to keep track of every minuscule detail - every conversation, every moment that would ultimately lead to avoidable conflict. Perhaps her notes would be used as references in the same way she found notes for her own studies. Perhaps when the seemingly inevitable war was over, she would be able to speak on the integrity of the situation.

She would never get to see it through. One week before war was officially declared against Voskivy, she would be found dead in a storage room on the top floor of one of the military bases she often frequented. Her cause of death was deemed a heart attack.

Xavier didn't believe it but had no grounds on which to question it.

All of her notes and research had gone missing, and Xavier never had time to look into what had happened; as soon as he was able to regain his footing, he was thrown into a war that he had no part in creating.

His history with the military and with the army and with the war was incredibly tangled. It had given him both the best and the worst in life, and he was stuck in limbo; to feel grateful or to feel resentment. And though he remembered some of what Daria had written, he was always too busy to immerse himself in her research and her notes. He knew that she had gone above and beyond to try and make sense of what was unfolding, and he knew that it was important to her that things remained honorable, but he had become so deeply occupied with his work that he hadn't taken it as seriously as he should've. He regretted not spending more time with her in her pursuits. He regretted not trying to understand what she had to say. All he could do was carry what he knew with him in hopes that it would help him, somehow. As she had made clear, history projects the future, and he was going to make sure he did as much as he could to allow her thoughts to be worth more than just words on a page.

He received the phone call from Eleri Roman late at night. He had just settled into bed, a cup of tea in one hand and a magazine in the other when the phone rang from across the room. He didn't normally receive calls at this hour. He was often busy during the day, despite having retired months ago, taking calls and writing out documents as a favor for some men he had worked with. He often spoke to Milton Haas, as well, seeing as he had taken over the position, and though he had his opinions on the man, he knew that there was no point in filing an appeal. His report probably wouldn't be looked at, anyway, now that he was out of service. It was something he seriously considered, though, after each painful conversation.

So when the phone rang as he had settled in, he could only assume it was Haas, asking him some stupid self-explanatory question again. He sat up with a huff, strode over to the phone, and placed it against his ear in a hurry, patience running thin.

"What?" he said harshly.

There was a beat of silence. "Captain Talon, Sir? It's Eleri Roman. If this is a bad time, I can call back -"

"*Oh,*" he chuckled, "Eleri, I am so sorry, my dear, I assumed this was someone else. Any time is a good time for you. What is it?"

"Thank you, Sir, I just... I was wondering if you would be willing to meet with me sometime soon. I have some things I want to talk to you about, and I don't think they're fit for a call."

Xavier smacked his lips together in thought. He had always harbored a sneaking suspicion that his calls were still being monitored, despite having left, and he was aware of the fact that even if ingoing and outgoing signals from his line were not tracked, those calling from within the base would be. He understood the implications of a conversation that was not set for the phone. He sighed.

"Is it urgent?"

"My life is not in danger, no," she said, slight amusement in her tone, "but it is very important."

He screwed his eyes shut in thought, trying to remember anything he had previously spoken to her about that may have led to this phone call. He hadn't heard from her since he left the army, and in all honesty, he hadn't expected to hear from her at all. She was respectful, and he knew that she loved and cared for him, but she was not sentimental, nor was she one to cling to the past, so the thought of her reaching out to him was so foreign that he understood that this was more of a request, and less of a question. If she was asking for his help, she truly needed it. "I can come down tomorrow," he said finally, hoping the answer was sufficient.

"You still have my address?"

"Unless you've moved, then yes, I've got it."

"Good, so I'll see you soon, then."

"That, my dear, you will."

He could practically hear her smile through the phone. "Good night, Xavier. I miss you."

"Night, El. You too."

She hung up quickly, sighing deeply, crossing his name off of her list. She was sitting at her kitchen table, looking at the names and contact information of everyone she wanted to reach, sifting through months worth of paperwork in a feeble attempt to get something together. No one from the resistance was answering her calls - not that she was surprised. She wasn't sure if it was because they knew it was her or because they weren't around to hear the phone ring, but she felt that she would have to start resorting to letters soon. She hadn't handwritten a letter in a long, long time, seeing as everyone she needed could be reached in person, but it was always something she would fall back on if need be. She was familiar with the process, but not in a formally treasonous sense; the thought of sitting down, writing a letter to Voskivy, and sending it off without it being intercepted was a difficult thing to grasp. She could never be sure of what people were doing, especially now.

She would try ringing each member whose information she had once more, again to no avail. She would ponder any other options for a moment, realizing there were none, and she would reluctantly pull out paper and a pen.

She considered typing these letters, but then printing would be traced back to her, and seeing as no one (with the exception of Xavier and Fyo) had ever seen her handwriting, sending a written letter with no return address would be safer than typing one out.

She could only stare down at the blank paper. She knew she could call Fyodor if she was desperate for inspiration - he was full of it - but she thought it best to keep him involved as little as possible. His contributions would no doubt be helpful, but as they had both agreed, this was not something he could safely be a part of until it was secure. It was already enough that he knew what she was planning, and she wondered if even that had overstepped the boundary they both knew needed to be set.

She thought of what Kassander may have told her to write in this moment. He was always a very righteous person. When he believed in a cause, he fought for it, and he would stop at nothing to make sure that what he thought was right would prevail - it was a trait that had undoubtedly rubbed off on her, increasing what sort of hero complex she already seemed to have. She knew that he would tell her that she had to write exactly what she was thinking. He would tell her that if she wanted a response, she would have to be honest. That people, especially those who already have a prejudice against her, would never take the time to respond to something that seemed superficial and shallow.

She tapped the pen aggressively against the table, rolling it between her knuckles, trying desperately to think of how she should start this. Hi? To whom it may concern? Every idea she thought of sounded stupid. She had to measure this very carefully - this was her first and only chance for interaction - and she already had a disadvantage. Surely, her reputation would precede her. Surely, they knew who she was. And surely, they'd want nothing to do with her.

She had gone back and forth about addressing each individual by name to start the letters, the only thing holding her back being that she wasn't sure if it would be seen as too friendly for someone who was coming from the opposing end. She didn't know what reactions the formalities, or lack thereof, would emit, and she didn't want to make the wrong opening statement.

She stood. She paced. She had a smoke. She came back. And she sat, putting her pen to paper without a second thought, beginning her series of letters.

She'd address them by name. She'd pretend that she had known them for her whole life. In a way, after all, she had.

Her letters were soft around the edges. They were very unlike how she spoke to people face to face. She couldn't scare them off. She knew the odds of her receiving a single reply were low, and she was not going to make it zero. She was beside herself as she sealed them - a handful of letters to a handful of people who most definitely hated her. She looked down at the pile of envelopes in her hands, taking one deep breath, before stepping out of her apartment into the hallway. The lights were dim, fading with time, and she knew someone would have to replace them eventually, or things would go dark. She ensured each corridor was empty before she committed to going that way. It wasn't that anyone in this building intimidated her (much the opposite - she was a superior and she was scary). It was more that she did not want to have any conversations. Not at this hour, when she was half asleep, when she'd just tried to make a dozen phone calls, and when she'd written pages upon pages of letters. She was spent, and though she could still slit any man's throat, she knew that her wit was not where it should be to talk her way out of a situation that may arise.

She reached the bottom floor of the building, sliding the letters into the mailbox that was provided before she turned on her heels and went back up the stairs without a second look. Her hands were folded over her chest and her head was down. She managed to catch a glimpse of a clock as she moved - almost three in the morning - and with a huff, she began to trek back up to her apartment. The metal steps were irritatingly loud, and she tried her best to land on her toes and put as little weight as possible on each one, but silence meant patience, and patience was not something she had left. She gave up, stomping up the stairs, ignoring the loud clanging caused by thick boots hitting thin metal, hoping that no one would wake up. In a time that felt both excruciatingly long and all too fast, she reached her door, lids falling closed as she took the doorknob in her hand, reaching into her pocket for her key, throwing the door open and slamming it shut. She kicked her boots off, and as if something in the air had shifted, she was suddenly wide awake.

Her brows furrowed, her hand finding her knife, fingers wrapping around the hilt delicately. She held it chest level, eyes scanning the dark apartment, moving slowly, this time ensuring that she wouldn't make a sound as she crept through the space.

She didn't know what it was that had set her off, but something felt *wrong*. The blood in her body felt as though it had drained, her hands cold, her eyes darting back and forth between anything they could find to land on. She was very unprepared for this. She didn't assume that she would have to be on alert at this hour, in her own room.

She walked through the kitchen - no one was there - and she continued through to the living room, looking behind furniture, peering onto the balcony, only to be met with empty space.

She turned her head. Her bedroom door was closed.

She was certain she had left it open.

She took a deep breath, paying attention to how the air flowed through her body. For a split second, she was at peace, and as soon as she began to exhale, she swung the door open.

There was someone standing at her window.

The figure turned, illuminated only by the moonlight. It was a familiar silhouette that of a male most definitely, but in her hazy mindset, she couldn't put her finger on it. It wasn't Fyodor; she was certain of it, but who else would let themselves in like this?

"What are you doing out this late?"

Her grip on the knife tightened. It was Milton Haas.

"What are you doing in my room?"

"Checking on you."

She stepped forward cautiously. He turned his body towards her, and even in the dark, she could make out the outline of his stupid shit-eating grin.

"I don't need to be checked on."

"Oh, but you do when you're making phone calls to people you shouldn't be talking to."

She scoffed. "What? I can't call my old superior to talk?"

He moved towards her. Her grip on the knife never loosened, and her gaze on him never faltered. She did not trust Milton Haas.

"You and I both know that is not what I am referring to."

The tension was thick. He was so close to her now, touching her, almost, as his tall frame loomed over her. He was staring through her. She hoped he was seeing nothing.

Unbeknownst to him, though, he had no idea that she was used to being the smaller one. She was almost always being attacked by men who were bigger and stronger than she was, and if anything, she welcomed the attempt to intimidate by size with open arms. It was her forte. She would never cower away from a fight, especially from one that seemed all too easy to lose.

"Don't you have things to do?"

"I'm doing them."

There was a moment of silence. It couldn't have been over a second long, but they both stood, unmoving, unspeaking, barely breathing. In that moment of eerie static, the gears in Eleri's head clicked. That moment of silence told her more than any words ever could. She was familiar with it. She had met it many times. It was the calm before the storm. It was the breath before the plunge.

It was the silence that preceded death.

Before either of them could think, Milton's hands had wrapped themselves around Eleri's throat, pushing her back against the wall. She haphazardly slashed his wrist with her knife, sending his one arm reeling backward, making his grip on her throat loosen, giving her the opportunity to kick him, causing him to stumble. He stood his ground as she pushed off the wall, regaining a breath that she lost all too quickly as he hit her in the face.

She felt the blood trickling from her nose onto her lips. She felt her head spinning. More importantly, she saw him moving towards her, quickly.

She ducked under his arm as he reached for her, appearing behind his back, and before she could measure her actions, her *killer instinct* took over. The killer instinct that had allowed her so many promotions in so little time. The killer instinct that made people fear their lives around her.

The killer instinct that saw her knife sink into Milton Haas' back.

She hadn't realized what she had done until he coughed. In the dark, she saw the viscous liquid escape his throat. It would stain the wall, she thought. She would have to clean it.

Then, as she removed the blade from his skin, he fell forwards.

He hit the ground with a thud. She stood still for a moment, preparing for him to bounce back to his feet, to call her stupid and pathetic for thinking she could do something like that to him. And as nothing came, she took one step, knelt down, and slowly turned his body to see his face.

Her heart skipped a beat.

She had killed Milton Haas.

Six.

There is a mountain near the home I grew up in that I used to frequent often with my parents when I was young. We had a dog for the first few years of my life, which, come to think of it, I haven't seen someone with a pet in years, but I digress... and my father used to take the dog and me on walks up Aloneia Peak. My dad and I were walking the dog once, on our way up the hill, as we normally did. It was always a tense walk, especially when mom wasn't there, and I can't remember what I did to set him off, but one moment we were walking along the ledge and the next, I was laying on my back, staring up at the seemingly infinite mountain. My head was spinning, and I felt nauseous, and there was blood coming from my side. My father had pushed me off in a fit of rage, and I felt too weak and tired to give him a piece of my mind. Eventually, I was told

I had two broken ribs, probably some semblance of a head injury, as well. My father obviously wanted nothing to do with me, and my mother didn't care enough to actively help, so I waited alone in my room for a few days until the pain was gone and decided I'd let my ribs figure themselves out as I went on. Somehow, the dog had died while I was out. I had my suspicions about what had happened, but that was not a conversation I was willing to get myself into.

From that day forward, I only went to the peak by myself. I only did many things by myself. I hadn't quite been old enough to wrap my head around what my father was like as a person despite how he always behaved around my mother, so the whole pushing me off a hill ordeal was a shock to me. I think, from that day forward, I may have assumed that everyone was going to push me down the hill - metaphorically, of course. I think that having that moment and the subsequent time spent alone only led me to realize that at the end of the day, all I have is myself. Maybe that's why I find it so easy to kill, or to plan, or to completely destroy. Maybe I know that there's nothing anyone can do to hurt me besides doing just that - physically hurting me.

And pain is no longer something I feel. So if they want to get to me, they'll have to have me dead.

- The Found Diary of Eleri Roman, p. 55

—

Fyodor sat in his apartment, head leaning back in one of his oversized chairs, a glass of alcohol in his hand, a cigarette dangling from his lips, some music from what had to have been over one hundred years ago playing softly through his speaker. Most of his nights were spent like this. If he was ever lucky enough to sleep, it would be in moments like these; where he was able to feel detached from the world, where the comforting music passed down through his family was serving as his blanket, where for a brief second, he could forget about everything.

He had a photo album somewhere that housed one single photo of each member of his direct family since the early 1900s. Imagine that - all of these people he would never meet were related to him, their pictures pasted in a book that was in his possession. Sometimes, on nights like these, he'd flip through it. He would think about what life was like all those years ago. He thought, in the deepest part of his heart, that it could not have been much different than now.

Other times, he would stand on his balcony and imagine that he was somewhere else, some song from who knows when guiding his mind to a place he would never know. He always had quite the vivid imagination, and the other wars his parents had told him about were often subjects of these fantasies. He wasn't sure why. Perhaps, he was trying to connect these people with himself the only way he knew how. He would wonder what it was like, and if he'd have survived back then. His sentimental side no doubt came from his mother - when she handed him a necklace and told him to take good care of it, explaining that it had belonged to one of his great-great uncles from way way back in the First World War. The notion was inconceivable to him. How long ago was that he'd asked, and with a smile, she replied.

Oh, only a couple hundred years.

He had looked at her in awe, the first and only time he put it around his neck. He'd never taken it off since.

It vaguely reminded him of the necklaces they gave him when he enlisted in the army for the war against Voskivy.

His sweet, loving mother. He always wondered what had happened to her.

His father was killed in action. This, he knew, because he received the letter saying so, to which he simply sighed and began to think about how to tell his brother. He remembered his brother wailing, and the only thing that would get him to come down was Fyodor's breaking voice - *mommy will be home soon.*

She never returned. They never got a letter. They never got a call. Fyo could only assume she had died, too. The only alternative was the thought that she had found something better and no longer cared for her children.

That idea was too much for his heart to handle.

So, he went with the easier and more comprehensible option - that she, too, was dead but that there was too much going on to receive the news.

He missed his family. He would never think of things like this outside of his moments of solitude, and for Eleri, who had a strenuous relationship with the people in her life, this conversation would be impossible. But sometimes, the longing and the hurt were overwhelming. His younger brother, who was so funny and so kind and so pure. He didn't deserve to only know war. He didn't deserve to know heartache at such a young age. He deserved to know more about their parents. His father, despite how closed off he was, had always been one of the strongest men Fyodor had ever known and so incredibly intelligent.

And his mother… his mother, who loved him more than anything, who taught him everything she knew, who gave him that necklace and showed him music and wrote him stories when he couldn't sleep.

He missed his family. So much.

He took another drag of his cigarette, took the final sip of his drink, and accepting the fact that he'd once again be getting no sleep, he went to go refill it.

The crystal bottle touched the edge of his glass gently, the sight of the deep bronze liquid bringing him a strange sense of comfort. He took a sip from the glass, then, after a moment of contemplation, set it down and took the bottle in his hand instead, as he walked back over to his chair.

Just as he was about to sit down, there was a frantic knock at the door.

For a moment, he thought his mind was playing tricks on him. He raised an eyebrow, turning to look at the clock that rested on the wall behind him. Squinting, he barely made out *three-forty* in the morning.

Who was at his door at three-forty in the morning?

He walked towards the door with hesitance, trading his cigarette for a small handgun, gently placing the bottle down on a table near the door after taking another drink.

He turned the handle gently, and before he had the chance to step away, someone shoved him aside, slid into the room, and closed the door.

He flicked on the light, squinting. "Eleri? What's going on?"

She pushed him into the house, closing his blinds, running a hand through her hair once before taking his face in her hands.

"I am fucked."

There was a silence that followed as she pulled away, pacing the apartment, lighting a cigarette. This uncharacteristic behavior was incredibly worrying to Fyodor. What had gotten into her? All these years, not so much as a sideways glance from her. And now, she was shaking, her eyes locked onto his, silently begging for him to come up with a response for a problem he didn't quite yet understand.

"I need you to tell me what's going on," he said finally, his voice soft.

She took a moment, closing her eyes, straightening her back. "Milton Haas is dead," she said finally. He opened his mouth to speak, but there was more. "I killed him."

"I was joking when I told you to plan his sudden and mysterious death, you know."

"Yeah, well, that's great. Too bad I'm not joking right now."

He didn't know if it was the alcohol or if it was the early hour of the morning, but for the first time in his life, he didn't believe her. "Eleri,"

"I stabbed him," she said, "and now I don't know what to do."

"Eleri," he said again. "What are you talking about?"

She reluctantly told him the story, sparing no details, and somewhere in the midst of the step-by-step recount of the events, his chest tightened, and he knew that she wasn't lying.

"I'm meeting up with Xavier today," she said, taking a drink from the bottle, finally settled enough to have a coherent conversation. "I don't know what I'm supposed to do."

"I'll stay over at your apartment," he said after a moment of silence. The only thing he could offer her until she thought of a plan was ensuring no one else would find out about what had happened.

She mumbled something then, barely audible, to the point of him almost missing it entirely.

"Come again?"

She put the drink down and pursed her lips. Somewhere, music was still softly playing.

"He's in the closet."

He blinked hard once. "He's in the closet?" He repeated.

"Where else was I supposed to put him?" She groaned, the bottle once again finding its way to her lips. "I already have to bleach everything. I couldn't just have him sitting there, you know, in the way... do you want me to throw him off the balcony next time?"

"There won't be a next time."

She looked at him with a frown, then a small smile emerged on her face, and suddenly, she was giggling. She leaned forward on the table, her head in her hands. She looked up at the bottle beside her.

"I'm becoming my father," she groaned.

He stood, ruffling her hair. "Your father would never stab his C.O., darling. You've got him beat there."

She sat at the table for one more moment before standing, walking over to Fyo's door. "Come on," she said, "we have things to do."

He switched off the music and followed her to the door, throwing his things on. "Where's your jacket?"

"I didn't bring one... I just kind of ran out of the house."

"Do you want one of mine?"

She shook her head. "No point. We're just crossing the street."

"You'll get cold."

Moments like these confirmed the one thing Eleri was insecure about. She was so sure of herself, and of her own decisions, and of who she was. She knew that when she made a plan, people would follow it, and it would succeed. She knew that when she lifted her knife to someone's throat, they'd melt, following her every command. She knew that whatever she wanted would be done for her if she was assertive enough in her demand.

But from a young age, she had learned that the only actions she could control were her own, and no matter what she did, everything else, ultimately, would be out of her hands.

That included Fyodor.

In the back of her mind, her single insecurity plagued her - it was a disease that could not be cured, it was red paint bleeding into a white canvas, it was the feeling of being struck over and over again until she was too weak to stand.

It was her worst nightmare.

She was unavailable. She was violent. She was commanding. She was every undesirable characteristic put into one person. She knew that Fyodor had to cling to her during the war. She knew that was the one thing she could hang over his head if she ever had to. For years, she was able to fall back on the fact that he needed her to survive. But now that it was over, there was no chain binding them together, and she was insufferable. It was bound to end, just as everything always did.

He was the only person she had, and she was almost certain that he'd have enough of her eventually.

But then, there were moments like this.

You'll get cold.

Such a small statement, said in passing, barely even any thought behind it. But it showed that he cared.

It was reassurance. She took it and held it to her heart.

"I'm okay, Fyo. Thank you, though."

With a shrug, he opened the door, letting her out before following her.

Fyodor's apartment was different from hers. His door led directly outside, onto a thick set of concrete stairs that would help them down to the ground. It had openings to the other apartment doors below his, leading each door right to the sidewalk outside. She shivered as they stepped into the road, folding her arms across her chest, and Fyodor, noticing her discomfort, opened his jacket and pulled her into his side, draping the oversized coat over both their shoulders.

She pretended to be irritated at the gesture. She appreciated it more than anything.

They spent the next few hours in her apartment. He forced her to take a nap, and he cleaned off her floor and wall as best he could. She woke only a few hours after she'd fallen asleep and he'd put together some breakfast for her.

"Your turn to nap, no?"

He gasped. "And leave poor Haas alone? Never."

She giggled. The knock at the door came then, and she, with one last glance at Fyodor, and tightened her ponytail and stepped towards the source of the noise. She opened it, whispering a quick hello to Xavier, and she followed him out into the hall.

Fyo loved her, but she was killing him. Sometimes, he felt like he couldn't keep up with her.

***

Eleri and Xavier had reached the restaurant fairly quickly. She studied his features, a warm feeling coming over her as she did so, remembering how on edge he always used to seem. He looked older, yes, but he appeared to be much more rested. There were no longer bags under his eyes, the creases on his forehead seemed to have faded, and his white hair had grown long and healthy. He looked content, for once, and despite the fact that she noticed the flashes of *something* in his eyes every so often, she knew, in her heart, that this was the best he had ever felt.

The conversation, at first, was light nothingness. How've you been? Life's been crazy. But staring down into the black coffee, seeing her distorted shadow over the liquid, she began to speak.

"Xavier,"

"Yes, dear,"

She took a breath, her finger tracing the rim of the mug, the chain of her bracelet dangling gently on the outside of the glass.

"How much do you know about the involvement of officers in the school curriculum?"

Xavier's dark eyes narrowed in thought as he ran a hand through his beard. His thick, golden rings glistened under the dim overhead lights in the restaurant, the scar running from his palm to his wrist visible as his sleeve fell.

"Why do you ask?"

His voice was rough and deep, the sound of honey and a campfire. Eleri knew that it was only the result of chain smoking for his entire life, but it brought her comfort that she had never felt. His voice was the feeling of a warm, wool blanket being wrapped around shaking shoulders on a cold day. He was the one person she looked up to, and he knew this. For this reason, whenever he spoke to her, he ensured he measured his words carefully. He would never raise his voice. He would never become accusatory. He had always wanted a daughter, but life became too busy too quickly, and suddenly the opportunity was taken from him. He saw her the same way she saw him, as the one thing he never had. And, as a result, he was able to see her as more than just an asset. He knew that he was incredibly lucky - for the Reaper to trust him as much as she did, he had clearly done something right - and he was uniquely positioned both in a tactical sense and in a personal regard.

"I learned some things," she said, her hand stopping its movement, now resting against the handle. "And I need to know more."

Xavier swallowed thickly. He knew *some* things, yes, and he no longer felt he had any obligation to keep them private now that he was out of work, but Eleri acted quickly. He knew she would not like what she heard, and he knew that when she didn't like things, she changed them. He just didn't know how drastic her actions would be in this instance. He was smart enough to know that now, with no war and no preoccupations, she would have all the time in the world to devote the abundance of energy she had to whatever cause struck her as important. The information that Xavier had readily available would more than likely change her entire view on everything she had been fighting for and against for her entire life.

He took a deep breath, his chest rumbling, and his gaze broke from hers. "I know enough."

She raised an eyebrow. She chose her words carefully. Deliberately. "Do you know about... amendments made to the history curriculum?"

He knew this is what she'd be asking about. He didn't know how the information had fallen into her lap, as he knew she'd never even been aware of any allusion to it before, so she wouldn't have gone in search of it. With her luck, the universe realized she didn't have anything to do and gave her another controversy.

"I've never known the extent to which it happens," he said, "but I know changes are made. I was never fully involved with it."

She frowned. "At your big position... you weren't fully involved?"

He shook his head. "No. It goes a lot deeper than anything I'd be able to explain. All that matters is that everyone unanimously agreed that I'd be unfit to perform in a setting like that."

She folded one leg underneath her body, perching on her chair. "So then, what? You know things happen, or you know *what* happens?"

"What I know," he said slowly, "is that children haven't had a history book with an accurate recount of events in over fifty years."

She took a sip of her coffee. "Children have been taught altered history for fifty years... here? Or everywhere?"

Xavier's hands folded into each other, the single word hanging off his tongue bound to change her entire trajectory.

"Here."

There was a heavy silence as Eleri attempted to process what she had just learned. Here. Here. Here.

The word rattled against her skull. *Here.*

She closed her eyes for a moment, and a feeling of disappointment that she had never felt before washed over her. She thought back to school, what she remembered of it, and how she was always deemed one of the smartest in class. She thought back to when she first joined this fight, how she was told how great she was every step of the way. How she fought for this army without a second thought.

"So when I was selected at fifteen for this thing because I was the best academically," she whispered, her heart breaking, "what they actually meant was that I was the most brainwashed."

He was silent. He could never argue this. The kids with the best grades were the kids who learned quickly, who trusted the state, who could take orders. The kids with the best physical were kids who had potential to be soldiers. The kids with both, much like Eleri, were gifts to them.

A chill ran down her spine. She took a deep breath, trying to calm herself. She had never felt sadness like this. "So everything I did," her voice was shaking. "Everybody I killed, every stupid trap I planted… *watching my friends die*… it was for nothing, wasn't it? We were never even invaded, were we? This wasn't a revenge war. This was unprompted, right? This was just… God."

Eleri hadn't expected the conversation to go this way. She expected Xavier to tell her who did what, to tell her what had been changed and what hadn't, to tell her what the purpose of it all was. She had come to this conclusion on her own, and she knew she wouldn't be able to *make* the conversation go her way, but this, in her mind, was not even in the realm of possibility. This was never even something she'd considered before.

She thought she was smart. She was dreadfully wrong.

Xavier wanted to be delicate with the situation. This news, to her, must've been earth-shattering.

"Milton Haas is dead," she said then, suddenly.

"Sorry?" It was his turn to feel dumbfounded.

She dropped sugar into her coffee, stirring it absentmindedly. She had become detached from this conversation. Xavier could see it.

"I killed him. Not on purpose, but I did it."

"Eleri, *I'm sorry*, what?"

She shrugged, taking a sip. "Doesn't even matter, really. He was annoying, anyway. Didn't know too much about anything."

Xavier watched her finish her coffee quickly and pull her jacket back on. "Let me ask you one thing," she said, buttoning the front. "All these years, when you *mentored* me, when you taught me everything you knew… did you do it as an act of service to the state?"

"It started that way but did not end that way. Of course, that is all it was at the beginning. That's how it is, because I am your superior, and I have to train you. But if it was still that way, I wouldn't have met with you today. I wouldn't have cared to."

She sighed, exasperated. "Xav, you knew all of this was happening, and you went along with it?"

"It's a lot more complicated where I stand."

She eyed him. "Yeah. Sure. You never thought to tell me?"

He wanted to salvage this. "El, I -"

"Why did this war start?"

"I think we should -"

"Xavier," her voice was brash. He had heard her speak in this tone to those in her group or to those she was commanding in her early I.O. days. He had smiled at the harsh intonation before, proud of how she didn't take what people threw at her, but this time, as it was directed at him, he felt his skin crawl.

"Why did we fight in Voskivy for *fifteen years*? Why was it that we fought to win or die, not to compromise?"

Xavier looked at her, as he did so, recalling all of the work his wife had done. *Wars are fought to gain power. Wars are fought to rule by fear.*

He remembered, vaguely, the papers she had written about the World Wars. The first - an assassination that started a chain of events that ended with war being declared everywhere. The second - a fascist dictator who wanted to wipe out an entire population. The third - the abduction and public execution of five world leaders leading to the deadliest war the world had ever seen. The fourth - nothing more than two world superpowers going head to head, for no reason other than what could be chalked up as insane nationalism, declaring war on each other and forcing their allies to get involved. Why do wars start? For power. Always for power.

He recalled the days, the months, leading to the start of the war. He recalled the hushed conversations he was once a part of before he was inevitably removed. The decisions were never his to make, but he would always have to face the consequences.

"Why do you think we've still got troops in there, El?"

She was silent. "I don't know."

Xavier had goosebumps along his arms. "We wanted their land. They wouldn't give it to us."

She pressed her lips together. "So we decided to just go take it?"

Xavier nodded slowly. "Their surrenders mean nothing. The only way to take what they have is to get rid of them entirely."

Seven.

When I was young, I had these horrible recurring night terrors. They happened so often that I was convinced they were normal, and I was sure that there was no possibility of sleep without them. At first, I would wake up screaming, but as time went on, I learned that there was no point in fighting the inevitable. I figured that if they weren't going to go away, I should just live in them. So that's what I began to do. I would live in these nightmares whenever I went to sleep, feeling every moment, seeing every face. They were always of some man murdering me. It was always on a rainy, dark night, with thunder and lightning crashing around me. There was always a struggle, and there was always pain, almost real enough to feel it. One thing I became thankful for was that having those plague me as a child only allowed me to feel less scared when bad things happened to me in real life. Any horror that occurred when I was awake was never nearly as bad as the things I felt in my nightmares, and I was able to get through a lot of horrible things in my youth by reminding myself that it could be so much worse. It could always be worse.

And then the war happened, and I was injured time and time again, and I watched the only people I cared about die in front of me, and the whole time, I just kept reminding myself that it could be worse. It could always, always, always be worse.

I was right. The first month after Voskivy's surrender, the month of the haunting lack of gunfire, and of the sound of children laughing reminding me more of death than death itself, and of standing on top of my building in the middle of the night wondering how bad it could truly be if I threw myself off... that was worse. That was the nightmare that consumed me.

I could fight off soldiers, and I could fight off dreams. I could never fight off my own mind.

- The Found Diary of Eleri Roman, p. 60

—

Fyodor had found a way to dispose of Milton Haas before Eleri had returned from her excursion (he preferred not to revisit it, but he could say in full confidence that he was glad there was no one around as he worked). He cleaned out the closet, made sure it didn't have any odor, and by the time she returned, it was as if Haas was never there. Fyo was always quick in cleaning up. He wasn't sure exactly why or how he had been graced with such a gift, but he was glad that he had been given that talent. It was pure insanity, but in a situation like this, it was a saving grace.

Eleri returned, immediately sitting him down, reciting everything she had just been told by Xavier, expressing her frustration, and explaining that she would no longer be waiting to learn things, instead finding them on her own. Fyo had expected some kind of outburst like this from her for a while, and if he was honest, he was surprised that it took this long to happen. A few months of working some fairly tame job, not commanding, not leading, not doing anything that she had grown so used to doing… it only made sense that something of this nature would happen, especially to someone like her.

Fyodor had come to terms with their reality, and he supported her hot-headedness wholeheartedly.

She told him that if no one called her from the resistance in a week's time, she'd just go in on her own. Who would stop her, after all? No one in their right mind would get in her way. She still had her reputation, and they still consumed the lies they were fed. It was exactly as it always had been for everyone but the two of them, and she was trying very hard to remember that.

He left her that night after they watched the sunset, as he always did. He asked her time and time again if she was alright, if she needed anything or if she wanted him to stay.

"No. Thank you. I'll come grab you if something changes. Have a good night. Be safe."

She sat alone in the dim light of her balcony. She looked down, her blue veins painfully visible against her wrist, her bones protruding, her skin translucent. She felt absolutely horrible, be it from the general lack of self-care or from the events of the day, she didn't know. All she could focus on was the pounding in her head and the knot in her stomach.

She lit herself a cigarette, trying to stop her hands from shaking. Maybe, if she had something to hold onto, she would relax a bit. But it felt different smoking on her own and the usual comfort that came from the stupid thing was nowhere to be found.

She dropped her head into her hands, taking a deep breath. She wouldn't cry. She didn't do that. She didn't even *understand* crying. What exactly did it do? It didn't help anyone at all, it didn't further any solutions, and it looked ugly. Even if she did cry, hypothetically, what exactly would she be crying about right now? The fact that she was lied to? Okay, but crying wouldn't change the past. The fact that she was scared for the future? Again, okay, but she'd been scared of the future for a decade now, and she had never let a tear slip before. What was she going to do now? Broken alone on her balcony in the middle of the winter? Laughable. Pathetic. What kind of *Reaper* did that, huh?

And if someone were to walk in, because apparently people other than Fyo felt permitted to do that, what would they think? They'd tell people, certainly. There was no doubt in her mind that word would spread like wildfire if someone were to see her cry.

With her head in her hands, she let out a strangled breath, her entire body trembling as the air escaped her.

Then, she sat up, taller than before, finishing her cigarette, crushing it under her boot, throwing it off of the balcony, stepping back into her apartment.

That was enough. That was more than enough.

Her phone rang the moment she stepped back inside.

She walked over to it reluctantly, almost debating if she should answer it or not, but the phone was at her before she thought it through entirely.

"Hello?"

"Am I speaking to a certain... Eleri Vera Roman?"

Eleri paused. "This is she?"

"You wrote to me. My name is Clover O'Caine."

Eleri's heart went to her throat. It had only been a day. Could the letters really have gotten to Voskivy so quickly? This was an opportunity unlike any other. Clover, as far as Eleri's research had shown, was one of the most important leaders of the resistance force in the main region. She had influence, and she had status, and she was *smart*.

Of all the people she had written to, she least expected a reply from Clover.

"Clover, wow, I didn't expect to hear from you. Thank you for reaching out, really. It means so much to me that you'd take this chance."

"What did you need to talk about?"

There was a pause. Clover was concise and cold in her phrasing - as expected from someone who had been terrorized by Eleri and her army for years. "I... there are some things I need to discuss with you. They're crucial, but... I don't think it's safe to talk over the phone."

Clover frowned on the other end. She pulled her lower lip between her teeth in thought. Of course, she'd heard of the Reaper. She had never come face to face with Eleri during the war, but she was constantly reminded of *some girl her age from Aloneia who was heading this attack.* Clove always felt slightly inferior to Eleri, despite never having met her. The relationship she had with the girl she'd never met was as complex as it was strange; any report about Eleri that Clove was able to see only helped to mold her way of leading. It was part of the reason she'd decided to call. She recognized the name, and before she had a chance to be advised not to, Clover was reaching for the phone.

But now, she realized she may have been moving too quickly and not thinking enough. This could be a trap or a ploy to take her out. Clove had her reservations about meeting Eleri, but she didn't want to pass up an opportunity.

Clover sighed, running her hand over her neck, anchoring it in her thick, coiled hair. "And why would it be unsafe to talk over the phone?"

"Because," Eleri's response was quick, "I am going to be very honest here, I don't know who listens to my calls, and frankly, if they hear some of the things we need to discuss... you will be in a much worse position than you are now."

"So why would you admit to knowing your wires are tapped on a call with me? Whoever is listening will hear that, too."

Clover swore she heard a chuckle. "I don't care what they do with me anymore. I'm looking out for *you*."

There was something in her words that made Clover believe her. Something so defiant in her tone, so confident in her small rebellion, that Clover wanted to bring her into her own home and hug her. She wasn't sure if this was the effect of years of hearing about her and finally speaking to her, or if it was because Clove was incredibly understanding and empathetic, but she believed every word that came out of Eleri's mouth, no matter how dangerous the woman was.

"Okay," she said, breathy, submissive. "What do you want to do?"

Eleri was very careful to measure the words Clover used. It was *what do you want to do, not what do you want me to do.* The difference was subtle but deliberate. Clover was keeping Eleri's power over herself, not letting it control Clove. It was impressive. It was the sign of someone who was a leader.

"I can come to you," Eleri said. "I can meet you past the border fences. There's no way you'll be able to get in here - not with all the border officers they've got out there. And there's no way they'll stop me from getting through to you. They wouldn't *dare*."

"How are you going to know where to go once you get through the borders?"

There was a lump in Eleri's throat as she responded. "Three months isn't too long. Give me a place, and I'll remember where it is."

Clover noticed how her voice dropped. She noticed how there was a layer of emotion that hadn't previously been there. She noticed, though she didn't want to, the implications of Eleri's response. "Do you know where the Sixteenth Building is?"

"I do."

"When will you be coming?"

Eleri pondered this for a moment. "When will you have me?"

Clover tugged on the chord that attached the phone to the wall as she thought. Somewhere, distant, there was a leaking pipe. She could hear it. "How does the 20th work for you?"

"It works perfectly. Are you good at around 10:00?"

"Yes. Perfect. I'll meet you then." and, after a moment, "Good night, Miss Roman."

Eleri smiled into the phone. "Good night. Take care of yourself."

Clover put the phone back on the wall, tugging at her curls in frustration. "Shit,"

There was a quiet knock at her door, followed by footsteps. Clover turned around, expecting to see someone with an incident report or with bad news, but her demeanor immediately softened when she laid eyes on the woman before her.

"You okay?"

Clover sighed, walking towards the woman, embracing her, placing a quick kiss on her cheek.

"Yeah, babe. I'm good." Clover took the woman's hand in hers, leading her to the bed, sitting down gently on the edge. "We have something big coming."

Clarissa was Clover's right-hand woman, her closest confidant, the only reason she had lived this long, and, to put it bluntly, the love of her life. The pair were inseparable. Clove and Claire were two women who - though they would never take credit for it - were the sole reason the resistance still existed. They were smart, and they were experienced, and they would never ask people to do things that they wouldn't do themselves. They were great leaders and even better people.

"Is it a good thing?" Clarissa's voice was soft, her deep green eyes peering into Clove's brown ones. Clarissa Silver was every kind of beautiful - thick, black eyebrows, raven hair down her back, deep, brown skin, freckles and scars lining her sharp features. But despite her intimidating exterior, Clove knew her differently. Clarissa was soft-spoken. She was the mediator. She was justice, and she had a heart that housed more love than anyone could begin to fathom. Clarissa never liked fighting. She could do it, of course, and she was *great* at it, but it was not something she prided herself on, nor a skill she wished to improve. Because of this, she was a strategist. She reported on whatever she could. Any casualties? Her job. Any new assignments? Her job. She *oversaw* everything. She was the backbone of this resistance.

"Eleri Roman is coming to meet me."

Clarissa's eyes went wide. Her eyebrows raised. She was shocked. "By force?"

Clove shook her head, pulling the letter out of her pocket, handing it to Claire: "I got this earlier today. I called her just now. She's coming here. She says there's something that she needs to talk to me about. You can come with me if you want, but I don't know what's going to happen."

There was a heavy silence in the room. Clarissa's fingers found Clover's. "I should," she said, "in case I have to do a write-up."

Clove smiled, pressing a quick kiss to her lips.

"What does she want to talk about?" Claire asked, standing, leading Clove out of the room. The pair had begun to make their way down the hallways of the safehouse, ensuring that everybody was inside and that the building was secure. They had done this nightly since they'd realized that the troops from Aloneia were not planning on pulling away from Voskivy. They had to make sure that if nothing else was left standing, that if nothing else would ever be habitable, that this building remained. They were directly housing about one hundred people and had access to about three hundred more, all of which were part of this resistance. They knew it would be better to have two buildings, and they understood the potential disasters that would come because there was only one space in which the majority of them stayed. They had weighed the pros and cons, and on multiple occasions, had considered kicking people out in order to ensure the survival of half of their people as opposed to the hypothetical scenario of none. They had looked time and time again for a building that would work as a second safehouse, but with troops lining the streets and with people being abducted in broad daylight, the chances of being able to assess an area properly and thoroughly enough to make a decision were next to none, and they'd not yet had an opportunity. They wouldn't know where to begin, either - the other small forces scattered throughout Voskivy were not affiliated with them, and any approach had the potential to be misinterpreted.

Clover waved at one of the younger boys who was running to his bedroom as she responded. "I don't know exactly, but I feel like it *has* to be important. You should've heard her on the phone, Claire. She was nothing like what I'd expected her to be."

Clover punched a code into the keypad beside the heavy, metal door that led to a stairwell to the basement. The door slid open slowly, with a loud screech, and Claire pursed her lips, taking note of it.

"What do you mean?" Claire asked as they stepped through, starting down into the second area.

Yellow light flickered above them as they traveled. There was still the sound of a dripping tap somewhere in the distance, hushed murmurs from behind walls, and every so often, a sneeze, laugh, or a cough.

Claire often thought about how these people were still in such good spirits. She had never brought the subject up with Clove; the woman was far too busy doing tough things, and Claire had only noticed it because of how much she spent in the safehouse, so to Clover, it would be irrelevant. It wasn't that Clove wouldn't care, more that she wouldn't be able to find a way to relate to or understand it.

"She sounded like… God, Claire, she sounded like *me*."

The statement took Clarissa back. "No one sounds like you, angel."

The pet name always made Clove's heart leap. She had thought it unsuitable, at first, because angels were *good* and *kind* and they *did not kill*. Clarissa, of course, had countered this. Angels are there to love and to protect, and that is what Clove did.

"You'd think so," Clove said, draping her arm across Clarissa's shoulders, smiling gently as they made their final rounds. "But I swear, I heard myself in her."

"You literally modeled yourself after her," Claire snickered, pinching Clove's side. "Your *idol.*"

"I did not!" She laughed. "I only thought that if she wasn't on the bad side, she'd be a hell of an addition for us." There was a pause. "Maybe that day is coming."

They had just reached the top of the steps, and Claire froze, taking Clover's arm. "What?"

"Look, I don't want to make any claims or get ahead of myself because I'll only probably be disappointed, but... she sounded really, really fed up. I don't know why. Maybe I'll find out soon, but she really did sound like she finally had enough."

They made their way to a hatch that led to the roof, as they did every night, to inspect the surroundings before getting a few hours of rest.

"So," Claire began, lifting the hatch, letting Clove through before following. "You think that maybe, there's some tiny possibility, that something drastic might happen?"

"Maybe."

"But have you thought that maybe, this girl is only pretending to act like this, and she'll come here and kill you? You know she's been keeping tabs on all of us, and you know her job was to make sure we didn't do anything too bothersome. If she comes here under the guise of having some big news, and the big news is just - *surprise, you're all dead* - then what was the point at all?"

They sat at the edge of the roof, overlooking the wreckage. "I have thought about it, yeah. But I don't know, Claire. Something about this really, really feels different."

The streets were quiet - the curfew that had been imposed along with the general fear of being abducted and put who knows where was more than enough to keep people inside for most of the day, even more so at night.

Claire opened her mouth to respond, but a voice from behind them made her pause her actions.

"Sorry to bother you," the voice said, "I just wanted to run a team by you for tomorrow morning's patrol."

Clover turned around, smiling, her eyes meeting a woman named Evginia. She was a bit older and was not native to Voskivy, but she knew a lot and had long since proved her loyalty to the cause. In all honesty, neither Clove nor Claire knew much about where this woman came from, who she was, or what had inspired her to join the losing team. All they knew was that she seemed to have a lot of answers to a lot of problems, and she never once stepped on their toes as leaders. Despite her ambiguity and her mystery, she was essential to the resistance. Evginia was incredibly well respected, often acting as the mother for many of the younger kids who had found themselves refuge in the safehouse and almost always being the mediator for stupid fights and arguments. She exuded love and peace, and that was something they all needed some of. Her blonde hair had begun to turn grey over the years but remained as thick and healthy as ever, tied into a braid down her back. Her piercing blue eyes were brighter than the world around them, her rosy cheeks and permanent smile bringing joy wherever she went.

"Yes, Genie, of course."

Clover stood, using Claire's shoulder as a support, and walked over to Evginia with a bounce in her step. Claire watched passively as Clover looked at a sheet, pointed at what she could only assume was a heading, and with a quick hug and a good night, sent her back down.

"I love her," Clover said, squatting beside Claire. There was a flare making its way through the sky somewhere in the distance. Claire leaned her head against Clover's leg.

"Bomb?" she questioned, watching the flare arc in the deep, dark sky.

Clove squinted, looking above it, then looking below. "I don't see any planes, so not by air if it is one." then, a dark laugh, "We'll have to wait and see."

One, two, three, four, five… the flare burnt out, falling out of view, and the pair sat with an eager anticipation, waiting to see if anything would come of it.

Thirty seconds had passed, and nothing seemed to be on fire or exploding, *damnit, I wanted a show*, and Clover stood, pulling Claire up with her. "We should go."

"Do you think," Claire said, as they made their way back to their rooms, "that the troops will pull out of here if Eleri Roman miraculously joins our side?"

Clover pondered this for a moment, her hand resting on the doorknob leading into her room. Her lower lip was pulled between her teeth, eyes cast down. Would they?

She found it laughable that they were talking about her *joining their team* as if this were a sport or a game. She found it laughable how desensitized they had become to everything going on around them. Even more, she found it *laughable* that the world knew what was happening, but none of them wanted to address what was not their problem. Fifteen years, not one lifeline.

"No," she said finally, "but she would give us a fighting chance."

Eight.

The day I was packing my things to head over to Voskivy was very, very strange for me. I had only ever seen the place with the intention to destroy it, and now I was coming in to save it. I thought, maybe, that I only really craved destruction and that I just loved causing chaos, so maybe this entire thing I was doing was only to start ruining Aloneia since I'd already ripped through Voskivy or something, but I knew I was just trying to rationalize in a strange way. I was trying to make myself believe that I was doing this on my own, without any external influence. That, of course, was not the truth, as much as I wanted it to be. At the end of the day, if I had never learned what I'd learned, I'd never be doing this. The struggle inside of me was one that I'd never vocalize - was I doing this to be benevolent, or was I doing this because I wanted to save my character?

Ruben Yorke would definitely be finding out about what was going on soon, Xavier Talon more than likely had a good idea of what I was doing, Milton Haas was dead, and I was going on some suicide mission to save a place that I'd been attacking my entire adult life. Because that's what rational people do.

I remember how I was carrying my weapons and this binder, and how I collected Fyodor, and how when we were walking down our street, for a moment, I felt like my old self. I was a machine, and he was my counterpart, and we were going to do what we did best: destroy, destroy, destroy. It was a very surreal feeling, walking through those borders with equipment and weapons that we'd not worn in months, but that still felt so normal to us. It was some sort of strange and horrific homecoming, but we had decided, after talking it over time and time again, that it would need to be done.

Out of the corner of my eye, as we walked through the gates, I caught Fyo absentmindedly tracing that horrific scar on his face. I pretended not to notice, but God did it pull at something inside of me.

I wondered if there was any recovery for either of us. We sure as hell didn't deserve it, but people never get what they deserve, anyways.

- The Found Diary of Eleri Roman, p. 67

—

Clover waited inside the building, sitting at a table, her fingers tapping against the flat surface. She had her weapons on her, and she had her girl at her side. She was ready for any outcome, for any turn. Her gloves covered her hands - no fingerprints - and she had already planted an explosive under the table.

Behind her, Claire was prepared to fight, even if she didn't want to. Her hand rested on Clover's shoulder as she watched the door, prepared for the worst.

Meanwhile, Eleri and Fyodor were navigating Voskivy as if they'd been born and raised there. They both knew the fastest, most inconspicuous way to get to Sixteenth. They both knew which paths would be filled with enough *shit* to hide behind. Eleri held a rifle in her hands, her three knives still against her thigh, a pistol on her hip, and a cover over the bottom half of her face. Fyodor, following closely behind her, was the same - save the knives for a second pistol - and as if they were back in an active warzone, they remained silent, communicating through glances and gestures.

The binder was in Fyo's backpack. It was somewhat surreal to him how quickly this entire situation had escalated. There was no way he could've predicted this when he showed El the document for the first time, but he wasn't angry about it. In fact, if anything, he was excited to be doing something important again. The mundane tasks they'd been assigned after the war was over were insufferable, and even if this would get them killed, at least they'd be going out on the right side of things.

They stood outside of the building for a moment when they finally arrived. Snow covered the path entirely, but fresh footprints leading in, not out, indicated the space was occupied. Eleri pulled her face covering down and sighed deeply.

"Well," she breathed, "it looks the exact same."

Fyodor could only nod in response. They had spent long nights in this building. It had been the place they always came back to - there was a sliding platform on the floor that led to a basement that locked from the inside. They'd hidden below these floors numerous times and made plans above them even more. Seeing it again with no immediate threat created a strange feeling, but the notion that they were now here for something that would have been inconceivable to them months ago was a rush on its own.

"Let's see if it's the same on the inside," Fyo responded in a breathy, unsure tone.

Eleri swallowed and walked up to the door, pushing it open before she had a chance to talk herself out of it. She stepped inside, looking up to the table at which she had sat numerous times, to see two women awaiting her.

"Clover?" She asked, her grip on her rifle tightening.

"Yeah. Hi, Eleri. Have a seat."

Clover motioned to the chair in front of her, and Eleri sat, laying her rifle on the floor. Fyodor stood behind her, mirroring the other woman.

Eleri stuck her hand out and Fyodor pulled the bag off his shoulders, handing her the binder.

"I know this seems strange," Eleri began, sliding the binder across the table. "But I have to do this."

Clover took the binder, staring for a moment, before turning to the marked page without being asked.

"What you're looking at is a proposed amended version of the history textbooks that will be taught in schools. If you look here," Eleri leaned forward, pointing at the picture of her and her friends, forgetting that she and Clover had only just met, "you'll find a picture of myself, and of Fyodor here behind me, and of four people we fought with, whose names have all been changed. If you read through the rest of the book, you'll find that every event that led up to the war has been changed, as well, and that it's been skewed so much that it seems like there was no other option than to fight."

Claire was peering over Clover's shoulder, scanning through the words on the papers, feeling her heart sink as she realized Eleri was right.

"Okay," Clove said finally, "what do you need me for, exactly? Because this doesn't seem like my problem."

"These troops that you're seeing every day... I learned that they're not planning on leaving until most, if not all of you are dead. And my fear… my fear is that they'll succeed, and they'll write you guys out of history entirely."

Clover's blood ran cold at that. "And you… what? You didn't know about this? You just now had this revelation after you won the war? After you personally saw to it that we were *fucked*?"

Eleri shook her head. She could get angry, but her anger nearly never resulted in a raised voice or an outburst of emotions. She had learned how to remain calm in situations such as these, despite any premature rage forming in her chest. "No. I didn't. I was fifteen when I started, and the only information we got was from our teachers in class, so I had no way of knowing. And now I do. So now I'm telling you."

Clover would've leaned across the table and slapped Eleri right there if not for Claire's hand planted firmly on her shoulder. The prospect that Eleri and Fyodor could both be dead in a moment was no stranger to anyone in the room, however, so the anger that flashed across Clover's face was not intimidating in the slightest.

Clover had a hard time understanding what it was that Eleri was telling her, exactly. How could she not have known what she was fighting for? How did she sign up for something without understanding what it was?

"And you expect me to believe that you just learned this?"

"No," Eleri said, "I don't expect that at all. Obviously, it sounds like bullshit. I'm expecting you to take what I'm telling you and realize what it means for you and your people."

"And so now, you've told me that you're going to wipe us out and then *really* wipe us out. We've established that. What do you want?"

Eleri took a breath. This was implied, sure, but she had never explicitly said it. Fyodor felt her hesitancy. She had never even admitted it to herself because that would only be admitting that she had been wrong all these years. But now, there was no other option. There was only this moment, and this moment that preceded the next could change the course of history forever. This moment, here, would be her biggest challenge. To put her pride and her ego aside.

"I want to help you make sure that that doesn't happen. If I had known what I was *really* fighting for this whole time... I'd not have done it." and then, quieter, "It's so hard to know you're being lied to when it's the way you've been raised. I promise you, outside of the people running this whole thing, Fyodor and I are the only two who have realized what's happening. I promise you everybody else has no idea. I'm sorry it got this far without people waking up. And I'm sorry that we have to be the ones to bring you this news."

Claire spoke from behind Clover. Her soft voice and even tone immediately brought the tension in the room down. "Eleri - I'm Clarissa, by the way - if you don't mind me asking, how did you come across this? Because, as I'm sure you can understand, this seems very, very strange to us. The fact that you were part of something for so long and just... never knew... is unsettling."

Eleri smiled at her. "Yeah, it is, isn't it? It was luck. It was Fyo who found out, actually," she said, tilting her head back to her friend, "and he just showed me. It started with the history amendment in that binder, and it led to me asking a lot of questions and stringing together a lot of answers. It isn't something I should know. It's unsettling to me, too."

"And so, do you think, looking back now that you know what you do, that you may have missed something that would have led you to this conclusion earlier?"

"If I may," Fyodor said from behind her, holding an arm out, "and I'm not defending anything anybody is doing or has done, but Eleri was right in saying it's hard to know you're being lied to when that's all you've been raised around. I think that for me... my mother was very big on history, but very much one to tell me to focus on school, as well. Maybe if I had taken into consideration all that she was telling me, it would have been easier to see that something was wrong. At the same time, though, I dropped out of school and was pulled into the army almost immediately after she'd gone and my dad had gone, and it's similar for a lot of us in that sense. You're swept up into the one thing that's been reinforced to you by everyone around you for your entire life, and at the tail end of your childhood, you're being raised by sergeants. When you're in it, it's all you know, and when it's all you know, it's hard to find the problems because you've never had something to compare it to."

There was a bit of a silence. Fyo was right in everything he had said. It was evident that it had helped them understand - even a little - where he was coming from. Clover closed the binder, standing.

"Come with me then," She said suddenly, handing the binder back to Fyodor, walking out of the building.

They stood, following without a word, as she led them through the back streets, explaining what each building was as they went, answering any questions they had. She was not friendly, but she was incredibly courteous, and any time things seemed to be getting out of hand, Clarissa would step in gently.

Clover was fiery. Clarissa was calm. They balanced each other, much like Eleri and Fyodor did.

Oil and water.

The building Clover led them to was one that neither Eleri nor Fyo had seen before, despite all the time they'd spent in Voskivy. It seemed to be only two stories, and it was quite thin and narrow. Clover turned to them as she reached the door.

"People are going to look at you, maybe try to talk to you." She said, facing them both with a genuine concern in her eyes. "Don't answer. Just follow us."

Eleri nodded once and the door was opened. Clover was right; there were stares from the people inside. Clover smiled at some people as she passed, Claire did the same, but walking between the two, Fyodor and Eleri remained neutral, eyes on each other or the ground, ensuring they didn't cause more problems than they already probably had. Eleri, unlike Fyodor, was fairly comfortable, despite all the stares and gawking jaws and hushed whispers. She got this a lot. The Reaper never went unnoticed. She wondered, for a moment, if fame and infamy were truly interchangeable.

"Are you two comfortable sharing a room?" Clove asked as she pushed through a pair of swinging doors.

"I mean, yeah. We've shared worse. What's going on?"

Clove didn't look back at them as she responded. "If you two are serious about helping, you'll be staying here for a while."

"You're just…" Fyodor paused, trying to find the right words. "You're just letting us stay here?"

"Is there any reason I shouldn't?"

"No, not at all. I just didn't expect it."

Clove giggled. "I may be a bitch, but I'm not evil. You'll have to provide me with a plan of action, though, since you two decided to come here with this whole mission. Claire and I already have enough to deal with, so it's on you two, if you're serious about this, to figure it out."

There was a pause, and Clove spoke up again. "Be aware, though, that you are dangerously outnumbered. Try anything, and it'll be the last thing you do."

The proposal was fair, and it would give them what was probably going to be their only opportunity to come up with some sort of strategy. Eleri's mind had already been racing, but without a full, comprehensive understanding of what they were working with or how many people they'd have at their discretion, it was difficult to create something that she was sure would work. Eleri had led a lot of missions, and she had come up with the majority of them on her own, but she was always aware of every detail that she would be working with, and she never had to share *anything* with anybody unless she felt it was necessary. She always worked on a need-to-know basis. She never gave any detail away to someone who wouldn't be directly involved with that specific aspect of whatever was happening. She never shared her entire plan with any one person, and most of all, she would never come up with an idea to appease someone else. Of course, she knew this was a different situation, and she was well aware of the fact that things were already going much smoother than she had anticipated. She didn't want to ruin it, but she didn't want to change a system that had worked so well for her in the past.

Clover had led them to a room; two small beds, a phone, a dresser, a window, and a washroom attached. Nothing special, but not much more than what was expected. She turned to them.

"I'll leave you two in here for today so you can figure something out." She handed Eleri a small, white oval with a black button on top.

"What's this?" She asked, turning it over in her hand.

"This is called a Deller, but you don't need to know that. All you need to know is that if you press the button, say my name, and flip it over, we can communicate through holograms. Watch."

Clover lifted hers to her mouth, *Clarissa Silver*, as Eleri and Fyodor watched, bewildered. Two lights began to project from each Deller, a small video of either person in the palm of each other's hand. "That's how it works. Simple. If you need anything, just call me or Clarissa, and we'll see what we can do for you two."

The pair turned to leave, Clarissa pausing at the door. "A woman named Evginia will most likely be by later to do a little questioning session with you two. We have to make sure, you know, that this isn't some inside job, and you're not here on some really elaborate research mission. She'll read you well enough. If you're planning on lying, don't."

Eleri smiled. "Looking forward to it. Thank you, guys."

They left, shutting the door softly behind them, as Eleri and Fyodor sat on their respective beds, facing each other.

"So, what's your big idea?"

Fyodor's voice was laced with amusement, just as it had been months ago when he was waiting for her briefings. He was always astonished by how quickly she worked and how sharp her instincts were.

"I'm going to call Xavier."

Fyo's face fell. He hadn't expected that. "What? Why?"

She looked at him with a faraway glance. "He's going to *hate me* for this, but we need someone on the other side, don't you think?"

Fyodor frowned. "Maybe we should think of a plan *first*?"

"We don't have a plan if we don't know what they're doing."

"But if we call him, he could just… I don't know, tell people what we're doing here?"

Eleri sighed. "He doesn't work for anyone anymore, though. Why would he do that?"

"You think he wouldn't?"

"I don't know. I don't think so. He already knows Milton Haas is dead, so if he's saying anything it's been done already." She fell backward onto the bed. "Mister Ruben fucking Yorke probably already knows we're here, anyway. He knows *everything*, the bastard."

"Okay. Look. We can think of something and sit on this for a bit, and then call Xavier if you want. But I think we should really *think* about it first. This is different than last time."

Eleri nodded. He was right.

"Okay. Fine." she sat up, facing him again. "What I was thinking is we're going to have to remilitarize this place. We don't stand a chance against so many troops, plus more of an army that's ready to go at a moment's notice. We can't take things lightly, and with the rate at which people are dying, or being abducted, going slowly would probably end with more of a loss than going full force would. At least, with that, they'll be a little stunned."

Eleri put the Deller down on the bed. Fyodor nodded. "That's what I was thinking, too. But how deep do you want to go with this?"

She bit the inside of her cheek. "We're going to have to make a mess, you know."

Fyodor looked down, hanging his head, gripping the sheets. His stomach was turning. Sure, after all he had learned, there was nothing more he wanted than to make sure that those in power were stopped, but he had a vision in his mind of how Voskivy looked at the end of the war, and applying it to the region in which he'd grown up broke his heart.

"Yeah," he said, his voice low, "I figured."

She felt his discomfort. Eleri hated comforting people, but she leaned forward, placing her hand over his. "Hey," she said, looking at him. Her hand once again found its way to his hair, her eyes trailing over the scar. "You still need a haircut."

He smiled sadly, leaning into her touch, taking a deep breath, grounding himself. "Sorry. Been busy."

She pushed his hair back. "We'll be okay, yeah?"
"Everything will be okay."

His heart was racing, anxiety pricking at his ribs and his neck and his back and his fingers. He knew she was right, but he couldn't shake the feeling that something was wrong. Maybe he hadn't quite anticipated something so dramatic. Maybe he wasn't quite ready to go headfirst into Hell again. All he knew was that he felt horrible.

"Do you need something?" She asked quietly, her grip on his hand tightening. "Do you need me to do anything?"

He shook his head, then, in one swift motion, pulled her into a hug.

The last time they'd actually *hugged* was so long ago that she barely remembered it. But she wrapped her arms around him, holding his head against her stomach, running her fingers through his hair with as much warmth as she could muster.

His breathing was labored, and there was a rumbling in his chest. He was struggling, and she didn't know how to help him.

With one deep breath, he pulled away from her, holding onto her forearms.

Before he had a chance to speak, there was a knock at their door, and it swung open.

Fyodor had moved his hands to her hips, looking down, eyes closed, trying to contain himself. Eleri turned to greet the woman.

"Hi, dears, so sorry to bother you. My name is Evginia - I'm sure someone must have mentioned that I would be stopping by - and I've just got to ask you a few questions, if that's alright."

Fyodor's grip on Eleri's hips tightened. *Something was not right.* There was something eerily familiar about all of this. He felt cold, his stomach doing backflips, his heart picking up speed again, rattling his ribcage, shaking his spine. He was sure he was bruising Eleri's hips, but he couldn't breathe. There was nothing else he could do.

He couldn't think. He had to remind himself he was alive. *He was here. And here… there was a problem.*

Eleri must've said something because the woman walked over, occupying the currently unoccupied bed. He felt the blur of her figure moving through the room.

"Now, we'll skip the formalities," the woman said, her voice silky. "Everybody here calls me Genie. You guys can do the same, no miss or ma'am or Evginia. Genie will do, just fine."

Genie. Genie. Genie.

All at once, Fyodor was alert, his chest ready to burst. His eyes shot up, past Eleri, directly to the woman who'd sat down.

And when he saw her, he knew.

He recognized it. He recognized the soft skin. The lively smile. His own piercing blue eyes staring back at him.

His mouth felt dry as he opened it. He felt his hands tingle at the thought - a single word that had formed itself in his mind with the ability to change everything.

He swallowed. He could barely hear himself think, let alone speak.

"Mom?"

Interlude.

Fyodor, my love, come over here.

It was a cool spring day, crisp, fresh, beautiful - the rain had stopped the night before, leaving dewdrops over the blades of green sprouting from deep brown. The orchard was full, apples bright red, huddled in a soft cushion, clinging to strong branches. Aloneia Peak sat tall and proud against the clear blue sky, a painting in the distance, so alive but so far away. A young boy with blond hair and blue eyes turned on his heels, his small hands gripping the handle of the woven brown basket, swinging it along his side as he returned to his mother.

The sound of bees and flies and birds filled the otherwise silent space. Flowers in rings around the trunks of the trees, life sprouting from the roots, planted firmly in the earth. He stepped on a white lily, accidentally, and he frowned. Such a careless action, such a beautiful tragedy.

His mother's hand touched his as he handed her the basket. She was standing on a foot ladder, her yellow dress the brightest thing in the orchard, not the flowers or the apples or the sun itself. She shone brighter. She always did.

Her smile was soft as she picked the first apple, handing it to her son, ruffling his hair.

He took a bite. It was the sweetest thing he had ever tasted.

***

Bring your brother, we're going on a walk.

A sweltering summer evening. There was rarely blistering heat in Aloneia, but when it came, it created a thick, sticky blanket. It would not be lifted.

He moved his baby brother - the soft, innocent boy - placing him delicately into the stroller, his hands clasping firmly to the handle, as if pushing it were the most important job in the world. Deep purply-pink skies, the moon, and the sun, both hanging down as if saying hello and goodbye to each other. Birds somewhere high overhead. Families out, despite the warmth. The chatter - ice cream - a rocky beach with crystal clear water.

He looked at his mother - a silent plea, a favor to be sought - and with a smile, she nodded towards the body that spread into the sky.

Go ahead.

She watched him from the shore, her eyes never leaving the boy, her second son in her arms, her heart full of light and love. The sound of soft waves and loud splashes. The joyous laughter of a child. The careless nature of his arms and legs.

He came back to her. He always did. His mother retrieved him a towel, wrapping it around his shoulders, walking him home, pushing the stroller, guiding him along.

***

Don't be home too late. I have something for you.

The trees were orange, the days cool, the nights cooler, but never cold. Comfortable. Homely. Lovely. The crunch of fallen leaves underneath his shoes - red and yellow atop black roads, the fire of a season changing falling onto an untouched canvas. It had rained in the morning. He jumped in a puddle. October was melting into November. The day was melting into night. School had begun, and the rhythm of structured life had returned, the pattern, the cycle, the thing he would be doing until he died.

He did not see the world with the wonder which he used to. He was bored. He had seen the sky. He had seen the earth. He had seen the water. There was nothing more. There was only this, and there was only death.

He stepped through the front door, a loud creaking, a bang as it was slammed shut, a call out into the space in which he resided. His mother appeared, a box in her hands, a smile on her face. She beckoned him inside, and he obliged. White walls, brown floors, windows in every room. Outside came inside. Safety faded into fear.

She sat with him on the couch. Black leather. Soft. Dense.

The box was opened with delicate care, hands clasped over velvet, fingers dancing around the chain found inside. Thin silver with two flat pendants. Rusted. Dented. A portion missing along the bottom. The vague memory of their creation marked only by the few dark indentations, indicative of a name.

Take good care of this. Remember where you came from. These belonged to one of your great, great uncles, way back in the First World War.

How long ago was that?

Only a couple hundred years.

He ran his hand over the necklace gently. Cool. Rugged. He could make out a name.

William Laine.

He gently pulled it around his neck. The pendant hit his chest. It gave him a rush. His mother smiled. It made him feel loved.

***

Happy birthday, bubba.

The blond boy smiled at his kid brother, trying his best not to cry. It was winter. Snowflakes falling softly, printing the windows momentarily before fading away. He supposed they were all like them in some way. Falling, only finding a place for a moment, before fading back into the nothingness from which they came.

There was only this. This, and death.

His brother hugged him. He returned it reluctantly, but the gesture was all he would get. With his brother in his arms, he peered out the window, fixating on the white blankets—layers upon layers of something that would soon be irrelevant.

His first birthday without his parents. Without his mother. It'll go back to normal soon. It'll be the same as it was before. Mom and dad will come back, and by this time next year, we'll be eating cake and telling stories. This will be my only birthday without them.

If only he had known to hold onto that fantasy a little longer. If only he had known that he would only lose himself as time went on.

Fyodor Kacer lost everything one piece at a time, like sand falling through his fingers. Even with a clenched fist, it would all find its way out.

The cycle would never end.

There was only this.

Only this, and death.

PART TWO

JANUARY 30TH, 2248
09:00
111 DAYS POST-WAR

Nine.

We once spent four days without food, sharing only one bottle of water. It was funny, really, because after the hunger and the cramps, there came some sort of second wave of energy, and that fourth day we were unstoppable. We almost never wanted to eat again. We had gone past the point of no return and thought we had become superior. We were absolutely delusional, and we didn't realize it until we finally got some food and some rest and some water.

Delusional. That's what we all were, and still are, in the end. Delusional to think that we could make a lasting change. Delusional to feel like we would somehow be able to break a cycle without falling further into it. Delusional to believe, with all our hearts, that we would ever be more than pawns.

Delusions create dreamers, though, and dreamers create legacies.

We will all die, one day, but we stay here for eternities if we build a legacy. Without one, we will be forgotten.

I will not allow myself to be forgotten.

- The Found Diary of Eleri Roman, p. 68

—

Fyodor Kacer had never experienced a moment in his life quite like the one he felt looking at his mother for this first time in fifteen years. There was nothing he could equate it to. It was the northern lights and the deep dark sky and throwing a bottle at a wall in a moment of pure, unfiltered rage. It was everything he could feel and everything he could not. There was so much he could understand and so much he never would, and in that single moment, he was a child, knowing nothing about the world, his body immersed only in peace. Looking deep into her eyes, he saw only a reflection of himself.

He saw that she was just as broken as he was.

Had she always been that way? Had he been too young to understand?

He only vaguely remembered the moments immediately after. A hug, her fingers gracing over the gash on his face - *where did you get this?* - her voice strained as she asked about his brother as if she already knew the answer. He remembered her saying she couldn't conduct this interview. A conflict of interest. She'd talk to Clove and see what to do. He only vividly remembered waking the next morning, Eleri sitting beside him, her one hand resting by his body, her other flipping through notes.

"Good morning," She said, not looking over to him.

He sat up, eyes opening slowly, adjusting to the light, readjusting to the space around him. The white sheets had been tossed off of his body, now in a pile at the end of his bed. The inside of his mouth tasted like metal - a hand raised to his lip, blood gracing his fingertips, a frown, a look to his left - Eleri once again responded without looking up.

"You were biting your lip in your sleep," she said, tying her hair back.

Fyodor stood, palms of his hands on his eyes, his brain foggy. "What happened?"

She scribbled something down on the back of a page before flipping again. "You and your mother had a nice reunion. I left, though, you know, give you two some privacy. I come back, she's gone, you're exhausted, I say, okay, go to sleep, and you're out for, like, fifteen hours. You missed a lot, too, but I wasn't about to wake you. I've called Xavier, I've spoken to Clover and Clarissa, and we - or I, depending on how you're feeling - have things to do."

Fyodor's throat was dry. He rubbed his palm against his neck. "Do you have any water?"

Eleri reached down into the bag that rested beside the bed, pulling out a bottle, handing it to him. She closed the binder she was looking at.

"What did you talk to Xavier about?" He said after taking a long drink.

She looked at him, and something about her demeanor took him back. In the past day, she had changed. Any fear or anxiety she'd shown had been eradicated. She looked, once again, like the Reaper who led a group of individuals into dangerous, *dangerous* missions and got them all through the impossible. He thought he'd never see this side of her again.

"Ruben Yorke is after me," she said with a small smile. "Of course, *he* isn't coming for me, he's probably sending people because I doubt he'd put himself in that position, but he knows Milton Haas is dead, and he knows I did it. Xavier says he didn't tell him, and you most definitely don't have a direct line to Ruben Yorke, so I guess it's that whole magical all-knowing aura in full force again. Xavier said that he can't directly *help us*, with Yorke or with - as he put it - 'whatever we've got going on over here', but he did say that he can update me on anything he hears on their side that seems dangerous to us."

Fyodor breathed out a sigh of relief. "He's on our side?"

"I don't think so. But I don't think he's against us, either. I think, honestly, he cares more about us and our safety as individuals rather than our noble cause, or whatever."

"That's good enough, right?"

"Right. So I spoke to Clove, told her we have one person who can give us intel from Aloneia and that genuinely, the only way to do this is to get people ready to fight. We... we came to a conclusion."

"That conclusion?"

Eleri pulled her jacket over her shoulders. "We're going to have a meeting now if you're up for it."

He put the bottle down. "Why wouldn't I be?"

"Your mom's going to be there."

He closed his eyes briefly. "Okay,"

Eleri gave him a moment before answering. "...Okay?"

"Yeah. Sure. Guess it's mother-son bonding time, you know, planning to overthrow your home, that normal stuff."

Eleri smirked, gracing his shoulder. "Well, get changed then. Come on."

She opened the door, stepping out to give Fyo some privacy. It was perfect timing for Clarissa, who had just come looking for her, as she reached out and grabbed her arm. "Walk with me for a minute."

Eleri obliged, following her down the hall, into a separate room. Clarissa's voice was hushed. "Did you know?"

Eleri tilted her head. "What?"

"About his mother. Did you know she was here?"

"No," she said. "I had no idea this person even existed - from an analytical standpoint, you know, I never had a file on her or anything - let alone that it was his mother."

Clarissa bit her lip. "This is so weird."

"What do you mean?"

"We've known her for years, Clover and I, and she never once mentioned having a kid."

"I don't know. Maybe -" a door opened and closed somewhere in the hallway. Eleri lowered her voice. "Maybe she just didn't feel like it was important? Maybe she thought it would jeopardize her opportunity here?"

Claire shook her head. "No, I don't think so. She told us about how her husband had died, so why keep everything else secret?"

The gears began to turn in Eleri's head. "Did she tell you she was from Aloneia?"

Claire frowned. "No, not explicitly, anyway. She, like, vaguely insinuated that she had been in combat a few times but never really said anything, and we never thought to push her. It didn't really matter to us, anyway, since she was doing all of our work."

The gears clicked. "So she didn't want you to know about her kids because that would put her in a vulnerable position."

Clarissa looked over her shoulder, into the hall behind Eleri, and then back to her. "Elaborate."

"Well, obviously, I don't know if this is true, but look past your bias towards her and your relationship with her. How suspicious would it be if someone whose kids fought in the Aloneian army, who was a soldier herself, decided that in the middle of the war, she was going AWOL and joining the resistance? Wouldn't it seem... I don't know... staged, I guess?"

Clarissa's fingers bounced against her leg. "You have a point."

"I don't know it all, but I know that even for *me*, I was so hesitant to send those letters." Eleri had decided, sometime overnight, as she was watching Fyodor sleep, that being honest would get her farther, faster in this environment. There was no point in trying to lie when she was already the odd one out. "I thought for sure no one would answer because why would you take that chance, you know?"

Clarissa laughed to herself. "Your reputation surely will outlive you, I can tell you that much."

Eleri smiled, looking down. "I know. Lots of hearsay, too." and then, in a mocking tone, "I heard she did this, I heard she did that, I heard she slits people's throats, I heard she kills her Commanding Officers -"

"I've never heard that last one," Clarissa interjected.

"Yeah, recent developments."

Clarissa did something that Eleri had never expected then - she laughed. A real, loud laugh, with a genuine smile and a hand over her stomach. Eleri smiled widely, watching her movements, feeling that some bit of the tension had melted away.

"You know," Claire said as Fyo emerged from the room to join them. "You really aren't so bad. Maybe we'd have been friends from the beginning if we'd known each other."

Fyodor reached them as Eleri spoke. "Are you planning on telling your *girlfriend* that?"

Clarissa smiled, a new light in her eyes. "Yeah, I'll let her know you don't bite."

They were led to a room further into the main floor - large, fairly decently furnished, definitely the most important room in the building. Eleri couldn't help but feel somewhat honored as she was let into a space that held a symbolic magnitude of which she would have never been allowed to reach in Aloneia, despite her work. She noted that, had this room been the only thing she had ever seen in Voskivy, she'd never have thought it was in the middle of destruction. It was beautiful, with high ceilings and grand doors, so put together that she nearly felt out of place. Knives on her leg, pistol on her hip, all-black combat gear. A uniform. Her second skin. Something that did not fit here.

Clover and Genie were already sitting at the end of the table, deep in a hushed conversation. Clarissa sat on the other side of Clover. After a moment of deliberation, Eleri sat beside Clarissa.

Fyodor sat across from her, beside his mother.

Eleri studied the two. The similarities were striking. Same eyes, same nose, same mouth - the only difference coming in their cheekbones, which led Eleri to the conclusion that Fyo had inherited his incredibly sharp structure from his father - and she almost felt herself smile. She was glad that he had some closure and even happier than he had found her alive. She knew how much she meant to him. Despite how Eleri behaved, she always listened.

Always.

She watched then as Genie's gaze trailed over to Fyodor, as her eyes widened, and as she grasped his hand.

"You still have it?"

The table was silent, all attention on the pair. Fyodor took a moment before his hands gently went to his neck, revealing a leather chord, at the end of which was a flat pendant.

"I had to change the string," he said quietly.

He pulled it over his head, placing it on the table in front of his mother's hands. She picked it up gently, as if she were scared it would break. Eleri had seen this necklace a billion times. She knew how much it meant to him, but despite that, she never knew exactly what it was. She was sure, somewhere in the back of her mind, that it was some familial thing, seeing as he was such the sentimental type, but the full explanation was never provided, and she didn't have the time to speculate.

"That's okay," Genie breathed, fingers tracing the pendant. "I'm glad you kept it."

He took it back, sliding it over his neck. He looked at his mother once more before speaking again, bridging the conversation. "Eleri tells me you've got some ideas?"

"Yeah," Eleri said, taking the line in stride, turning to Clover. "Remilitarization."

Claire stood, pulling a folder from a box against the wall. She returned to the table, opening it, laying the sheets down. "This is a timeline of the past three and a half months, starting after our surrender."

Eleri took a look over the pages, each day detailed with specific fatalities, how many people were missing, how many people were found, and any recount of what had happened that they could give. Testimonies, allegations, and detailed descriptions - all of which painted a picture so vivid that Eleri felt as though she had lived each event. She wondered if someone had ever kept track of things with this much detail in Aloneia, especially pertaining to the seemingly missing history. She blinked hard, focusing, as Claire proceeded to unfold a larger paper, revealing a map. "Yeah, a map, I know, Medieval, but it's the easiest way to do things. From what we're able to gather, anyone who is being confined is being confined somewhere here."

Her finger dropped onto a part of the map that Eleri and Fyodor both vaguely recognized as a space close to the border, but a sector in which they'd never personally had to venture into.

"Is it… a building? Do we know?"

"We don't know exactly because no one's stories line up," Claire said, a hint of aggravation in her tone. "some people who made it out said that they were in trucks, others say they were in a room. I don't know for sure, but the one linear thing is the whereabouts. Approximately."

"Eleri," It was Clover speaking, "do you think that you could maybe lead some sort of search in that area?"

She pursed her lips. "I can try. I don't know what word has gotten out about me and how far it's reached. It wouldn't be a big group, though. It wouldn't work."

"That's fine. I'll have some reinforcements near enough to the space, and we have the Dellers in case anything goes wrong."

Eleri nodded. "And so, hypothetically, we find that this space is a building or a transport point or *whatever*. We have two options; we either get people out or, on the chance that we and the prisoners are outnumbered by some huge mass of soldiers, we cave the place in."

Genie's eyes went wide. "You'd just sacrifice all those people? We're already thin, don't you think it's a little harsh to do something like that?"

Eleri shook her head, but Clover spoke up first. "I know that it seems that way, but one thing that made Eleri and Fyodor so effective against us *was* her planning and her ability to make decisions that would cause other people to stumble. We talked about this for a long time yesterday, and we wouldn't love to just destroy the place, so it is our second option, but that still means it is an option. She'll make that call when it needs to be made. You have to trust it."

"After that," Eleri said, ensuring there was no room for debate, "there are some things in Aloneia that need to be destroyed, and we're going to have to move quickly."

"A breach in their systems will no doubt be reported," Claire said, making sure she made eye contact with everyone in the room. "And Eleri already has people looking for her. This means that we already need to be on high alert, even from now. So, we need to remilitarize anyone who is able to do it."

"If we get to this location by tonight, by tomorrow we'll have a huge step up." Eleri said. She turned to Fyodor. "You know how slowly news travels at night. No one will care enough at, like, midnight, to look at reports or flashing lights, especially not when the war is over."

Fyodor nodded in agreement. "So tonight, around sunset, Eleri and I go?"

Clover shook her head yes. "You two go, you keep us updated. You tell us what happens. I trust that you'll make the right decision when you get there, and either way you choose, we'll support it. And then, you get back here as soon as you can."

"We assume that when we demolish, or at least, ruin whatever they're using to hold people, they'll be too preoccupied trying to figure that out for a few hours in the morning. Fyo, this means no rest for us. Tomorrow morning, we leave here, we bring Clover and whoever else was rounded up for military efforts, and we go straight into Aloneia." Eleri added.

"What about the troops here?"

She sighed. "They're not here for active warfare. They're equipped with rifles, sure, but most of these guys are young, and haven't seen combat, and are doing this out of some heroic mindset they've built for themselves. I don't think they're a threat, and even if they are, we have Claire and anyone else in the building who didn't come with us to Aloneia to help out. That's the lowest possible number, too, because assuming while we're out, they're able to round up people who don't live in the safehouse, we've got even more than we expected."

Fyodor nodded, folding his arms over his chest, leaning back. "We have the resources for this? The weapons?"

"We have a bunker a few kilometers south that hasn't been touched. We should have enough in there." Clover said firmly.

"Is there a plan of attack once we're in Aloneia?" Fyodor spoke again.

"I'm planning on making a call to Xavier before we leave, seeing what the overall situation is over there, and we can assess as we go, but as far as I'm concerned, we're going in, and once we're in, we have three stops."

Eleri looked directly at Fyodor as she spoke. She knew that this would be difficult for him, but she also trusted that when the time came, he would put his life in her hands, as he had time and time before.

"First," Clover began, "is your administrative building."

Fyo nodded. He figured that the place that employed all of their Commanding Officers and any other superiors would have to go first. He had nearly no attachment to it. He didn't care.

"Second," she continued, "is your ministry district."

"The whole district?" Fyo asked, bewildered.

Eleri took the reins. "Fyo, think about it. It's composed of four buildings, and they take care of *everything*. Education and research, military and defense, labor and employment, science and environment - all of it is in one place, and all of it directly relates to everything that's going on here. If any stay, we have no hope."

"When you all get to that stage, El will assign groups to each building. We will all most likely be split up, but once we destroy everything, we need to reconvene and go to our last post." Clover said.

It was not lost on Eleri that Clover had not referred to her by her full name. That was the first time, and she made sure to remember it.

"Our last post," Eleri said, with a sigh, "is the housing area that we lived in."

Fyodor felt his heart stop. His mind went back to his record player. "What?"

"I don't like it any more than you do," she said gently, reaching for his hand across the table, "but think about it. There are so many things in those buildings that have to be destroyed, and we won't be going for regular civilians, only the sector for soldiers. Imagine, you and I alone have so much compromising evidence in our rooms. I would assume everyone else is no different. We have to make sure none of that gets out."

As much as he didn't like it, he knew she had a point. There was always a method to her madness. If he didn't have his own things in the space, he would have had no objections. He saw her logic, and he understood it perfectly. Even before this, the thought of people finding some of the things he had stashed away in his room ate him up inside.

"Is there any opportunity for me to go in and grab a couple of things?"

Eleri ran her thumb across the back of his hand before retracting it entirely. "We'll have to see, but don't bet on it."

Fyodor nodded. He was not happy with this, but he knew what he was getting himself into. He knew or at least had a vague idea of what this would entail. He just hated that his suspicions were being confirmed.

"We have some people that we need to get in our sights," Eleri continued, to the table this time, "dead or alive."

Clarissa sifted through the papers, placing one on top of the rest. "Here,"

Fyodor took it in his hands, reading it over.

HOLLAND, Oliver
YORKE, Ruben
DIMIRNO, Alex
TALON, Xavier

"Oliver Holland, I understand." Fyodor began. Oliver was the only person above Ruben Yorke. Both of them were, in their essence, ghosts, but they were deadly, and anything they said would be the final word, always.

"Ruben Yorke, obviously, I understand. Alex DiMirno, I get it." Alexander was one of the most dangerous operatives, with a reputation that made Eleri's seem soft. He was well known, well respected, and had a lot of power. If he ordered an airstrike, unfiltered, over all of Voskivy, it would be done in the blink of an eye. Everybody was in much more danger with him around. "But Xavier?"

Eleri bit the inside of her cheek. "We aren't going in with the intention of killing him," she said gently, "but if we have any suspicions... if he gives us any reason to believe he's lying, it has to be done."

"But, he's done so much for us-"

"One thing you need to understand, Kacer," she said, her eyes locked on Fyodor's, her voice strong and forceful. He sat up straight, almost instinctively. This was not Eleri, his best friend, this was Lieutenant Roman, and he knew to respect that. "Is that our personal relationships mean nothing in the grand scheme of things. Just because someone has shown us the utmost kindness and grace does not mean that they behave in that manner with everybody. I did not say we are being sent to assassinate Xavier Talon. I said we are keeping an eye on him and ensuring the appropriate measures are taken. Understood?"

"Understood."

"Good," she said. She looked at Clover, then stood, turning her attention back to Fyodor. "You know how it works. Details come as they're needed. We have to get ready."

Fyodor rose to his feet without another word. Genie spoke up. "Don't you think he deserves to know more of what he's getting himself into? Doesn't that seem unfair for you to know and for him to have to find out? What if you die? Then what? He has to guess?"

"Mom -"

"With all due respect, Evginia," Eleri began, smiling tightly at the woman, her eyes full of rage - *how dare she question me when I led her son through more than she did - as she spoke with a sharp tone and a thick venom.* "I don't die. And your son is a grown man who has fought under my command for a long time. I think I know not to underestimate him. I think you should learn to do the same."

Eleri turned on her heels. If Evginia had reacted, she had no idea. She didn't care to see it.

Fyodor looked back at his mother, only once, before following Eleri out of the room.

Ten.

I never had a particular issue with control. I could let go of it if I needed to, and I could stay silent when someone else knew more than I did. I never claimed to be the smartest in the room, nor did I claim to have all the answers. I always knew that there would be people who opposed my decisions, and I was more than willing to have a conversation with anyone who didn't see my logic. I was fine with explaining myself. One thing I never tolerated, though, was people directly - or indirectly - insulting or questioning my intelligence or practices.

I did not make it this far to be talked down to or to be perceived as weak or stupid, and I most certainly did not make it this far to let people get away with that.

Some people say that I have an attitude. I just think that I have self-respect.

- The Found Diary of Eleri Roman, p. 70

———

Eleri's eyes strained in the dark, the dim light only coming from the moon above and whatever streetlights hadn't been destroyed. This was where she was comfortable, as eerie as it may have seemed. This was where she was most at home. With the familiar crunch of snow beneath her feet and the weight of the world on her shoulders, she felt at peace. She felt as though she was back in the only environment which allowed her to be truly, fully, unapologetically herself.

Fyodor trailed close behind her, his eyes only ever leaving her silhouette to scan the area. He, despite the anxiety he had felt as they were getting ready, was incredibly calm. He knew that this was something he had signed up for then, even more so now and that this was what had to be done to ensure that they wouldn't live the rest of their lives in guilt.

Even bigger than this - he now understood that this was what he had to do to ensure that an entire population wasn't written out of history.

He followed behind Eleri, listening carefully for any communications in his ear. They had adjusted the Deller to fit as an earpiece, not only for the convenience of not having to hold it but also for the fact that the hologram would create a light that would expose their location immediately. He hadn't heard a word yet. He wasn't sure if he wanted to. He wasn't sure what they'd be told.

Eleri followed the directions they'd carefully laid out before leaving. She had memorized the map perfectly - every turn, every corner, every line - a gift she had, the thing that made her the natural leader in transition. She was guiding Fyodor quietly, carefully, around the outer border of the region, ensuring they would run into as little trouble as possible. Clarissa had told them that most of the troops out at night lined the streets, ready to take unassuming people who were on their way home. They normally didn't go into backyards, or onto far corners. They thought there wasn't a great enough reason to do so. Eleri was eternally grateful for their ignorance.

She stopped in her tracks, holding her arm out behind her, signaling for Fyodor to do the same. Her eyes searched the area for any movement, tracing the outlines of buildings, looking for any abnormalities in the ground or the trees.

And she saw it. A single gleam, no doubt accidental, behind one of the trees. Someone who didn't expect to be seen by an enemy.

An *enemy*. The idea was still so foreign to her, even though she was living it. She didn't expect the shift in mentality to come quickly, but it was proving to be much harder to accept her previous brothers and sisters and friends as enemies than she'd anticipated.

She stepped forward slowly, Fyodor, from memory, remaining still. As she approached the tree, she saw the gleam again, making out the shape of an arm. It was a watch, or a bracelet, or reflective tape of some sorts, peeking out.

Eleri moved, walking sideways, ensuring she was always facing the tree. She caught a glimpse of a back and of legs, and she slowly, *slowly*, set her rifle down. A shot would be far too loud, and she couldn't risk bringing attention to herself this early on. This had a time and a place.

For once, she was thankful for the snow, cushioning the rifle. She exhaled, her breath dancing in the wind, as she focused on the man standing by the trunk.

Her hand traveled to her leg, fingers gracing three knives, settling on the lowest one, closest to her knee. She pulled it out gently, its curved blade glistening in the moonlight. She stepped towards the figure, leaning down, watching him. She gauged his movements. He was taller than her, but he was thin. He would fold.

When she was close enough, her movements became quick. One, two, three. Hand over the mouth, knife to the throat, set the body. A rhythm. Something she'd been practicing for years.

He only choked, not perfect, but much quieter than it could've been. She watched, for a moment, as the snow became red, paint bleeding onto the canvas.

She retracted her steps, not turning her back to the body, picking up her rifle. She made her way back onto the path, motioned for Fyo to continue on his way, and began to walk.

He stepped beside her, walking in stride. "Hey," he whispered, "Clove said they're going to the bunker now. They'll be available if we need anything, but they've got things to do."

"No worries," she said, under her breath, "I think we're here."

She slowed to a stop, Fyodor following suit. Her eyes went wide, the sight before her one she'd never seen and one she most definitely ever wanted to see again.

Both reports were right, in their own respects - there were trucks, yes, most likely used to carry those who had been abducted. There was also, though, some sort of makeshift structure - tarps and cloths strung up, leading to the door of a building that was barely visible behind all the additions. She was able to see the frames of two large light fixtures hanging over the camp, turned off. She took a breath, fog seeping through her lips.

"Do you have a smoke?" she whispered, kneeling behind a fence.

"Now?"

"Yeah."

Without taking his eyes off the camp, Fyodor reached deep into his pocket, retrieving the light and the cigarettes, lighting one in his mouth, handing it over, before lighting his own.

"What's our plan?" he breathed gently, shoving everything back where it came from, holding the cigarette between his teeth.

She scanned over the space once. "Do you have explosives?"

He tapped his chest twice. "Right here."

She tilted her head up. The sky was empty. She moved slightly, scanning over the entire space for a second time, before turning to him. "We go from the top."

"The top?"

She nodded. "Absolutely. Look,"

She moved so that Fyodor was directly in front of her, able to see exactly what she was looking at. She motioned vaguely towards the trucks, and Fyo squinted.

"Right past the trucks. Look carefully at the tents."

Fyodor was trying his best, focusing but seeing nothing.

"Movement," she mumbled, prompting him, "you can see shadows moving behind the tarps."

He tried again, and this time, he barely caught a glimpse of a silhouette of a body, only for a moment, and it was gone again.

"So we go up," he whispered.

"So we go up." She repeated. She pointed to the side of the building - the only visible piece of concrete, the only area not covered by tarps. "If we go there, we can find an opening on the roof. If we don't, we just blow the roof off."

He frowned. "That wasn't-"

"We don't have much wiggle room. See," she said, pointing far in front of the trucks, "people are all over there. We can't go through the front, if we're on the roof for too long, they'll see us, and we can't see what's in the back or on the other side. This is our only chance."

Fyodor took a final drag of his cigarette, putting it out with his gloved fingers, dropping it in the snow. "Okay," he said, "let's go."

Eleri flicked hers to the side, her rifle against her chest. She looked once - a sweeping stare, taking in everything before her - as she began to walk. Her steps were featherlight, her finger resting on her trigger in the event of being seen. Her heart hammered in her chest as she finally reached the side of the building, slinging her rifle over her back. Using a pipe lining the outside of the single-story building and a pile of snow that had been moved to the side to make space for a truck, she swung herself up. Turning back, looking down at Fyo from where she crouched on the roof, she motioned for him to follow. He did so, quickly, landing with grace and ease. They stayed low, moving across the space, looking for anything -

They almost missed it. If not for Fyodor's extensive knowledge on hidden doors, they'd have blown the entire building to bits. But he grabbed Eleri's arm, leading her to a section of seamed metal roof with a strip that seemed a *little* too dark to be a coincidence. He brushed his fingers over it, looking back at her.

She nodded, and that was all it took for him to press down, the hatch popping open, a square of roof swinging down.

Eleri jumped through without a second thought.

She landed with a soft thud, wet boots on the concrete floor, and she took in the surroundings. Makeshift fences lined the walls, people filled into the sections. Fyodor followed, landing behind her, gasping.

"Holy shit," he said, his eyes wide.

Eleri swallowed, blinking hard, walking to the bars of the closest cage. "Hi," she said gently, a girl about twelve years old standing inside. "Do you know what's going on here?"

The girl looked at her, fear written across her features, dried blood on the side of her neck and the inside of her wrists. She shook her head. "I - I just got here today. I don't... I was walking home and I - they just put me in the back and took me here. There are more people in the trucks than there are in here. I don't know. I'm sorry."

She nodded, reaching through the bars to hold the girl's hand. "Hey," she said, "it's okay. Did you see how many soldiers are here?"

The girl shook her head. "No. No. There's a lot - at least, there were when I got here, and I don't know who they are or what they want from me." There were tears in her eyes. "They won. Why are they doing this?"

Eleri's heart broke. She knew, in part, that she was exactly who this girl was scared of. "I don't know, but it's okay. We're going to stop them, okay?"

The girl nodded weakly, her lower lip trembling. Eleri squeezed her hand as she spoke. "What's your name, beautiful?"

"Sevyn,"

That stung.

"Beautiful name. You know, one of my best friends is named Sevyn. She's so pretty and so brave… just like you. I need you to keep quiet for me, okay, Sevyn? Just for a bit?"

The girl nodded desperately, hopelessly. "Okay," Eleri whispered. "I'll be back for you."

She pretended not to notice Sevyn lurch forward when she let go of her hand.

She motioned to Fyodor, who had been making his rounds through the space. He appeared at her side, looking at her sadly. "I saw outside," he said. He looked to the floor. "There are too many of them."

"I figured there would be," she said, tapping his chest twice, brushing against the explosives, mirroring his action from earlier. "Near the front door."

He nodded, slowly moving his hand to the pocket on his chest, opening. "Are you going to lure them in here?"

"Yeah. Just say the word."

They walked to the front of the space, where the building stopped and the tents began. The mix. The meeting point.

Fyo unraveled the explosives, planting them around the space, stepping back, holding a small machine that would set them off. "Roof?" he asked.

She nodded. "Yeah,"

She climbed one of the thick beams below the entrance they'd come through, Fyodor following closely behind. She made eye contact with Sevyn once before she was out as she swung herself back through the hole. She hoped the girl would somehow survive this.

She walked to the front of the roof, taking the pistol from her hip, firing it once towards the general area of the trucks, hearing the immediate commotion and fear.

"For a top-secret building," she said, her voice carrying in the wind, "you guys do a horrible job at securing your shit."

One man turned first, the rest quickly following suit. The group immediately began moving towards her, and she pushed Fyodor back towards the door they'd found on the roof. That was a *lot of soldiers*, and despite all she had done and the experience she had, there was no way that the two of them would be able to stand their ground against this group for even ten seconds, no matter how talented they were. She jumped directly off of the roof, onto the ground outside of the building, with Fyodor following, hoping it looked *enough* like they'd gone back inside through the hatch to lead people into the space.

She stumbled further away from the building, and their eyes only locked for a moment as Fyo pressed the button.

The explosion shot them forward, their bodies falling to the ground, snow and dirt covering them. It took a moment. She had to catch her breath. Her head hurt. Her heart was pounding. There was blood coming from her temple. But once her ears stopped ringing, she got to her feet and ran back towards what was now a pile of rocks, the sight reminding her of all those stupid, destructive missions they'd gone on years ago. She didn't know if Fyodor was following her - she didn't care - as she returned to the approximate area where she'd found Sevyn.

And she was there, stuck under some debris, bleeding from her chest and her head and her mouth.

Eleri moved the large piece of metal which had trapped her, and Sevyn let out a piercing scream. "Hey, hey, it's okay, you're okay."

She held the girl's body in her arms, blood covering her suit, the sound of crying filling her ears. Sevyn's voice was thick and strained.

"What's going on -"

"Fyodor!" Eleri called, "Get over here, now."

He ran to her side, flicking his lighter, shining the flame over the girl's face, giving Eleri a better view, cutting through the darkness and illuminating the damage. Eleri felt her heart grow heavy. She held Sevyn's head, hands on her temples, fingers pressing against a wound that was bleeding profusely, *just try your best, okay, that's good*, the poor child's blood getting all over her. Eleri looked to Fyodor. In the wake of a silent plea, he extinguished the flame. He understood.

"Why did this - please, please," Sevyn murmured as she spoke, each syllable barely distinguishable from the next. Eleri didn't know if it was saliva or blood or tears seeping backward into Sevyn's throat, but it was causing her worlds of pain. Eleri could only imagine how the girl's lungs were burning. "I can't - don't want to -"

"You won't. You just have to keep still. Watch me, okay? Look into my eyes. Don't look away."

Sevyn coughed, blood splattering across Eleri's face, but she didn't flinch. She held the young girl, combing through her hair. Sevyn raised a shaky hand, placing it against Eleri's blood-soaked cheek, a desperate attempt for comfort or life. Eleri covered the hand with her own. She could do nothing but watch as Sevyn coughed and cried and kept trying to speak -

"Hey," Eleri said gently, leaning closer to her face. "Don't try to talk, okay? You're okay. We've got you."

The wail that escaped her was crushing, almost only overshadowed by the horror of the scream that immediately followed. Eleri pursed her lips, gently turning Sevyn's head to the side, trying to get the blood to drip out of her mouth instead of back in. She did this with unconscious bodies to prevent their tongues from falling back into their throats and choking them. She hoped it would somehow help Sevyn.

Eleri held her, looking into her eyes, not blinking, never diverting her attention. Sevyn's grip on Eleri tightened then, her body lurching forward once, another cough escaping her. Eleri watched, whispering a mantra of love and safety, as the light in the girl's eyes dimmed, dimmed, dimmed…

And it was gone.

"El," Fyodor said softly when he noticed she wasn't letting go, "it's done."

Eleri was still holding Sevyn's head in her hands, blood caking her fingers, thumb tracing circles on her temple as if she were easing her out of life. She felt Fyodor's hand on her back, patting gently. "We have to go."

"The last thing she ever heard in her life was a lie," Eleri said bitterly, swinging her rifle back into her hands as she stood.

"At least she wasn't alone." Fyodor tried, a hand brushing against her shoulder. "You did good, El. You did good for her."

Eleven.

I sometimes think about God. If he exists, why would he create us? Surely, someone as benevolent and all-knowing as him would never purposefully subject us to this Hell.

But then maybe I've got it all wrong. Maybe this is truly Hell. We already lost our chance, didn't we?

- The Found Diary of Eleri Roman, p. 71

—

"You should not be calling me," Xavier's tone was not harsh, but it was painfully strict over the phone.

Eleri figured he would say something like that. There was no reason for him to want to speak to her again, especially with rising tensions, but the fact that he had answered this early in the morning told her all that she needed to know.

"Are they onto us?"

Xavier sighed. "Yes, Eleri, of course, they are. For this specific incident... not yet, but there won't be any other suspects once they come to terms with what was done. If you're going to move, round up your people and do it now."

She took a deep breath, looking briefly at the others in the room. "Okay."

"Take care of yourself."

The comment took her back. "You too."

"I'm serious. People have died trying to carry out this same mission you've begun, on smaller scales, no less. You and anybody you're with... you're all in a lot of danger. I hope I'll see you again."

"Thank you, Xav." she hesitated. "Goodbye,"

"Goodbye. Good luck."

She hung up, sighing deeply, turning to Clover. "He says to go now. He says they don't suspect me for that incident last night, yet, so we'd better start walking before they do."

Clove nodded. "I figured. Come on."

They walked through the building to the main entrance, at which they were met with a large group of people - of *soldiers*.

Eleri felt herself smile. "Oh, wow. You got all of them? How many are back for their victory lap?"

"Most of them, honestly. They heard what we were doing, and they wanted in."

"God," Eleri laughed, "this is incredible."

"It's been fifteen years of being a part of this mess, most of them are thinking, what's one more?"

They found Claire, Genie, and Fyodor standing off to the side, in conversation with each other. Claire looked up, smiling at the two, and conversation halted.

"Are we ready?" Clover asked.

Clarissa nodded. She stepped towards Clove, her hands cupping her cheeks. "Don't die."

Clove pressed a kiss to her lips. "Never."

They hugged once, a final goodbye, and they faced out to the crowd. Clover cleared her throat, pulling her rifle off of her back into her hands, standing in front of the group.

"Can I have your attention!"

The chatter in the crowd halted immediately, all eyes on Clover. Fyodor and Eleri had found their way beside her, standing, looking at all these people, none of which they knew, who were now under their command.

"I am going to make a couple of things clear, and I am only going to go over them once, understood?"

A chorus of yes, ma'am, and Clover nodded.

"Good. First and foremost, thank you for your bravery, for your courage, and your willingness to be a part of something that will be remembered forever. Each and every one of you is so valued, now especially, and we cannot thank you enough." She took a small pause, smiling, before continuing. "Secondly, we do not know how long this will take, but we hope to make

this as smooth as possible. That said, you take orders from *three people* and only three people. Myself, Eleri Roman, or Fyodor Kacer, tell you to do something, you *do it,* no questions asked. Anybody else asks you to do something, even if they say we told them to tell you, you *do not.* Understood?"

Yes, ma'am.

"Good. We will almost never ask you guys to do anything on your own, and on the off chance that we do, know it is absolutely necessary and there is no other option. We will be taking care of the individual portions of this for as long as we can. Anything immediately life-threatening, we will lead. We know this is already a very dangerous thing that we're doing, and we want to keep you guys as safe as possible, given the circumstances. That means you have to listen to us, okay? Next. You see an Aloneian soldier? You kill them. I don't care who they are or where you see them. If you can, you get rid of them—no two ways about it. Make everything a lot easier. And finally," she paused, taking a breath, "If, for any reason, you are separated, or things do not go to plan, or we run into some unexpected catastrophe, worry about getting yourself safe, and once you do so, go back to Voskivy. We will not come looking for you. We will not send out a search party. As harsh as it is, in a situation like this, if you're on your own, you are truly on your own. Expect nothing. Is that all clear?"

Yes, ma'am.

"Good." She pushed through the crowd. There was a knot in her stomach. "Follow us."

The march through Voskivy proved to be fairly uneventful, which everyone was grateful for. The conclusion drawn was that whatever Aloneian troops were still in Voskivy were too preoccupied with the explosion to focus on what they were doing. This, in combination with the fact that they had laid out a route around the border, the opposite side of where Fyo and Eleri had walked yesterday, meant that their odds of having a run-in were decreased significantly. They were fairly close to the Aloneian border as it was, and as long as they stayed away from what was left of the town square, they would more than likely be fine until they crossed over.

Voskivy, by all means, was a beautiful region, even with the destruction. It was the complete opposite of Aloneia, despite their close proximity. Voskivy was valleys and rivers and long stretches of fields. Through the years, Eleri had tried to reconstruct an image in her head of what it may have looked like before everything began, and her idea was one that she would've loved to be in. It seemed peaceful and welcoming and so unlike the industrial sterility of Aloneia.

Voskivy seemed like a dream in comparison.

Of course, every dream came to an end.

The sun was a piercing white, the winter at its peak. The early morning briskness, its frost and its wind, was unforgiving, leaving no room for comfort. The anxiety floating through the group was almost tangible. They had all - Fyo and Eleri included

- been equipped with Dellers, but the easy method of communication did little to ease their worries. Eleri understood how they felt, and though she wished there was something she could do, she would have to wait and allow them to move through their own emotions, their own feelings, their own realities, alone. She couldn't speed up their process, she could only be there to lead them through it.

The Aloneian borders looked incredibly different from this side.

There was graffiti littering the walls and fences, garbage scattered over the ground, a mix of dirty snow and caved in roofs painting the remnants of a life that would never be found. Eleri thought of how it looked coming in from the other side - tall, proud, like Aloneia had something to say. A statement. A message.

We are superior, and we will ensure you will never forget it.

It was something she had never noticed before, and she wondered how all these people from Voskivy, who more than likely had never seen Aloneia before, would feel stepping into an entirely new world, only to destroy it.

She tried to recall how she felt doing that same thing.

She couldn't remember a thing.

She stepped forward, ahead of both Clove and Fyodor, looking at the border for what she knew may have been her last time. One sharp breath and she was marching over onto the other side, clutching her weapons, counting her knives, looking to see if there was any immediate danger.

She turned back to the group, nodding once. They proceeded.

"Our first order of business," she said, addressing the mass of people, "is potentially our most dangerous, but no doubt our most important. We will be taking down the administrative building, and we will be doing so successfully. From what I understand, you have all been assigned one of us as your Commanding Officer. From this point forward, if one of us says a command, it is for the group who has been assigned to us to follow, not for our entire army to do. Clear?"

Yes, ma'am.

"Good. Fyodor and I will lead you all to the administrative building, but that does not mean this is a leisurely excursion. Make sure you are paying attention. Anyone could give new orders at any time, and your failure to do so could result in our failure as a group. Clear?"

Yes, ma'am.

"Good. And so we proceed."

Fyodor and Eleri took the lead, taking the group through the streets of Aloneia. They shared a mutual mix of emotions - not only did this place look so different now, despite their absence being so short, but the feeling of walking through with an army backing them felt absolutely surreal. Their lives had changed exponentially, all because of a binder, and they didn't fully grasp the magnitude of what was becoming of them. They couldn't. They more than likely never would.

***

The sound of boots hitting pavement was not lost on Ruben Yorke, nor on Oliver Holland. The vibration was familiar to both of them, and although they had a gut feeling that something like this would happen, they didn't want to face it.

Ruben sat at his desk, on the top floor of the administrative building, watching Oliver pace back and forth before him. They knew that they had two options: to stay and to die or to call some sort of drastic action that would likely cause more damage than they were prepared to fix.

"We can call airstrikes, can't we?" Ruben asked, leaning back in his chair, chewing the end of his pen. His brown hair was pushed up from his forehead, grey eyes staring directly at Oliver, who was still moving around, unable to contain himself.

"And get what from that? Everyone's dead, then. No point."

"So we sit here and die?"

Oliver shook his head, hair glistening in the light from the rising sun. Goosebumps trailed up his arms. "No. No. I sit here and die. You get out."

"Don't be an idiot, Oli. You know I'm no good at this without you."

"You're the one who spoke with Roman. You're the one who's been seeing this through. If they want to kill us, fine, but at least give yourself some time."

Oliver was set on his offer. He was higher up than Ruben, but that was only a technicality. That would never be the case if not for his experience on paper. Oliver was written up to be a *lot* more than he felt he was, and he knew he was never the leader people wanted him to be. Ruben, on the other hand, was younger, and smarter, and a quick thinker. He had experience in the field, acting as a commanding officer before finding Oliver. They were fast friends, and they had an unspoken agreement that as Ruben would make the decisions, Oliver would make the announcements. They were both fine with it, and it worked flawlessly for years.

Neither of them, despite their time together and apart, would have been able to predict something like this.

"We should have just pulled the troops out of Voskivy," Ruben mumbled, placing his pen back on his desk.

"We could never have done that, and you know it. You saw how the COs responded, and you know that pulling out would've made the entire war pointless."

"If we pulled the troops out, we wouldn't have this rag-tag team of half-dead Voskivian soldiers marching through our region. I'm just saying."

"But if we did, people like Haas -"

"Milton Haas is dead," Ruben snapped, "because of us not pulling the troops out. Besides, he was an idiot and a pawn. You said so yourself."

Oliver peered out the window. "So, fine, he was a fool. He got too ahead of himself. He tapped the wire of our greatest asset and got so mad about her conversation that he snuck into her room and was somehow never seen again. Whatever. Moving on. You still need to go."

"Oli, I'm not going to leave you here. What kind of martyr are you trying to be?" He laughed. "You and I are both going to Hell, anyways."

Oliver shook his head. "I don't know how to argue with you about this because it shouldn't be a fight. Ruben, you have to go. You have to."

"I won't."

"You will," Oliver said, his voice breaking, "it's an order."

Ruben rose from his desk, stepping towards his superior. "And do what? Go and die somewhere other than here? Go and kill the Reaper, only to have her whole army turn on me? What's the big plan, Oliver? Go *where*?"

"You go, and you find Alexander DiMirno. You find someone who can take her down."

"The goal is still to take their land?"

"It's *always* been the goal. And if I die here, knowing you'll see it through, I die happy."

"And if I can't get to her? If I can't get rid of her?"

Oliver sighed. "Then you did all you could, and I still died happily."

Ruben linked his hands behind his neck. He blinked slowly. "I have no choice?"

"Not this time."

He looked out the window once, seeing the mob of people approaching, and he nodded slightly to himself as he picked up his pistol and walked to his door. Oliver stood, watching, knowing that his last minutes living would be spent completely, utterly alone. Had he done something to deserve this? No, he had only ever been following orders, executing a vision that had been thrust upon him when he was put in this position. He had only been doing his job. If it were an evil job, or a cruel job, or a job that was malicious, surely, he'd have understood it. Surely his parents would have never given him the burden.

They loved him too much for that.

Right?

Ruben reached the door, turning back to look at Oliver.

"Thank you. For everything. I'm going to miss you so much."

Oliver nodded, tears welling in his eyes now, his throat all but sealing shut. "I'd say I'll miss you too," he said, with a small smile, "but I won't know."

Ruben laughed. It was sad. "I'll see you on the other side. Save a room for me in the eternal fire."

Oliver nodded. "Of course, buddy."

With one last glance, Ruben stepped out the door, closing it behind him for the last time, knowing he would never see his best friend again.

They used to conduct executions in prisons, he had read once. He wondered if the feeling that had planted itself in his chest now was similar to that of someone who knew they were being sent to die.

***

Eleri was the first to reach the steps of the building. She turned to Fyodor, checking her watch. "It's only seven. Nobody should be here yet, I don't think, right?"

Fyo shook his head. "Maybe one or two people somewhere, but the actual work hasn't begun."

"Okay." She stood on the steps, a makeshift soapbox, and she turned again to the crowd. "Fyodor and I will be going in here. Within the next fifteen minutes, people will start coming to the building to start their shifts. It is up to all of you, under Clover's lead, to… address the situation. Understood?"

Yes, ma'am.

"Good."

She nodded to Fyodor, and he followed her as they made their way into the building. He entered the passcode into the door, waiting for it to slide open, and as they stepped inside, he exhaled. "It's a lot nicer than I remember it, don't you think? Did they refurbish the place?"

Eleri slapped his arm. "Come on."

They walked into the elevator, hearts racing. They worked in tandem, as always, almost never having to communicate verbally. Fyodor placed one explosive on the ground in the elevator as the pair made their way up to the top floor. He drummed his fingers over the device in his hand for a moment before passing it to Eleri. "You're sure you want to be the one to do this?"

She nodded firmly. "If you die, your mom's gonna kill me."

He snorted, handing it to her, stepping out of the elevator onto the top floor, Eleri following. Equipped with their rifles, they walked into the section which they'd only seen a handful of times, large rooms and big windows, a space much more beautiful and put together than the rest of the region, reserved only for the top of the top.

Eleri nodded her head to the left, indicating the route she would take, and Fyo turned to the right. They were to do one sweep of the space before the beginning of the demolition.

Fyodor stepped carefully through the corridor; one, large, circular floor, peeking into each office with care. The red carpet beneath his boots was exceptionally clean. The wooden walls seemed to be glistening, gold accents adding to the grandiose of the entire picture. It was a slap in the face, he thought. He hated this floor. He felt like these higher-up superiors were just rubbing it in. They were, and would always be, more important than anyone else, regardless of the sacrifices people like Fyodor and Eleri had made.

He assumed that his radicalization had only increased in the past few days, but he had to admit to himself that it was always there, even if only slightly. He had always pushed away any feelings of confusion and distrust for fear of what might happen to him, especially considering how he'd been on thin ice for most of his life. Maybe it was that situation that had started it all. He was sure that if he sat down and really thought it through, at some point, he'd be able to piece together exactly what experience contributed to what mindset. As a whole, he'd always believed that the five years spent with that team of six had done it to him, almost entirely forgetting that he was a person before that as well. If he really, really reached into that vault of memories, he was sure he'd be able to truly piece everything together.

He stepped out of another room, stopping in his tracks. That sickening, heavy feeling in his chest had returned.

Something wasn't right.

He heard the voice almost at the same time as he heard the gunshot.

"Good morning, Fyodor,"

If not for his instinct to drop, the bullet would have gone right through his skull. He threw himself back into the closest room, closing the door behind him, calling Eleri over the Deller.

"Someone's shooting at me," he said, hushed tone, "Room 910."

He took a breath, swinging the door open again, seeing the man. Fyodor shot, low, at his legs, as to injure him but not kill him, and within a second, the man fell to the floor.

Eleri was around to Fyo's side of the building by the time Fyodor has knelt over the man's trembling body.

She rolled her eyes. "I always do."

She walked him back to the elevator, holding the device in her hand. "Sixty seconds and she blows, whether you're out or not."

Fyodor nodded, the doors closing. "I can make it in thirty," he said with a wink as the doors closed.

For the first time in years, Eleri felt utterly alone. She wasn't scared, not at all, and she knew that there was a high chance of her escaping the building, but nothing was ever certain. Fyodor would have to go down, and he would have to clear everybody out as far as they could go, away from the administrative building, away from her. She was perched, watching the clock directly above the elevators.

She gazed on with intent as it ticked. Her eyes were locked onto it, finger hovering above the single button that would start the downfall of everything that this place represented.

Tick. Tick. Tick.

Eleri was never one for dramatics, contrary to popular belief, but she knew she would need some sort of miracle for all of this to work properly. She had run over the escape plan hundreds of times - the bombs would take about thirty seconds to detonate, there was a window leading out on the fifth floor of the south stairwell, and if she ran, she could make it there and jump, landing on either snow or concrete (irrelevant), thereby surviving. She was sure this would *hurt*, but she also knew she was the fastest and, apparently, the one with the biggest death wish, so this was truly the only option.

"What are you doing, huh?" Fyodor asked, a scowl graci his features.

Oliver Holland smiled menacingly. "If you truly believe tl you are going to win, you are *wrong*. People like you don't c to win against people like me."

Eleri was standing, looking at Oliver from over Fyodc shoulder. "You're bleeding out on the floor of your o\ building. I don't know how you see yourself winning here."

"My sweetheart," he breathed, "always so *obtuse*. Thi about what I said, yeah? I said people like me. I know it m be hard for you to wrap that pretty little head of yours arour the concept that, unlike you, we *have* a system n dependent on one person. Sit and think about it for a whil It might start making sense to you."

Eleri cocked an eyebrow. "Wow, Oli. Really hitting n where it hurts, huh? That's what you want to go out with?"

He scoffed but dropped his head back against the floc "Fuck you, Roman."

"Big words from the big man. Wouldn't expect anythir less. Godspeed," she said, and in one, swift motion, her rif was up, and the bullet was through his forehead.

Dead.

Fyodor stood, not taking his eyes off of Oliver Hollanc body. "Did you see anyone else on this floor?"

She shook her head. "No. So start heading down."

He nodded, his gaze lingering for a moment longer thi usual. "Get out of here, okay?"

Tick. Tick. Tick.

She had never realized how long a minute was. She could hear and feel everything, and she could only hope that this was going to work. If she died here, she would die with the comfort of knowing that her best friend and one of the most capable leaders she had ever met were heading the rest of this mission.

Maybe she'd see Oliver Holland in Hell. Maybe they could fight it out there.

Tick. Tick. Tick.

She stood straight, watching the last ten seconds tick down. The hands moved almost painfully slowly, the clock refusing to line up entirely -

Until it did.

Without a second thought, her finger pushed down on the button, and she ran.

The door to the stairwell swung open and she moved, jumping over railings, trying her best to get down to the window.

Thirty seconds.

She had tried to time herself, but with the rush of adrenaline and the anxiety and the chaos, she had lost count almost immediately. All she knew was that she wasn't going fast enough.

There was no way.

Eleri Roman reached the window just as the building began to go up in flames. And, in what was expected to be her last moment, she caught her own reflection on the glass, reminiscent of her picture staring back at her in the lake, and somewhere in the back of her mind, she noted that this was the first and only time she had seen herself truly seem at peace.

Twelve.

Death, as far as I am concerned, is only a part of life. Everything is a cycle, whether we like it or not, and death is only the most dramatic form of this. You are born, and you die, brought from nothing, given to nothing. I think, in a way, it is very reflective of the life we live, at least here and now. It's some kind of big, sick joke all of it, isn't it? You come from nothing, you fight for nothing, you die with nothing. All of it is worthless in the end, whether you live to see it or not. And don't get me started on the stupid fucking 'stages of grief'. There are only two: you hear that someone dies, and you move on. It's no surprise that people don't live forever, so there's no point in mourning over someone who will never know that you're missing them. I wonder if people will rejoice when I finally take my last breath.

- The Found Diary of Eleri Roman, p. 72

—

Fyodor sat with his head down, Clover's hand on his shoulder as she knelt in front of him. "We have to go."

He knew this, but he couldn't. He didn't feel whole, here, without Eleri. He was surrounded by people, and he had a mission and a purpose, but he felt alone. He had to wait; surely, she'd come out eventually, that stupid smile on her face, laughing at him for thinking she could ever be slow enough to die. If he waited it out, even a little bit, everything would work itself out, and the lump would leave his throat.

He vaguely felt the ghost of Clover's hand rub his shoulder once before disappearing.

She stood, turning to the group; anyone who was under Eleri Roman's command will now be under mine, everyone else will remain under Fyodor's.

He didn't care. What was he supposed to do? She was everything to him, and she had been ripped away in the blink of an eye.

He never prayed, but he did then.

He should've been the one in the building. She was the leader. She was the glue that held them together. She was the one who knew what to do, who had that stupid killer instinct, who was able to get anyone out of anything. He should never have agreed to it. He should have talked her out of it. He knew that if she didn't get out, he never would've either, but he was a much more disposable asset, and of the three - now two - of them who were leading this group, he was undoubtedly the weak link, in his mind.

This was his fault. Maybe not entirely, but at least a bit. He knew this was preventable, and he couldn't handle knowing that he could've been the one to stop it.

I always do.

He pulled his head from his hands, standing, knowing El would've undoubtedly run her hands through his hair, which he still needed to cut, and smiled at him once before pulling him to his feet. She'd never let him wallow like this.

Stepping over to Clove, he was only a ghost of himself. She noticed, of course, but said nothing. To her, this was a situation that she had no right to interject herself into. Not only was she planning to kill these people only days ago, but now, she had essentially taken the place of the woman who he had been leaning on for years. She knew there was nothing she could do or say, especially considering how little she knew about him, to ease his pain. So she let him walk ahead of her, leading her to the second aspect of this mission, marching her through the streets of a region that had given him everything and now taken it, too.

He was bitter. Why had they chosen to do this, anyway? This was not their place nor their job. There was no reason for it. There would have been no consequences had they allowed what was happening to take place to continue. They were not conducting it or overseeing it or part of it to any extent.

It was his fault, all of it, wasn't it? Had he just left that stupid thing on the ground, they never would've seen the textbook drafts, and none of this would've happened. They would never have even felt guilt for staying static on something like this, *because they would have never known it was happening.*

He tried to even his breathing. This entire thing was stupid, all of it. Every last part. He needed a smoke.

He reached into his pocket, retrieving one, lighting it, handing it over.

Right. The pattern, the system, out, up, right, was gone. It was only one at a time now, he supposed. At least his things would last longer.

He held it between his teeth, not even smoking it, waiting for it to burn out on its own. He had no idea what he was doing, nor did he process how much ground they were covering until they found themselves just a block away from the ministry district. He flicked it to the side, pausing his walk, waiting for Clover to come stand beside him.

Even the sun seemed dimmer.

He felt the woman's presence beside him, and he spoke. "The left, here," he said, pointing to two of the buildings, "is education and science. Those two, on the right, are military and labor."

"Okay," she said calmly, eyeing the buildings. "Do you want to take your group to education, I'll go to science, and then we can reconvene and figure out how to take out military and labor?"

He nodded. "Yeah. Military is going to fuck us over, though."

"It is what it is at this point," she shrugged. "We're fucked either way, no?"

He smiled lightly. That sounded like an answer Eleri would've given. "I'll drink to that."

Clover smiled, then turned to the group. "First and third, on me!"

With one final nod, she began to walk to the first building, SCIENCE AND ENVIRONMENT written above the large, swinging doors in thick, gold lettering that stood out obnoxiously against the grey concrete.

He waited for a moment, watching as she led them into their uncertain future. Work had begun by now. People would be in the buildings, and he knew that there would be blood spilled. He didn't have the capacity, yet, to consider how they'd be taking out the military building, given news had already most likely spread and that they were far more equipped than he was. He wanted to think that far ahead, Eleri would, but he could only focus on the task at hand. He couldn't seem to think past it. It frustrated him.

Perhaps that was why she had always kept him on a need-to-know basis.

"Okay, second, on me!" he said, his voice coming out much steadier than he had anticipated, as he began to lead them into the EDUCATION AND RESEARCH building directly beside the other.

His heart was beating out of his chest. He knew that by the time they were out of here, if not, by the time they were out of the next two buildings, they'd be in a full-fledged warzone. He wondered if Clover had anticipated this, as well. He wondered if Clarissa, his mother, and the others would join them or if something had happened back in Voskivy. It seemed to him that every single possibility was much too overwhelming to consider in-depth, so he did all he knew how to do and thought about none of it, only focusing on his breathing and his heart, which he wished would just give up.

***

If Eleri Roman was any stupider, the gun against her head would have scared her.

The feeling of the barrel bruising her already bleeding temple should've sent shock and fear coursing through her veins. Instead, through a bloodied mouth and a broken nose, all she could do was laugh.

This was much worse than death. *Much worse.*

Unfortunately for her, she was smart, and because of it, she couldn't even get the temporary rush of fearing for her life. She knew she wouldn't die. She knew that they wouldn't kill her - not now, anyway - and that they would live to regret it eventually.

She leaned into the gun slightly, *challenging them*, raising an eyebrow at the man standing before her as if to say do it. *I dare you.*

If he wanted to pull the trigger, it would be anybody's loss, but not hers.

Ruben Yorke was leaning on a desk on the other side of the room, watching the scene before him unfold. He didn't want to kill her yet - he was certain of the fact that she wasn't sure how she'd gotten out of that building or what had happened immediately after. In truth, all Eleri remembered was waking up and wishing she hadn't.

The man before her, Alexander DiMirno, was not quite as intimidating as she had expected him to be. He was scary, sure, but with his reputation, she expected a lot more flair, she supposed. She held back a laugh as she considered that could be what people thought when they met her for the first time.

Alex licked his lips. *She could've sworn his tongue was blue*, one hand going to hold her by her chin, she assumed to force her to keep her eyes on him (which was stupid, in her opinion, because she hadn't once looked away, anyways), a scowl across his face.

Scary looking, maybe. Intimidating, no. Not to her.

He was a lot bigger than she was, and as it always did, the evident outcome of her death and his life fueled her.

"Give me a good reason why I shouldn't kill you."

She rolled her eyes. "If I die, you don't get the pleasure of seeing me suffer, darling. That's what you both want, isn't it? After all the problems I've caused? After killing your friend?" She said, looking past Alex, directly at Ruben.

Alex hit her against the head with the gun, the pain manageable, all things considered, and she turned her attention back to him.

"I think that you want to kill me because you believe that I'm the only one who knows what to do, don't you?"

There was silence in the room, the gun pressed into her temple again, and she knew that there was one of two situations unfolding: either she was right, or they were playing the silent game with her in hopes of her oversharing.

If, in fact, they were going for the latter, they *severely* underestimated her. It was almost offensive.

"Newsflash," she said, "everybody under my watch knows what the plan is."

She smiled sweetly at Alex, leaning against the gun as if it wasn't going to crack her head open. Her face, otherwise, was unmoving - no sign of pain, despite how much she was bleeding, despite the fact that she probably had a concussion, despite the fact that she could die any second. It was something she had perfected over the years - the act she always put on so well, the act of indifference.

"Go ahead," she challenged, again, out of pure boredom. "Do it. You'll see."

The silence that hung in the air was heavy. Alex took one step back from her, dropping the gun only slightly, so it was now pointing at her neck. He leaned forward and spat. "You are a fucking bitch."

"Yeah, well." she agreed, shrugging, taking it as a compliment, "thank you."

***

Clarissa had the reserve troops up and going the second she heard her Deller go off. She wasn't sure exactly what situation Eleri had found herself in, and all her attempts at communication proved to be useless, so all she could do was sit back and listen. As soon as she realized what was happening and that it was *not good*, she got everybody she could and began to march them into Aloneia.

This was not a glamorous feat at all. From what Claire could tell, Eleri's Deller had been broken, and the locator was not working as well as it should have been. It did, thankfully, still give her approximate location, and Claire knew that she had to take what she would get. She hated leading combat - she hated seeing it at all - but she understood that things were out of her control. She wouldn't ruin this because of her own predispositions.

Genie stayed back with the younger children in the safe house - God forbid she went with any of these people into combat and died. Eleri, Clove, and Clarissa had decided that Genie, under no circumstances, would be seeing the front. They didn't tell her, of course, as the protest would have been too much to handle, but Clarissa knew that at the speed she was moving to get people out of the safe house and with the magnitude of the situation ahead, telling Genie at the eleventh hour that she would be staying back would be much easier.

Genie coming to Aloneia now would mean leaving all of the children alone, and her motherly side would never allow that to happen.

Clover had instructed her team to sweep the floors - no prisoners. She knew that this would be difficult for many of them, given that Voskivy was built on the principle of peace, and even at the height of the war, when bombs were being dropped and people were being murdered in broad daylight, there were still Voskivians who found it hard to do what had to be done, but this time she made sure to be very clear in her direction: there was no other option. She had to be strict. She had to remind people that their single millisecond of hesitation could cost everyone else their lives. She had to make them all feel the guilt for an action they'd not yet done. It was the only way to be effective, and it was the only way to be strong.

She, herself, was sweeping the basement. She knew that the odds of finding someone there were high, and she knew that, from what Eleri and Fyodor had told her, most of the important materials were stored there.

She had already killed two people in the elevator. The ball was rolling now.

As she made her rounds, she began to consider how much was truly unfolding. She had taken everything in stride, understanding and navigating it all, but the sheer speed at which things were moving seemed too good to be true. She wasn't sure how they'd maintain this pace, but she knew that if they let up, even for a second, it would be worth gold to the Aloneians. And as heartless as it sounded, which is why she kept this thought to herself, they had already put themselves in jeopardy at their first stop waiting to see if Eleri would make it out. She entertained the thought briefly, for Fyodor's sake, she supposed, despite her better judgment. She knew they had to go.

She wondered if those few minutes would be the ones they'd be begging to get back when it all came down to the wire.

Thirteen.

My mother's favorite color was purple. Growing up, it reminded me of flowers and of gems and of beauty. I always attributed it to comfort and safety, stupidly. I wish, sometimes, that I could go visit my younger self and slap her across the face. I was such an idiot, when I still tried to find the good in people. A tragedy in itself, no? The good in people, as if that exists.

I'd like to think that human beings are neither inherently good nor evil because we ourselves decided what is constituted as good and what is constituted as evil, but I would be a fool to think that human beings aren't inherently selfish. At the end of the day, we will always save ourselves before saving others. I think if it comes down to it, and if we don't, we have trained ourselves not to do so.

My mother's favorite color was purple. Growing up, it reminded me of flowers and of gems and of beauty. Now, it only reminds me of bruises and of pain.

- The Found Diary of Eleri Roman, p. 74

—

Genie knew what was coming. She knew that things were going to end poorly. She knew that there was nothing she could do to stop it, and she knew that the more she hesitated, the harder this would be.

She had two options: to hide the children or to try and get them out.

The former seemed dangerous. She had seen the Aloneian troops making their way over to the safe house and she knew they were not coming to have a civil conversation. The thought was terrifying. She didn't know what she was supposed to do. Hiding the kids in the basement, in locked rooms, might spare their lives *if* the troops didn't choose to completely destroy the building. If they came for her, and only her, the children would stand a chance. She, of course, had no way of knowing what their motivations were and what their plan was. She didn't want her decision to be the wrong one, and she didn't want to look back with regret.

For a brief second, she appreciated the mindset that Eleri Roman had. That girl, in all her absolute delusion, would've made an entire plan in the blink of an eye. She'd never deliberate like this. She'd never waste this time. She would have an instinct, and she would go with it.

The other option, to try and get the kids out, seemed incredibly risky, as well. She would have no idea how to explain to them what to do and what was happening. She knew that the older ones - those who were thirteen, fourteen years old - would have some sort of grasp on the situation, and despite the fact that she, as a human being and as a mother, felt that they were entirely too young to have to face something like this, she trusted that they would be able to lead the group somewhere safe. Perhaps, she would send them to the bunker. Perhaps, she would flee, too. She wasn't sure, and that was her problem.

The only thing she was sure of was that she had to do something quickly.

***

Eleri had grown disinterested in the situation unfolding before her. She determined that Alex and Ruben weren't going to do anything to her once they'd learned that there was no point in killing her. She knew that they were making it up as they went, now, and she didn't care for it. Part of her - a *large* part of her - wished that they would just shoot her and get it over with. This was exhausting, and it was boring, and she hated this silence that was meant to be intimidating but only gave away their inability to change course of a plan on the spot. They were not adaptable, nor versatile, she decided. They were used to getting things their way and didn't know how to change their approach when they couldn't.

Alexander had turned his back to her as he spoke under his breath to Ruben, whose eyes were on her, unblinking. Neither of them approached her, but she knew that they'd be quick to do so if she so much as breathed too loud.

She'd found her way out of the binds that were holding her hands clasped behind her back, linking her fingers together to remind herself not to move too much. She knew that Clarissa was coming, with at least some people, and she could take both Alexander and Ruben down if she *really* wanted to, but she didn't know where her rifle was, and she had no idea why they'd let her keep her knives. They had to have some sort of backup plan if they were so ready to leave her with her favorite weapon. As much as she wanted to underestimate them, she could not. She knew better.

Ruben was panicking. He didn't know what to do. His fear was not of killing her - that would be easy and, honestly, fun for him. The fear was nestled in the notion that if she died, others would be angry. News would spread. People would become vicious, and he did not want things to escalate more than they already had. Alexander was pushing it - *come on, just do it, we're fucked, anyways* - but something inside of him said a firm *no*.

Alexander wanted to get it done and quickly. He was irritated - Ruben had unearthed him and begged him to come get this girl, and now that they had her, they weren't doing anything. It was infuriating for him. He said he wanted to stay out of all of this since the war ended, but Ruben seemed so desperate, and when he'd heard that Oliver had died, he reluctantly agreed. Now, he regretted that decision. If this were up to him, he'd not have come at all, or she'd be long dead by now. This game that Ruben was playing was a dangerous one, and there would be some sort of end point eventually. Alex knew this, and he could only hope it would end on his terms.

Eleri heard the noise before either of the men did if they noticed it at all. It was subtle, her overly exerted, military trained, alert at all times side picking up on it. The ghost of a sound, a small clanging noise, metal on metal. There was no ringing, someone had stopped their movements before the sound had the chance to travel, but the millisecond was enough to tell Eleri that they were not alone here.

Her instincts took over in that moment. She shifted, so subtly, in her chair, unlinking her fingers, cracking her wrists behind her back, loosening up her stiff limbs as much as she could without drawing attention to herself. Something was changing, and she'd be stupid not to notice it.

It all happened in a breath.

One moment, she was sitting, eyes ahead, watching Ruben and Alexander trade glances and whispers. The next, she had pushed the chair back, knives in her hands, Clarissa and two others bursting through the door.

Eleri moved like the ocean - a sheer force so adaptable and strong - as she charged towards Ruben and Alexander. There was no plan at this point. There was only the mantra that she had been trained to remember, the words that were engraved into her mind since she was fifteen years old. There was no compromise. No negotiation. They were to win or die trying.

Ruben fell to the floor. Eleri didn't see how it had happened, as she was too preoccupied with Alexander, but she heard the shot and the thud shook her to her core. Her focus split - one half of her mind attempting to process the fact that *Ruben Yorke*, of all people, was laying on the ground of a concrete building, struggling to breathe, just inches to her left; the other half desperately trying to stay occupied with wrangling the mass of a man that was Alexander.

She managed to wrap her arms around his throat from behind, her boot coming to the back of his knees, kicking in, bringing him down to the floor. She held him in place, guns trained on him by Claire and the others from in front, as the thought of using the knife in her hand became increasingly desirable.

She smiled. Claire noticed. It was slow, and it was *evil*.

Claire felt herself adjusting slightly in anticipation of what might've been coming. Sure, she had grown close to Eleri in a short period of time, but she continued to be an enigma. The Reaper's reputation was still, even now, playing in the back of her mind. She had heard the stories, and she took them all very seriously.

From what Clarissa had gathered thus far, she wasn't sure how many of the allegations were true, but she was incredibly certain that Eleri had the potential, and the will, to do any of the things she had been accused of. She never restricted people from violence, she encouraged people to do their work, and she supported most aggressive behaviors. Eleri was almost a textbook example of the image that preceded her, and Clarissa was somewhat *anxious* to see what would happen in this setting, with a man who outranked her after such an act of rebellion *already*.

Wordlessly, Eleri moved to his front, wrapping her hand around his throat, nails digging into the sides. She was careful not to cut his breath. Claire noticed this. Eleri wanted to remind him that she was in charge, but she didn't want to restrict him entirely. Not yet.

Ruben coughed on the ground behind her. Eleri, without averting her gaze from Alex, reached into her side, retrieved her pistol, and shot him.

Clarissa's eyes went wide as Eleri returned the gun to her side, trading it for her knife, tapping the blade against Alexander's head. "Are you planning on telling me what your goal is here, now that we've established that I do, in fact, have my shit together?"

She was twirling the knife between her fingers. She was shooting daggers with her eyes. Anyone in their right mind would've been scared to death. Unfortunately, Alexander was never in his right mind. He felt that this was funny.

The laugh that escaped his throat was evidence of that.

"Yeah, didn't think so."

Eleri adjusted her hand ever so slightly, and suddenly, Alexander was gasping for air, her fingers digging into his neck, drawing blood, her faces inches away from his. She pressed harder, and he was sputtering, his hands trying desperately to grasp something, to ease the tension, but falling onto air. Eleri did not flinch. She only turned her head to the side, a small smile forming on her lips, the pads of her fingers bruising his throat.

She dropped him then, giving him the luxury of breath, only for a moment, before kneeing him back up as his head dropped forward in anguish.

"You sit up when I'm speaking to you."

He was bleeding - from his head, from his neck, from his nose.

Eleri gently dragged her knife up his temple, collecting blood onto her blade, holding the piece of metal in between them.

"I think there may be a lot more where that came from," she whispered menacingly. "Wanna find out?"

She moved the blade to his throat, gently, until the first bead of crimson appeared on the skin. Clarissa was both unnerved and intrigued at this interaction. She *knew* how to use a weapon as more than just a tool.

She, herself, was a weapon.

She pushed the knife in slightly, holding the back of his head in her free hand, ensuring that he did not move away from the pain. She wasn't killing him like this. If she removed her hand now, he would be bleeding, sure, probably for a few hours, but he wouldn't die. He would make a full recovery. If anything, the bruising would prove to be more of an issue than the cut would.

There was something inside of her that was burning. Was it the pent-up jealousy that she'd felt for years, knowing that there was someone more feared than she was? He wasn't even *all that*, now that she thought about it, considering how easily she'd attained the upper ground. Was it because she wanted to show Clarissa exactly why her reputation wasn't going anywhere? Maybe, but she was also sick of it, to an extent, so furthering the agenda of those around her would not be in her best interest.

She refrained. If he was going to die, he was going to die painfully.

So instead of moving the blade further in, she moved it further across, dragging it gently around the side of his neck.

That was it.

He let out a cry. She heard Clarissa beg her to just kill him, to get it over with, and in one motion, understanding the magnitude of her actions, she did.

He fell to the floor, eyes full of fear in fresh death. Eleri had taken no pity on the man. She did not care to do so. He deserved every second of that as much as she knew that she, herself, did.

She stood fully, cleaning the knife on the edge of his shirt, placing it back onto her leg. She turned to Clarissa. "I don't have a rifle."

Clarissa nodded. There was an evident discomfort on her features, her eyes still trained on Alexander's body, voice trembling slightly as she spoke. "That's fine. Someone can give you theirs once we get out. But, El..." she took a look around the room, gesturing with wide arms, "Where exactly are we?"

Eleri took a deep breath, looking once again at the space around her. "You won't believe this, but I have no clue." Then, a smile. A soft one, unlike the one she wore to face Alex. "We can always find out."

Eleri had noticed how unfamiliar the room looked when she'd first been able to focus on her surroundings over the pain in her head. She had been into every room of every building she'd been into at least once, so whether or not this was a place she knew but a room she didn't was out of the question. She had tried to reason with herself, that maybe since she was out of it, there was something that would normally click for her that simply was not under the circumstances, but the longer she spent there, the longer she knew that was simply not the case.

She led Clarissa out of the room.

"We came in through there," Clarissa said, pointing to a door ahead.

Eleri nodded. "Do you want to go out? I think I want to figure out what's in here before we leave."

Claire shook her head, turning to the soldiers she had entered with. "Go back outside, tell them what's going on. We'll be out in a second." then, back to Eleri, "let's make this quick."

Eleri led Claire into the first unlocked room they found. It was relatively small, with only a few shelves lining the walls.

"It looks like a janitor's closet. Let's go." Claire said, frowning at the unremarkable space.

"No," Eleri said, trying to channel Fyodor, trying to think of what he would be doing in this all-too inconspicuous space. "It's not."

She stepped towards the back wall, hand dragging along it until she felt a ridge. She looked, her eyes focusing on a small square that seemed darker than the rest.

She flipped it up. The wall slid backward and rotated to the side, revealing an entire library full of boxes and files.

"Shit," Clarissa breathed, eyes wide, "we don't have time to go through all of this,"

But Eleri, as if something was pulling her, as if forgetting what was going on entirely, stepped into the room. Her eyes traced the outlines of the files, landing on names, and on titles, and on dates -

Until one caught her eye.

27/09/2247

It was a date that Eleri remembered all too well and would forever. The 27th of September, exactly fourteen days before Voskivy's surrender, the day her friends died.

"El, we should go -"

Frantically, Eleri opened the folder, met with pictures and reports of all six of the people in her group, herself and Fyodor staring back up at her as she flipped through the papers, notes and references and quotes littering the pages. There were clips holding sections of research together, one on each member, one on their tasks, one marked the date of the fatal explosion.

She pulled it out gently, only to find a reference number.

"Eleri,"

"Wait," she said, voice laced with a certain desperation that Clarissa thought she was incapable of.

It was enough to let her have a bit more time.

Eleri located the number on the paper against the drawers on the lower half of the walls fairly quickly, sliding it open after unlocking it with a key she found hanging against a shelf within arm's reach.

Her heart dropped to her stomach.

Inside the drawer were personal belongings of each of her friends, ones that she and Fyodor were specifically denied possession of - something about it all belonging to Aloneian authorities. Rings and necklaces and patchwork and *Kassander's green jacket.*

Her heart broke into a million pieces as she removed it from the bin, placing it over her shoulders. Allowing herself to sit in it for a moment, she moved her hands down, feeling something inside of one of the many pockets, swallowing hard. Her heart was hammering as she reached past the fabric, hand clasping around whatever the object was, hesitant to remove it.

His golden cigarette case, the image of the angel dancing with the devil engraved on the front, as familiar as if she had seen it the night before. She cracked open the top, revealing the red leather interior, a photograph of the group of all six of them tucked away beneath the three remaining cigarettes.

She left everything untouched as she closed it again.

She knew Clarissa was growing impatient, so she did what she could. She slid the rings and necklaces into his empty pocket, took the file of papers that was pressed to the bottom of the drawer, and closed it.

She returned to Clarissa.

"Let's go," was all she said.

Clarissa, always the curious type, wanted to ask. She wanted to understand what exactly had happened, to have a better grip on the aspects of this situation that she had never heard of before, but she knew better. Eleri's walk was tall, rigid, and that of a woman who did not want to be analyzed.

Eleri began to lead the group towards the Military building, knowing that they'd leave that one for last if they were taking out the rest. She had retrieved a rifle from someone else in the group, throwing it over her shoulder, *over* Kassander's jacket.

She had established that the building they'd been in was one she had seen many times but never entered. As far as she knew, it was co-owned by Oliver and Ruben, but its purpose was always irrelevant to her, and she never cared enough to learn about the specificities of the establishment.

She wished she had, though, reading through this file about her friends, leading a group of strangers into her own region in order to destroy her buildings. And she did not want to believe what she was reading. She probably would've rationalized, too, if not for the last statement, written and underlined, on the second page.

ALL SIX MEMBERS MUST BE DISPOSED OF.

She was no fool. She knew what this meant, and turning the page hesitantly, her suspicions were only confirmed - maps, layouts, directions, markings - all leading to the time and place that took the lives of those around her.

With a deep, full breath, calming her nerves, she folded the papers, pushing them into the jacket, flipping the rifle into her hands.

They lied. About *everything*. And all she did was stand by and watch.

Fourteen.

Days go by far too slowly given what is going on. Every single available second seems to be full of chaos. This should be a rush, considering everything we're doing. Things should all feel tense, yes, but I feel like it should be flying by. There should be more of a struggle, no? Besides my own personal... experiences... I don't think there have been too many setbacks. And it seems strange, given who we're up against. During my time with Aloneian forces, everything seemed so well organized and so well prepared. But then again, I never got to see everyone work as a whole - I was normally only with my own people. Maybe that makes a difference. I guess I'll never truly know.

The longer things go on, the more I realize how little I ever truly knew, anyways. My entire life, I spent every day under the *assumption that because of my position, or my record, or my service, I was relatively aware of everything. It was embarrassing how little I knew and how naive I was, especially as I was insulting people with that same quality.*

Was I thankful for the revelation? Maybe. But if anything, I was grateful to get revenge.

- The Found Diary of Eleri Roman, p. 78

—

Eleri arrived at the ministry district just as the buildings began to come down. She watched, a smile growing on her face as the education building crumbled onto itself, falling straight down as if it were made of paper. She heard some sort of screaming, barely audible over the sound of destruction, but it was enough to send her marching forwards, boots on concrete.

Thump. Thump. Thump.

Clarissa was beside her. She knew this without looking, the feeling of her presence strong enough to absorb even through all the smoke and flames. Eleri was certain that if they hadn't already, the rest of the military would be mobilized. It was far too late in the day for them not to be.

She watched as groups of their makeshift army ran from the building. Her eyes scanned each face, quickly, carefully. She saw Clover but wasn't sure if Clove had seen them amidst all the movement. She kept looking: no, no, no, yes.

The group had assembled far enough away from the building. Clover reassigned tasks, and Eleri watched as Fyodor stood beside her, that stupid scar on his face bleeding *again*, a bruise forming on his lower lip. She waited, unwilling to interrupt until Clover called the groups to action. People moved quickly, heading straight into the next buildings, not a second thought, not a moment of hesitation.

Eleri looked at Claire once and turned her attention to the group. "Fyodor!"

He turned, almost reluctantly on his heels, as if he was severely disinterested in whatever was awaiting his attention. But the moment he laid eyes on her, his demeanor changed. Even from the significant distance at which Eleri stood from him, she saw it. She saw his eyes widen, his smile grow. She watched as he threw his rifle over his back and as he ran to her.

She laughed, *a real laugh, Clarissa noted*, as she opened her arms to him. His body crashed into hers, arms around her waist, lifting her, holding her against his chest. His hand found the back of her head, rooting his fingers in her hair, keeping her pressed against him in fear of losing her again. For the first time in her life, she understood. She hadn't been considering what he was thinking as she was missing. She hadn't thought about how he more than likely had thought her dead, selfish of her to do, but the truth nonetheless. She settled on the thought that to him, it truly did feel like she'd be gone again forever if he let her go.

There was a certain steadiness she felt through her body as she knelt onto the ground in her room, pulling back a carpet, revealing a door. With a soft sigh, she opened it, revealing one rifle and one pistol and her only hope at survival. She pulled them both out, the knowledge that her time was running out weighing on her mind excessively. She knew they were coming; she'd never be able to understand what was going on by the time they arrived. She didn't have time to focus on that. She only had time to focus on the immediate future.

She was scared, but there was no place for fear in a time like this.

Genie walked in large strides to the front of the safe house, sitting down on the steps with the pistol on her hip and the rifle across her lap. She thought she would never be in a position like this again.

But knowing her son…

Fyodor had always been strong-willed and determined, even as a child, and from a young age she noticed that he had a mind of his own unless being influenced by someone he truly held in a high regard, like his family, or, evidently, like Eleri. Genie was sure that she had a much stronger influence on this decision than Fyo would believe. She thought, in the back of her mind, that Eleri was to blame for all of this - that the stupid girl's impulse got them into this extremely avoidable mess.

She wanted to see her son again, though. And without her impulse, they may have never been given the chance.

Genie sat tall as she watched the rush come towards her, knowing there was nothing she could do but accept her fate. She wondered if they'd kill her, or if she'd be taken prisoner, or if they would talk to her first.

She wondered if anyone would recognize her.

From what she knew, most of the Aloneian troops in Voskivy were young and would have joined this army long after she had gone. But, according to Clover, the vast majority of those troops had been taken out in the explosion caused by Eleri and Fyodor. This would only mean a full remilitarization of whoever else was off duty back in Aloneia.

And many of the men who were off duty right now in Aloneia knew her very, very well.

She thought, briefly, about her husband. She only ever wanted to remember him in flashes. The entirety of the memory - any of them surrounding him - was too painful to take in full. Only in doses. Only ever in doses.

He was everything she could have ever wanted. He was quiet, and he was stoic, but he was good, and he loved with his entire heart. That was what mattered to her.

Had she been more fortunate, he might've been here now. Missing in action for three days before his body was found. She assumed he'd been killed in combat. She'd never know, though. That was what pained her.

Her one regret was not sending a letter to her children. Her one regret was allowing some stranger to write about the death of their father instead of doing it herself. She was a coward in that moment, and she was a coward for not apologizing to her son in what may have been her only chance. She was not all that he thought she was, and though she wished she could be, she knew that if Fyodor knew how disappointing she had always been, he would hate her.

She wondered if he had already begun to figure that out.

Genie fixed her grip on the rifle in her lap, her knuckles white, her leg bouncing. She was scared. Her breath was slow, each inhale seemingly hours long, but her heart was racing. If she was going to be paralyzed in fear, she didn't want to exhibit it at first glance, and she could only hope she contained herself enough to seem unphased by the horror unfolding before her.

The rumble of their approach was akin to that of thunder in the dead of night. All that Genie could do was close her eyes, only for a moment, to try and see the lightning through the dark before the storm inevitably came.

***

Clarissa squinted, eyes focusing on the group of people making their way towards her. It was just people. It was just movement. It was nothing to be alarmed by. But the seconds went by, and the people never passed over the hill, the group only seeming to become larger and larger.

It was just people. But God, there were a lot of them.

There was something inside of her that seemed to be pleading with the universe. She couldn't place it - the feeling nor the proposal - and it was so subconscious that she barely realized that she was doing it.

Clarissa turned to the buildings behind her. She couldn't be sure how far along her friends were, and she knew asking would only alarm them, perhaps making them go too quickly. She and Clover had, through the years, led some unfathomable expeditions. They had come together and created some of the strongest forces their side would ever see. They were so incredibly smart and skilled, and for the most part, they knew what they were doing.

This, though, was something else entirely. She kept trying to put it into perspective. Claire was very rational, and she thought very intellectually. Her decisions were never emotional, always calculated, but despite an entire lifetime of thinking in numbers and codes, there was nothing about this that seemed to click for her. Nothing about it - not Eleri, not the plan they had made, not the speed at which they'd done it - felt right to her. And it wasn't a lack of faith. No. Never that. Claire had instilled in herself a mindset of determination, and of possibility, and of the very real option they had to go against this oppressive government. She always had faith.

She just knew that it didn't matter what documents she wrote, or what projections she made, or what numbers she pulled together. Her research, her planning, and her critical thinking were irrelevant. She would never have been able to come to this conclusion. She would never have been able to guess that she would be here, on this day, on the verge of something bigger than all of them.

"Hey," she said, a hushed tone, to no one in particular.

A girl stepped up beside her. Claire had seen this girl multiple times, always at the front of groups and always first out the door. Over their time in the safe house, this girl was always going around making sure people were okay. She would stop and talk to everybody, she would get food for people if they weren't eating, she'd tell stories to the younger kids, and she always seemed to bring light into the rooms she entered.

Clarissa didn't know if Clover had ever gotten around to talking to the girl, but she knew that she, herself, had not. It wasn't a lack of desire, but Claire was always *so* busy. This girl could only truly be three years younger than her, at most, and the intrigue was always there.

Frankly, though, things were never that easy. It seemed like lazy reasoning, but between the night watches and the papers and death always looming overhead, Claire never had the time.

But now, though, almost as she should've expected, this girl who seemed to be everywhere was once again at her side.

"Ma'am?"

Claire smiled, turning to face the red-haired girl. Deep eyes shone in admiration, the freckles littering her cheeks like the splatter of a paintbrush, thick eyebrows framing her delicate face.

She looked every part of how she behaved. She was warm, and she was kind, and standing to her left with the rifle in her hand and the straps across her back, she was the biggest contradiction imaginable.

She was a dark blade cutting through the petal of a rose.

"Claire," she introduced herself, folding her arms over her chest. "Your name, soldier?"

"Delaney," she said, then after a moment of silence, "Delaney Bishop."

Claire took a deep breath. "You know," she said, turning back to the girl, "Clove and I wanted to talk to you. We just never got around to it. But now, Del, now that we're here, I think I can say I want to trust you with something."

Her eyes seemed brighter, a blush creeping into her cheeks, pink between white and brown. She nodded, slightly, with a smile, and Claire noticed a scar across her neck.

She said nothing.

"I want you to help me lead this inevitable charge," she said, a light playfulness to her tone, a sinister voice that she rarely ever found herself using, "when we split this group into two."

Delaney turned behind her, looking at the rest of the soldiers they'd amassed, and then back to the horizon. "We have enough people?"

Clarissa swung her own rifle into her hands. She shrugged nonchalantly. Delaney, bless her heart, was trying to take cues from her. She was trying to understand her place and the feelings and the thought process behind this. She had always admired Claire and Clove - since they'd first been semi-appointed, semi-forced into these leadership roles - Delaney had always been incredibly in awe of how they took everything and created something better out of it. They planted seeds in a desert and had turned it into a rainforest. She had always thought about what it might be like to work with them, to become a part of this elite duo that always seemed to have it all together. She had always imagined that one day, luck would be on her side, and she would prove herself.

She never thought it would be like this, but hearing that they had noticed her and that they wanted to reach out but never could only solidify that she had been doing everything right this whole time. Delaney was honored, and she was humbled, that they had seen her and that Claire, who had not spoken two words to her before now, was ready to put full faith in her.

"We have more than none. That's always enough."

Delaney swallowed. She had a feeling that something along those lines would be spoken, but she didn't know how much of it was based in truth and belief, and how much of it was based in Claire not wanting to cast fear.

She quickly realized she had no time to debate this. Regardless of what it was, she had a job to do.

Claire pointed to the group in front of them. "They won't be long," she said, "and our guys still have shit to get done. I'll split the group. You take one side, I'll take the other. You go up, I go in."

"Up?" Delaney questioned, biting her lower lip.

Claire tilted her head to the side. Delaney followed the direction, eyes locking onto a bridge not far from where they stood. "Up. They come to me, you stay above them. Worst case scenario, they get through us, but you still have the higher ground. Literally."

Delaney looked back to Claire. "We have time to get up there, you think?"

Claire nodded once. "You have time to do anything you want. You just have to focus on it yourself. You can't factor in how fast these people are moving or how long you think it will take you to do it. You just *go*, and soon enough you're there."

***

Clover had only just set down the last of the explosives in her building when she heard the gunshots. Her head snapped upwards, staring directly ahead instinctively, waiting for more noise.

When it came, she rose to her feet, detonator in hand, running to the closest window. Peering outside, she saw something she feared but expected - the chaos, the combat, the direct fight that had begun. Unorganized.

Second nature - she held her rifle firmly in one hand, dropping it to her side, rushing through the halls of her building, calling on anyone she saw to get out. She knew that this was going to be messy. It appeared to her that this event would be unlike any other she'd ever experienced. There was no strategy. There was only the tangible notion of cheating death.

Teeth were sinking into the wound that had already been cut. The bite was from an iron jaw, the grip so secure, so strong, that there was no way out. The mouth had been open for a while, though - predator watching prey, the flytrap waiting for the bug, the smell of blood and taste of metal lingering - and Clover knew this. There was a wave of white noise and of paralyzing fear, and behind that chaos would be the sun. She knew this, too. It was a fact. She had been banking on it for her entire life, that one day the jaw did release, and when the wave fell back into the ocean, there would be peace.

But unhinging the jaw and pulling the tide were both tasks that she wasn't sure she'd be able to complete.

Clover had never felt doubt in her actions, but as she walked out of the building, thumb on the button of the detonator, the impact of the explosion almost immediate, she wondered for the first time if she had dug herself a grave, not a foxhole.

Fifteen.

A military state, it was called, apparently. Interestingly enough, I hadn't come to this conclusion on my own, Fyodor had told me the term that made so much sense. As smart as I felt I was, I felt so stupid in that moment. OF COURSE, it was a military state. We were run not by a government but by an army.

That changed my perspective on many things. I had always prided myself in my influence, but never understood, or at least was able to grasp, that it was because of my position in that military, and subsequently, the government. It had all gone over my head for far too long. Fyo had only known because of something his mother had taught him when he was younger. It was one of the many tidbits he seemed to have collected over the years; ones which he always assumed were common knowledge but were frankly individual to him. I told him, when he had talked to me about what a military state was, that this was something everybody should be aware of. That order and freedom shouldn't be mutually exclusive. It opened my eyes to something that I still tried to ignore. I wanted to spread the word, but with people like Milton, I was scared for my life. The truth was there to be found, but not exploited by me.

If I were an honest person, I would talk to people about how horrid everything was. But I am not an honest person. All I do is lie.

- The Found Diary of Eleri Roman, p. 81

—

Xavier Talon's fingers drummed against the desk, the pen in his hand gently tapping the sides of the table, falling between his knuckles, side to side. The imbalance was fun in theory, irritating in practice, as many things were, and Xavier curled his hand around the pen, stopping his ministrations, as he looked down at the sheet in front of him.

He could sign off on it, right? There was no reason he couldn't. It was a simple order. He wouldn't even be doing the killing, himself. He had done this time and time again. He had spent years signing papers just like this one. He had never, however, felt this knot in his stomach or this tug at his chest before. This would only take a moment. It would only take one drag of the ink across the line on the bottom of the page. And this was an emergency for all Aloneians. It was, truly, something he had every ounce of control over. He had his entire region to take care of, now, and he was shying away from the task.

A task that was so simple. A task that would require nothing more than this from him.

And yet, he could not find it in himself to do it.

He had never fully stepped out of his role. He, of course, under all technical umbrellas, had retired, but now considering everything that was happening, his ties to everyone who had been killed - Milton, Oliver, and he assumed Ruben, amongst others, he was sure - had put him in a position of power once again.

But, this time, there was a lot more on the line than he would've liked to admit.

He knew, though he pretended not to, that if his wife was here, she'd scold him. She would remind him that, in fact, there was no more on the line now than any other time he had ever signed a paper such as this one. It was the same situation, only for different people. She would've told him that he had to make up his mind - to consider if this was something he could morally do, or not. This should not rest on the shoulders of who is on the other side of the paper now because it never did before.

And she would be right. She may have not even let him make his own mind up. It grew increasingly evident that her guidance was something he was missing, even after all this time.

One executive order would fully mobilize every on and off-duty soldier in the region. One executive order that would allow for any action to be taken under the name of this emergency. One single sheet of paper, one single stroke of a pen, that would give full power over to each individual, that would dismiss any crimes committed during this period of time.

It would, surely, put an end to this *revolution*, if that's what they were calling it. He didn't see it as such, he saw it as more of a point trying to be proven, and he would never entertain the idea of acknowledging it as a revolution - that would imply that there was a reason to revolt, and he would never outwardly admit to his heinous behavior in such a way. However, he did understand that whatever it was, it was a strong movement, and he would have to sign off if they wanted to have any chance of stopping it.

But it wasn't just some random soldiers from Voskivy this time. It was Eleri, and it was Fyodor, and they were still, by all accounts, the closest things he had to kids. And sometimes kids acted out. Maybe they just needed a moment to collect themselves and they'd stop.

But you don't have a moment. You have now.

He heard the knock at the door behind him but didn't turn back as it opened. Instead, his eyes trailed up, in front of him, to the window, gazing outside at the peace that laid before him. His window faced the vast nothingness that he had never ventured into. The trees and the river always waited to engulf him, but he never stepped through. Something about the plausible, infinite calmness felt wrong to him. Maybe that was the same moral preventing him from signing off on this order.

Maybe he couldn't do it. Not in good faith or conscience.

But it wasn't about him; it was about *them*. If they weren't there, if this had all happened organically and two of the most important people in his life hadn't turned into the opposition, maybe this would have been infinitely easier.

He scoffed. Eleri always managed to find herself in the middle of everything.

***

Genie stood as the first man approached her. A cigarette hung between her lips, she had lit it sometime between fearing for her life and accepting her fate, the rifle in her hands still feeling all too heavy for her comfort.

The first man who approached her was older, and Genie *knew* that she had seen him before. He took his hat off of his head, tucking it under his arm, setting his rifle down. His eyes were hidden by dark glasses, the frown on his lips almost undetectable.

"I do not have my weapon on you, Madam Farrow-Kacer. Please, don't act like this."

The voice was familiar, too. She couldn't put her finger on it. She couldn't place it, and as it had been years since she had seen any of these people, but she knew that this man was someone she was familiar with.

She knew because he used her hyphenated last name. She had stopped using her own maiden name and had only gone by Kacer shortly after she joined this fight. That meant that this man had to have been there from the beginning, or at least had to have been around people who were.

She dropped her rifle to the side, setting it against the ground, taking the cigarette from her lips between her fingers.

"Can I help you?"

"You were presumed dead."

"What is it, exactly, that you are referring to?"

Genie was not an idiot. Sure, it had been some time since she was in a position like this, having a less than comfortable conversation, but she still remembered important things. For example, she would never say *I don't know what you're talking about*. That statement was vulnerable and could be used against her in a number of ways. It was the subtle difference between claiming she wasn't sure what was being spoken about and asking the other person to elaborate more. To the person asking, they meant the same thing. To the person receiving the question, they were two entirely different statements.

"I think, Gene, that you know what it is that I am referring to."

That was the second indicator. *Gene.* Not Genie, not Evginia. *Gene.* Only a handful of people called her that. Those who she knew well. Those who she was close to. Those who had worked with her before everything went to absolute shit.

She kept her face straight. "I'm afraid I don't want to be making guesses. I don't want to *interpret* what it is that you're saying." She licked her lips. "If you have something to say, it has to be said."

There was a beat. Silence. The man raised a gloved hand to his face. "No," he said, removing his glasses, "I don't really think it does."

Her breath caught in her throat. Bullet grey eyes. A menacing venom. The skin was swollen around his left eye, bruised and cut and tender, but the fire behind it was strong all the same. The pieces fell together. He looked much older than when she had last seen him, granted years, especially in this environment, did change a person, inevitably. She noted that something about his demeanor seemed different than how she remembered him. He seemed so *broken.*

She didn't think her voice would be so quiet as she spoke. "Ruben?"

***

Delaney was thanking herself over and over again for having decided to pack her scope with her upon their departure. She didn't think that she would be using it, in all honesty, but now, crouching on top of the bridge, it was the only thing that would help her. She had always been a sniper - now, in the midst of the actual war, even before then when she would go hunting with her uncle - and it was truly what made her feel most comfortable. She hated close-range combat of any kind - hand to hand, knife to knife, using a pistol as opposed to a rifle - despite the fact that she was good at it. It was here, it was the bird's eye view and the composure she felt looking through the glass, where she knew she would do her best work.

She wondered if Claire had known this or if it had just been luck. She wouldn't have been surprised if she or Clove had created a file about her or, at the very least, had heard about her. They seemed to know a bit about everybody, despite having a personal relationship with them or not, and she was sure that Clarissa was calculated enough to have done so out of desire, not chance.

Delaney felt oddly at home with the weight in her hands. Steady breaths, calm demeanor. She had organized her side quickly, directing people to spread along the bridge in small groups, ensuring that they had as much area covered as they could. She could see Claire fighting on the ground, her movements light, quick, concentrated. She could see the masses of people falling and the groups who were fighting to stay alive. She knew that they only had a few minutes, at most, before the Aloneians turned their attention to the bridge. There was no doubt in her mind that they could take it out in seconds, if they wanted to, and she and everyone else on top of it would be seriously injured, if not dead. Delaney had fallen into the leadership role fairly quickly, without realizing it, and she had taken it on her own shoulders to ensure that the people under her command made it out, even if she did not. She hadn't yet absorbed the pressure of the sentiment, but she understood it in an analytical sense, and she knew that if someone was going to die, it would be her, not them.

Del, though, unlike Clove and Claire and seemingly everybody who lived in the safehouse, had her reservations about Eleri and Fyodor, even more so now that she knew that Genie was his mother, and she wasn't eager to take their side. The greater picture, now, was something she could put above her own biases. The thought that these two may have been their only hope at coming out of what had just been bestowed upon them was something that she didn't want to admit, but she knew it was true in every aspect. She knew, based on what she had seen and heard, that as much as she trusted Clarissa and Clover, the two would never have taken the final step of putting any plan into action had Eleri not reached out and offered an olive branch. She'd heard from others in the safehouse that they had discussed it before, but the risk was too high given the occupation in their region, and they felt that it was too soon after the war to revolt. It wouldn't make sense. Everybody was on high alert, on both sides of the equation, and the Aloneians would have anticipated some sort of movement or change. It was obvious, and going into it guns blazing, head on, would be dangerous, so she understood their hesitance.

Eleri, though, still seemed suspicious to her.

She had never spoken to the girl, nor had seen her in real life, but stories outweigh memories when there are none to be had.

Back before Del had gone into active combat, she had been writing a report on the group that Eleri led. She, being younger than most of the people already established in the force, had to work her way up to their positions. As one of her final tasks before becoming part of active combat, she was ordered to amass all the information regarding Eleri Roman and this group of five other individuals. She studied all of the attacks and murders and destruction that could be linked back to this group beyond a reasonable shadow of a doubt. She looked for patterns, and for consistencies, and for anything that may have been an indicator of where they were going or what they were planning on doing next. Delaney fell deeply into the case study, leaving no stone unturned, leaving no corner unsearched. She took witness accounts, she went to the now abandoned sites of these events, she spent all her time creating this file, trying to understand what it was that was going on. She found it so incredibly unbelievable that these people could go around like this, and that they were yet to be caught. She knew that if they were out of the picture, Voskivy would have a significant advantage over the Aloneians.

Delaney had concluded, at some point in her research, that they were the spine of the force and that had they not been so good at what they did, this would be a much easier war to win.

The problem, though, for Delaney was that she could not draw a pattern. She tried charts, but everything seemed like its own outlier. She tried sorting, but everything seemed to only fit in an individual category. There were nowhere near enough trends, nor consistencies, to be able to anticipate what was going on with this group. She was someone who liked knowing. She liked having answers. She liked being able to understand things. But when it came to Eleri Roman, there was nothing she could do. The girl was wicked. She was unbelievable. She would only ever leave her tracks uncovered if she wanted people to see them, and she would disappear into thin air if she wanted to hide.

In a way, Delaney admired her. Through her studies, she found many leadership qualities in the Reaper that she could only wish to have herself. Del knew that so much of what Eleri could do would never be quantified nor explained. She was graced with these gifts and abilities and unmatched clairvoyance from birth, as it seemed, and Delaney was *obsessed* with it. She had heard once, many years ago, that leaders were born, not made. She often disputed this claim. She wanted to believe that anyone could become a leader if they were hungry for it. But after looking at Eleri for so long, she could no longer dispute the claim as long as it was amended.

Leaders could be born, or they could be made. There was no strict guideline. There was no good nor bad. Anyone could be a leader, despite their cause, despite their stance. A leader, if not a leader for her, was a leader for someone else. Opposition did not dictate the stance of someone in power, it only gave them someone more to attempt to rule over. Leaders could be made by all means.

Villains could only ever be born.

Sixteen.

We turn each other into weapons but become angry when we kill. Why become angry at successfully completing the only task you've ever been given?

- The Found Diary of Eleri Roman, p. 84

—

Eleri had a suspicion that a decision like this would have to be made eventually. The moral dilemma. The worst thing that she could ever do.

One of the things that she regretted most about her reputation, about who she so harshly painted herself to be, was that she was supposed to act like this moral dilemma was not something that impacted her. It did. It always would. But that didn't matter to anyone else, and it would not matter to her.

Her decision was made all at once. It only took a moment for all of the pieces to tie into each other.

She knew it as the military building fell. She knew it as she saw another wave of people over the horizon. She knew it as she watched a sniper on the bridge and soldiers in the streets. Someone has signed an executive order, and the registry in her mind could only allow her to land on one person, despite how little she wanted to. She found herself, unlike her usual thought process, scrambling to find an alternative. But Xavier's name was the only one that stood clear in her mind, both on first instinct and after reflection, and she was very much aware that this was indisputable. Eleri did not want to believe that he would do this to her. She would want to believe that of all people, Xavier would be the one she could trust to put the pen down. To not go through with it. She thought that he, given their relationship, would struggle and would choose her life over his orders.

She was naive to do so. Her naivety would end here.

Between the chaos and the noise, she had told Fyodor her suspicions, and he agreed - *I told you not to talk to him, shut up, he's still the one who gave us information* - telling her that they would need to figure this one out on their own.

Eleri found Clove, who had asked where the hell all of these new people were coming from, and upon her brief explanation, the mutual understanding and agreement was brought to fruition with only one phrase.

"So you know better than we do," Clover said, "that you need to go fix it."

And so, with her blessing, Eleri and Fyodor broke away from the group, as they so often did, as they were always more comfortable doing. Rifle. Hands. Knife. Thighs. Straps across her back. Necklaces draped from his neck. The jacket over her shoulders. The scar on his face. All of it was so familiar. If she closed her eyes, she could almost imagine them back with their team, on their way to complete something else that they were overly qualified for. The storm that waged inside of her had been a mellow thunder for so long, but the hurricane and the tornado seemed to be building and she was scared that she would no longer be able to contain it. Eleri had never felt so much, let alone all at once, before. She was full of pure, pointed rage and of deep, dark sadness. She was buzzing, she was focused, and she was absorbing everything the world had to offer. The snow beneath her feet. The sun shining cool overhead. There was a new life in the world around her, and her sick and twisted mind could only attribute that to the task at hand.

Fyodor, despite his attitude, felt a crushing weight on his shoulders and in his heart. Of course, something like this would come their way. Now that they had learned and grown and decided to fight for something that was right, now that they were able to see past the lies and deceit and manipulation, now that the gaslighting didn't leave fog in their minds and they'd pulled the wool away from their eyes just in time to see the slaughter, they would be thrown back under the rocks and crushed by those walking above them.

Now, Fyodor was smart. He was much more intelligent than he gave himself credit for and possessed a sort of intellect that Eleri did not. Because of all that he knew, he had semi-anticipated (or at least, had not been too shocked and bewildered at) a lot of the events that had unfolded over the past few days. In that regard, he had a sneaking suspicion about Xavier, and his gut had been telling him that something would happen with the man. Despite this, though, he would have never anticipated it to happen this way.

Eleri couldn't help but think back to Sevyn - not her friend, but the girl she had watched die in that explosion. She had killed before, but never anyone she had felt a connection to. Never had she watched the light leave someone's eyes and felt *guilt*. She had gone her entire career, she could say, without having put herself in a position to fully see and process the wreckage she had created. She moved around. She had things to do, and feeling pity was never one of them.

Now, though, things were changing, and she knew it. She knew that less-than-desirable decisions would have to be made if she chose to immerse herself in this endeavor, and she'd told herself it did not matter. She, for once, would be doing something right after years of committing to the wrong thing. She rationalized it. A few hard choices for the sake of saving an entire population. To essentially help stop a genocide.

A genocide that she helped to start.

She hated it. She hated everything she had done in the name of something she never even understood. The conflict was growing, and it was consuming her. The sky met the sea and disappeared into itself, only leaving behind the shadow of what was once structured and comprehensible; the sun falling behind a veil of its own light, the wind picking it up and throwing it away. Nothing made sense to her anymore, no matter how hard she tried to push past it.

Fyodor and Eleri walked through the place they once called home with a new hatred towards each building, each street, each window. There was the water. There was the sky. There were all of the things that once stood for peace.

There was the conflict. The moral. The conscience that she never had.

She wondered what it would be like to be a decent human being.

***

Genie and Ruben stood far away from the safehouse as it was searched. He leaned against a tree, hands in his pockets, eyes locked on hers. She stood directly in front of him, hands clasped together in front of her, her thumb running over her knuckles as a distraction.

"Gene-"

"Save it."

Ruben breathed deeply, a rumble in his throat and chest. Part of him felt bad that this was how they would meet again, but at the end of the day, he had made his decisions, and she had made hers. He held nothing against her personally, and he could only hope she felt the same.

"You know, you could've-"

"Shut up, Ruben. Please." She rubbed her hand across her forehead. "You don't really think you're going to prove a point to me, do you? Because after what you did, you should know how little I care for what you think."

Ruben Yorke and Evginia Farrow-Kacer worked together when things had first started to come undone. They, at first, played off of each other in a way nobody had seen before. They seemed to fit all of each other's missing parts, knowing exactly what the other would say before they said it. It was a partnership that, in the early days, would prove to be a great asset. Their combined knowledge of history and the current state of the world was unrivaled, and they knew how to use that in a way that no other skill would balance.

Of course, all good things come to an end.

Evginia blamed herself for her husband's death. She also, equally, blamed Ruben Yorke and his thick skull.

Their first, and only disagreement, turned out to be something that they both deeply regretted. Genie had been out in combat more often, going from mission to mission as they all saw fit, knowing that while she was valuable on the field, she was equally valuable in administration. It was when Ruben had organized an incredibly dangerous field operation, her husband on the force and Genie herself left off of it, that she became angry. Ruben explained that the reason she had been left off was that they could not afford to lose her.

That was his first mistake.

His second mistake was assuming that she would take this and digest it. She did not. She was repulsed, vehemently opposing. Pain was something she had grown to know as part of herself, but she was not prepared for what she knew would happen if this was truly as dangerous as it was made out to be. And, from what she could gather, it was far worse than what they were letting on.

Ruben hadn't *wanted* to put her husband on this team. He had tried to choose alternatives, but his skill set was unique, and even if they chose someone who was close to him in terms of ability, they would never *be* him, and for that reason, he was irreplaceable. He was the perfect soldier, and if he wasn't able to complete the job, no one would.

On paper, it was simple - a screening and a possible abduction, not something that hadn't been done before. Easy, with proper planning and the right group of people. The issue here, however, was that the team had minimal information on both the specificities of the location and who would be there. It was not a necessary task, but it would help them unequivocally in the future.

Genie remembered the day in three parts.

The first was defying the orders she was given. She and Ruben were equal in position, and though it was mutual respect that allowed them to follow each other's direction, there was no written reason for it, and Genie knew this well. She'd never thought that she would *truly* do it. She never thought she would feel the need to go against the word of her closest advisor. But as she slid the black gloves over her hands and pulled her hair back behind her head, she knew what she was doing had to be done. Ruben had found her scanning over documents one last time in the basement where the files were stored. He stood at the door only for a moment before walking over to her in long strides, removing the papers from her hands and pointing his finger in her face. "You are *not* going on this mission."

She pushed past him without a word, exiting the room. *He has no right.*

The second - the chill of the day turning to night.

She wasn't sure why she remembered it so vividly, but there was a single moment in which the sun had set behind the hills and a wind picked up only for a moment. It was harsh and cold, and she shivered. Her husband's hand rested over hers, only for a moment, before they continued their march towards the building. She knew that he would do no more. She didn't care. It was all she needed.

The third, and final, was the moment she revisited so often - the moment of his death, the last time she would ever work with her own region's army. She knew this was a bad idea, and if not for her, there would have been more casualties on her side than just him. His death struck her, and she often found herself wondering if there was a way for her to have been able to save him and, perhaps, leave one of the other members of the team. She *hated* the thought - it made her feel selfish and disrespectful - but she didn't go a week without replaying the day in her head and wondering where she could have stepped or what she could have done differently to make sure *he lived*.

She blamed herself. But she blamed Ruben Yorke, too.

She was not one to hold a grudge. It had been years, and she had, to some extent, come to terms with his death, but she hadn't anticipated this interaction, much less in this way. Some of the anger she felt came back. Not all of it, and not as strong, but it lingered beneath the surface, a fire burning under her skin, dangerously close to piercing through.

"You know I'm sorry," Ruben said, looking at her with intent. She scoffed, but the sincerity in his voice was evident. Ruben was incredibly transparent when he spoke - at least with people that he trusted - and that was one of the things she had always admired about him. For someone with as much power as he had, vulnerability was something he should not have been so comfortable in displaying. She could never be sure if Ruben was this way with everybody or just with their circle, but regardless of what the truth was, she appreciated that he trusted her enough to show her the side of him that was nothing other than a window. No smoke, no mirrors - only his true, authentic self.

She was surprised, frankly, that he still trusted her.

Maybe he didn't. Maybe he just knew how to act.

"What happened to you?" She said, her demeanor calming greatly knowing that she didn't seem to be in any great threat and that the kids had to have been in the bunker by now. She motioned to his face. "I've seen you look better."

"Well," Ruben shrugged, laughing lowly, "you can ask Miss Roman. I'm sure she'd be delighted to tell you."

Genie mentally scowled. She should have known that Eleri had something to do with this. It only made sense. "And? What would she tell me?"

Ruben took a breath, tilting his head to the side. His eyes narrowed slightly as he looked at Genie, taking in her features. She, too, had aged. She looked tired and hurt, and though he could see that same sparkle of wit and intelligence, he didn't know how much force was left behind that. He didn't think of her as a threat, nor as an ally. He didn't know what she would do with the truth, and he didn't know how much her son being friends with the Reaper would cloud her judgment.

Family did that to her before, and he was sure it would happen again.

"Are you a fan of Miss Roman's, Gene?"

Genie shrugged, curling her lips into a small smile. "I respect her abilities and her talent very much, yes. I think that she has capabilities that are only found -"

"Not as a Commander," he said gently. "Take your professional lens away, for a second. I didn't ask you if you would've recruited her. I asked you if you were a fan of hers. Do you like the girl or not?"

Genie felt her walls coming down before she was able to process it. She knew she shouldn't have told the truth, that it would only serve to put her, or her son, in more danger. She knew that this was something that she would regret, but she didn't realize she had spoken until it was too late.

"No."

Ruben smiled down at the ground before looking back up at her, a new sense of pride in his voice. "Then you'll be delighted to know that she believes she's killed me."

Interlude.

The piano was horribly out of tune.

Eleri had not played in years, but her fingers knew where to go. It was something strange - some song that she knew from her childhood, a combination of notes that brought some peace over her body. Her breath was even, heartbeat the metronome, the music ringing out in the space beautifully, despite the flats and sharps.

The rifle was slung over her back. One of her boots was untied. Her hands were caked in blood and the bandages over her wrists and knuckles were dirty and peeling. There was a tear in her sleeve, right by her shoulder, the fabric cemented to her skin by the blood from her cut. She was in a pain, so immeasurable, that she could no longer feel it. She could not articulate nor quantify what it was that she was experiencing. Her limbs burned with every movement, tears stinging at the corners of her eyes, but despite it all, she played.

The wallpaper was peeling.

The room around her seemed to be a projection of her innermost thoughts. Once something so stable, now crumbling with the slightest wind. The wooden floor was cracked and thin, the window above the piano broken. The ceiling had caved in, sunlight peeking through, illuminating the flakes of dust and ash and dirt in the air.

She heard footsteps behind her. She did not look up. She continued to play.

"Hey,"

It was Kass. She recognized his voice, tearing through the pain and the noise and the hurt. She couldn't take her hands off of the keys. The ashes. The screams outside. The blood coming from her fingers.

She didn't respond. She closed her eyes, a split second of vulnerability, before opening them again, locking her gaze onto a feather that had caught itself on the jagged glass of the window. There was something so ugly about it - the soft feather, the broken glass, the image of peace and chaos joining together. They were both inanimate objects. They knew nothing, but the fear and pain and hurt she felt overwhelmed her, and that stupid feather couldn't fly to wherever it needed to be because the glass was holding it down.

The piano sounded like shit, but it was a sound much more desirable than the reality beyond the walls.

"What are you playing?" Kassander asked, walking over to the piano, standing behind it so he was facing Eleri.

She let her fingers drop into the keys, making a harsh, loud bang, a noise that was strained, one that this old instrument was not meant to play. She was exhausted.

She did not respond immediately, her eyes focusing on the way her fingers rested in the valleys of the keys, pressing them further into the wood that was meant to support them. White. Black. White. Black.

She heard a bomb go off somewhere in the distance. It rattled her spine, but she stood in place. It seemed so far away. It was right there, she could step outside and grab the remains of what had been hit, but in her mind, right this minute, it seemed like a dream.

She was a liar. She was a liar, a fraud, and she was nothing like what they wanted her to be. She wondered if anyone had noticed.

But then, looking at Kassander before her, looking at her bruised hands, looking at the destruction that she had caused, she knew that nobody had. She may have believed herself to be weak and unfit for this role, and she may have thought with her entire soul that she would be better suited elsewhere, but she would never allow herself to be compromised by letting someone know that. She was too smart, and frankly, too proud, to back out now.

"I don't remember what it's called," she said finally, looking at him with intent, ensuring that she spoke with a level tone and moved without wavering. "Some song from when I was young."

"Yeah?" Kass smiled. "It's horrible."

She narrowed her eyes. "It's the piano, not me."

"Yeah, a bad workman always blames his tools." He tapped one of the keys, the sound horrifying, and he recoiled. "Maybe not this time, though."

"And you had the audacity to doubt me."

He came back around the piano, tapping her shoulder just above the cut. "We're heading out. You need help with this?"

She shook her head. "No. Don't feel it."

Something in the way he looked at her changed, only for a moment, before turning back around and walking towards the door, which rested on its hinges. "Do you ever wonder who lived here?"

The question caught Eleri by surprise. She hadn't ever wondered that, no, not at all. The notion that someone once lived here, or in any of the other buildings in which they'd rested or destroyed, was so far beyond her that she could barely even wrap her mind around it. She had actively pushed it out of her realm of comprehension when she first started seeing the wreckage, knowing that she had to remove her morals and her conscience, knowing that she had to take any humanity out of the people and the places she saw. It had been years since she thought of this place as once habitable, or these people as humans. It had been even longer since she had ever thought of herself as such.

For her to remove humanity from others, she had to take it from herself first. It wouldn't make sense otherwise. So, as she had laid it out in her mind, she was an unforgivable monster, and they were worthless scum, the common ground being that they were both soulless and both going to die, anyway. She would die a villain, and they would die without having mattered. It was dark and sinister and an incredibly cynical outlook, but it was the only way she could bring herself to do anything she was doing.

They were bad. She was worse.

"Not really," she said, turning to follow Kass. "Do you?"

He nodded. "Let me show you something."

Kassander led her down the hallway; white walls turned brown, brown floors turned red, stopping to open a door. Inside was a bed, a few articles of clothing that had been forgotten, and a dresser with drawers pulled out. Kass knelt down, putting his hand gently under the bed, emerging with a wooden frame. He handed it to Eleri. "Look."

She took it gently, brushing the dust and dirt off of the front, looking down at the smiling faces staring back at her.

The glass on the picture frame was cracked. It reminded her of the window.

"They probably lived here, then. Or maybe this was someone else in their family." Eleri said finally, coldly, the

three children in the photograph appearing so incredibly joyous and carefree that she almost felt envy.

Kass nodded. "That's the thing I think is interesting. Everything here, like, belonged to people, at some point. There could've been things in here that they never wanted anyone to see."

"Yeah, well, look around. Now, no one ever will see it."

He frowned. "No, I guess not."

Eleri put the frame back down, brushing her thumb over it once more, before swinging her rifle into her hands and exiting the room. "Come on, let's go."

Kass followed behind, watching her movements, mind reeling. "El?" She paused, turning to him. "Do you really believe in everything you say?"

She bit the inside of her cheek, looking him up and down once. "If I don't, no one else will, either."

PART THREE

FEBRUARY 3RD, 2248
14:00
115 DAYS POST-WAR

Seventeen.

Love is a stupid, stupid thing, to any extent. It is the reason things do not get done as they should. It is an obstacle. It is a distraction. I hate it. Every part of it. And I try to put this to practice - I try not to love many people. I try to be selective about it. I like a Hell of a lot of people, sure, and I hate even more, but I would never be stupid enough to love more than I need to.

I have only ever loved three people. One of those three is dead, and another will be soon.

- The Found Diary of Eleri Roman, p. 85

———

The rage that Eleri felt had not subsided, so as they reached the building they were headed to, she wasted no time in bursting through the front door. Fyodor, anticipating this, followed close behind her, rifle up, watching for any disturbance.

The house was silent, aside from their movements, and Eleri put her head down and began to search every room she could. He had to be in this place, somewhere. Sure, she didn't know where, but his coat and his books and his glasses were thrown across the room. He was in here. She knew it. She felt it.

He found them before they had the chance to discover him.

"Roman? Kacer? What are you two doing here?"

She turned her head to look at him, where he was standing at the bottom of the staircase, and she scoffed.

He was scared of her - scared for his own safety - for the first time in his life.

"Did you sign off on any executive orders recently, Xavier?" Fyodor spoke, his voice soft, inviting Xavier to respond honestly.

"I can't disclose -"

"Bullshit," Eleri said, laughing. "You breached *how many* protocols during your official time serving, and now that you're some prosthetic to this entire thing, you want to do it right? Sure."

Xavier did not move towards her as he would have normally. He stood his place. These were his kids, his own children standing in his home with their guns trained on him. These were the two people he cared about more than anything, ready to take him out. And with Eleri's ruthlessness, it was very, very possible.

"Things are a little different now," he said, eyeing her with intent.

She knew what he meant. They all did. Eleri and Fyodor were the enemy now. Of course, he would not disclose this information to the enemy.

The trigger beneath Eleri's finger felt *so, so tempting.*

"You signed a paper for our deaths. Is this the same as what you all had planned for our little team? Huh? Is this you finishing what you couldn't do before? Is this you getting the remaining two?"

Fyodor's brows furrowed. "What?"

Xavier's face went blank. "I don't understand -"

Eleri removed one hand from the weapon, moving to her pocket, pulling the papers out to show him.

Xavier swallowed thickly. He recognized the document. He recognized her jacket, too, now that he thought about it.

"I'm not an idiot, and neither are you, so let's not pretend that we're lost here, Xavier."

Fyodor thought it best to stay silent. He, evidently, had no idea what was going on. He trusted Eleri, though, with his entire being, and if she had a point to make, he would let her make it. He knew she'd explain later. She always did.

"Do you want to sit down?" Xavier asked, his guard completely up.

"Do I look like I have time to be entertained?" She snapped, still holding the sheets in front of her. "How about you tell me what you've been doing, and we can get this over with. Did you sign off on that order this morning or not? Because, in case you've forgotten, we know what it looks like when someone signs off on one of those, and frankly, I'm running out of other options."

He breathed deeply. "I know."

"You seem to know a lot, huh? And yet, you still pretend to be confused. I asked you a question, and when I ask questions, I expect answers."

She was a monster. He was worthless.

The shift in her mind had been made almost effortlessly, the moral dilemma causing no issue for her. Was it the rage she felt from knowing the one person she treated as a father figure had killed her friends and wanted to kill her?

Yes. It was.

Poetic.

Eleri threw the papers to the ground, her hand finding the rifle again. Xavier put his hands in front of him, begging for peace and calm and *mercy* all in one motion, staring down the barrel of a gun held by a woman who he had taught to shoot.

He'd be killed by his own hand. Always.

The silence was so incredibly audible. He knew that Eleri would not speak again with words, that her next message would be through action, and he knew that he had to measure what he said very carefully. He had a lot of questions - namely, he needed to know how exactly she had found these documents - but he knew he was not being awarded the time or space to ask them. He knew that even insinuating a question would be perceived by Eleri as being mocked or as being doubted, and that would end poorly - *painfully* - for him.

He watched as she lowered her weapon again. Her hand made its way to her leg. His breath caught in his throat as he watched her fingers find the shaft of one of her knives, sliding it out of where it rested.

Fear.

"This isn't the sequel to that document if that's what you're asking." He said finally, eyes locked onto her hand.

She stepped forward for the first time, knife in one hand, rifle in the other, fury in her eyes he had never seen.

"So how about you explain what it is, then? Because, as I'm sure you can appreciate, *Sir*, this looks a hell of a lot like you trying to finish what you and your stupid friends started."

Xavier took a breath. "This decision wasn't made because you were there. You just happened to be there when the decision was made."

She shook her head, kissing her teeth, smiling to herself. "Not good enough."

Before either man could process what was happening, Eleri had swung herself behind Xavier, sliding the blade against his throat, watching him fall to the floor before pulling the trigger she had refrained from touching earlier.

He was lifeless, the red shadow below him expanding onto his clean floors. She felt nothing but disgust for the man she loved so much. She was glad that she would no longer allow herself the luxury of naivety.

The blood began to seep onto the documents and she stepped over his body, collecting the papers, shaking them off. She looked over at Fyo, with his wide eyes and parted lips, and she carefully, almost timidly, moved towards him.

She slid her knife back into its place, not bothering to clean it off, and she patted his cheek twice. "You're going to want to sit down to read these."

It was only a moment before they all heard Genie's voice in their Dellers.

It caused Claire to pause her movements. It caused Clover to shake her head, thinking she was hearing things. Fyodor heard it before Eleri did, seeing as hers didn't work properly, but he took his out of his ear, allowing it to play audibly, as the conversation came into their realm of understanding.

"But, my son…"

"He didn't know you for so many years, Gene. It won't hurt him."

"No fucking way," Eleri hissed. Fyodor, desperately trying to pay attention both to the conversation over the earpiece and the girl in front of her, raised an eyebrow.

"I swear to God, I thought I killed Ruben Yorke," she said, eyes wide.

"And if I agree? What happens then?"

"Well," Ruben sighed loudly, "I guess it would only be fair for me to say I'd stay away from them. All of them. I can't promise what anyone else would do since we've got confirmation to be able to do as we see fit, but you and I both know how much pull I have, and I won't touch them. I won't be involved at all."

There was silence over the headset. "What's going on," Fyodor mumbled, playing with the papers in his hands.

"So, all you want me to do is... leave?"

"Essentially, yes."

Shuffling. Movement.

"And I wouldn't get to say goodbye,"

"No, unfortunately. But, listen, you'd be helping him. Trust me on this one."

"What happened last time I did that, huh?"

"I know. But this is different. I'm taking danger away from him, not putting him in a worse situation."

Eleri, at some point, had led Fyodor over to a couch, sitting him down, watching his movements as she tried to make sense of the conversation.

"Did they know each other?" Eleri asked, quietly, as if Genie or Ruben would hear her.

Fyo clenched his jaw. He shook his head. "I have no idea."

"Okay." She breathed. "Okay. Yeah. I'll do it."

There was more movement, rustling, static, and then silence. Complete and utter silence.

"What the fuck," Fyodor said. He tapped twice on the earpiece. "Evginia Kacer," he spoke.

Nothing. He tried again.

Silence.

"Hey, hey," Eleri's tone was breathy, soft. She was making a strong effort to convey some sort of stability through her tone. "Here, let's give it a second. I'll try."

Her hand rested on his shoulder. She watched him for a moment as he breathed deeply, closing his eyes, nodding.

She took his earpiece and tapped it twice. "Evginia Kacer."

Nothing.

Then, in a quick moment, she tapped again. "Clover O'Caine."

"Eleri -" Clover's voice came over the headset almost immediately. "Christ, I was about to try and get to you. Did you hear all of that?"

"Yeah, what the fuck? Do you know what it was about?"

"Negative. I - *shit* - we'll have to figure it out, though." Clover spoke, trying to be concise, trying not to put herself in any more danger. "Did you do what you had to do?"

Eleri looked over from the couch to Xavier's body, which was now pale and had already begun to sag. "Yeah. Xavier Talon is dead. That means no more executive orders, for now, at least."

"Okay," Clove breathed, "Okay. I'll see you."

Eleri looked back at Fyo, who looked as though the life had been sucked out of him. His expression was blank, and she tried her hardest to imagine what he was feeling. He had lost his mother, gotten her back, and now had lost her again. Only recently, the first two of those steps had happened with her. She assumed he was picking up on the pattern and that he was scared. She also assumed that he was worried that something worse than he could imagine was happening to the woman he loved. He had no idea what was going on, and that caused him unimaginable anxiety.

It was *different* when Eleri was pulling something like she just had with the documents - Fyodor had known her and grown to trust her more than he trusted himself, and even when he didn't know what she was doing, he knew it was for a good reason - but in a situation like *this*, where he didn't know or trust Ruben Yorke, and he barely even knew his own mother, he couldn't feel anything but helplessness and defeat.

He had just reconnected with her, and she was gone again.

He should've known it was too good to be true.

"I don't know, Fyo." Eleri said, moving closer to him. "I'm sorry. Are you alright?"

Fyo shook his head slightly, looking down at the papers in his hands, thumbing the corner of the document gently. He opened his mouth to speak, closing it only when he concluded that there was nothing he could say. Eleri frowned. She hated when he was upset, and she hated not knowing what to say to him to fix it.

It was hard.

"These papers," Fyo said finally, his voice hoarse, tension laced through the syllables, "What are they?"

"I found them when I found this jacket and those necklaces," she said gently. She didn't have the heart to tell him that they had to go, that they had work to do. He needed a minute, and she appreciated that. She didn't want to walk him through this entire document - not now, after what they'd just heard - but she was smart enough to know that this may be the only time he would have to retain this information in its entirety. Fyodor was interesting like that - he was much more receptive to bad news when he had already experienced something upsetting. He would always listen and always try to learn, but he had an inherent philosophy that led him to further understand and want to process new information as a distraction for what had already hurt him. He would pile it all on, only focusing on the top.

Did Eleri think it was in his best interest? Absolutely not. But who was she to judge other people's coping mechanisms, especially considering her own?

He scanned over the first page, turning it over, his reaction similar to hers upon her first look.

He read through quickly, scanning for headings and subheadings and bolded statements that would mean something to him, before dropping the papers beside him and turning to his friend. He rubbed his hands over his face.

"Just... Can you just tell me what I need to know? I can't-"

"Yeah," Eleri said softly. "Yeah. They... uh... the people in power, Xavier included, I guess thought that we would find out about this entire backhanded project and these... motives that they had for declaring this war. They wanted us to do our job, and they wanted to get rid of us before we had a chance to go into the world on our own. I guess... they knew the war was coming to an end the day that things all happened, and they figured it would be a decent time to get rid of us. We had helped them. They didn't want us to get in the way."

Fyodor closed his eyes briefly, sighing, standing, pinching the bridge of his nose. "Okay."

"Okay?"

He shrugged, looking down at the document, picking the paper back up, handing it to her. She took it slowly, folding it back into her pocket, away from the light.

"Yeah," He said gently. "That's what they wanted to do, then that's what they wanted to do. They were right in trying, anyway, right? Look at us,"

Eleri squeezed his arm, slinging her rifle back over her shoulder. "All we do is cause problems, huh?"

The laugh that escaped Fyodor was dry and bitter as he agreed. "All we do is fuck shit up."

Eleri stepped over to Xavier's body, emotion rushing through her once before escaping as she exhaled, and she kneeled down to touch him.

She pulled him onto his side as she reached behind his neck and unclasped the necklace that she knew he always wore. She put it into her pocket without another word. She traced his body with her eyes once more, then took the used knife out of her pocket. She wiped the blade on his clothes, cleaning it off, before wordlessly stepping outside.

Despite all that she felt, she found her mind wandering. She hoped that if there was some sort of afterlife, that Xavier was resting easily.

At least, then, he wouldn't be coming back to haunt them anytime soon.

Eighteen.

We were a democracy, once, apparently. I don't really understand how that would work, nor do I understand what I'd be doing in that situation. There was a coup d'état, I was told. Something about a few very strong, very bold men, organizing an entire underground, illegal military movement, killing Prime Ministers and any civilians who stood in their way. They, from what I was told, had presented themselves as saviors - that there were very serious, horrible things going on within the democracy that had to be eradicated. They presented their arguments so well that killing those in power seemed justified.

I want to understand it, but it was so far before my time that I can't even begin to imagine choosing who is in power, let alone having someone outside of the military to run this entire region. It doesn't seem like a fathomable idea. A random civilian running something this strong seems so flawed. But then again, how much better are we doing now? I won't know what things could have been if they haven't been. So I try to imagine. And I think, maybe, that having every person contribute to who leads may be a good option - even if we amend the idea a bit and pick someone who's in the military. But then, if I'm imagining, I want to imagine something more obscure. I want to imagine something entirely different. Imagine someone who was chosen by the public in power - great. Imagine, though, being able to function without someone in power? Where everyone was equal, without having to worry about a decision being made on their behalf. No one leading another, everyone coexisting in a way that meant we were all truly equal.

But, of course, this is something I am imagining. This is not something that can be achieved, at least not in my lifetime. Maybe one of these days, when people stop being so dependent on a system that will dispose of them in the blink of an eye, we can see something change.

- The Found Diary of Eleri Roman, p. 87

———

Ruben Yorke could not have been more grateful that he had worn his protective gear underneath his clothing. He was lucky - *God, he was so fucking lucky* - that he had escaped the Reaper. It would be so easy to take it for granted. It would be so simple to use this to raise himself, to make himself feel more powerful, but after losing both Oliver and Alex, he knew that he had no right to do that. He *was* lucky. He wasn't stronger than her or smarter than her, and though he had his suspicions over the years, he could see reality now, clearly, confidently, and unfortunately, it was not the picture he had wished to paint. Ruben had struggled with the idea that there was a possibility of her being more than he was. The thought of someone easily towering above him, both in theory and in practice, was one of his worst nightmares. It was part of the reason that he had organized the plot to kill her and her friends - presenting the concept under the guise that she was untrustworthy and would ultimately be their downfall, all the while developing it for his own personal gain. If he could've gone back, he would've tried to make sure that she was the priority. Hell, he would've made it an assassination if he had to. If he had truly known the turmoil she was going to send them all into, he would have started this project much earlier.

If he'd been smart enough, he would never have brought her in as a child to begin with.

But, much like everybody else, that stupid Kind baby seemed like a great idea. Even Ruben would admit that when she first arrived, when he first interviewed her, and questioned her on her outdated documents, and directed her through the facilities, she seemed so polite and eager. She seemed like the miracle they needed.

And, to an extent, she was. But, of course, every miracle has a catch.

You have the highest technical scores of anyone born in your year and the second-highest physical. We do not want to let a talent like yours go to waste, however, we will not hesitate to do so if you can't get yourself together.

He remembered the conversation. He remembered how her hands rested on her lap. He remembered how she watched him look through her documents. Most of all, though, he remembered hoping that they were right about her. It was not his choice to recruit her at all, but he had settled on watching over her every movement if she were to be brought onto the team. He was the one responsible for all that she did; all of her promotions and demotions, and tasks were orchestrated by him and were delivered through the surrogate of Xavier Talon.

And it almost worked. All of it almost went exactly as they'd planned. Ten years of obsessing over one woman, ten years of understanding that she was the key to their victory or their defeat, all for it to unravel in the eleventh hour. He hated it. He hated knowing that he had wasted all of this time. He hated knowing that he created her.

Especially now, with the conversation he had had with her, telling her to stop monitoring in fear of a revolution. Telling her that there were still troops in Voskivy. He thought, stupidly, that as she had spent her entire life fighting alongside his beliefs, she would follow his direction without question. He thought that ten years would have corrupted her enough for her own mind to be his property. There was no reason for him to believe otherwise, either - she had always followed orders and completed tasks. He could not begin to understand what was different this time. He didn't know where he had misjudged things, but he felt *horrible* about it.

He figured that Gene wouldn't tell him about Eleri or Fyodor to save her own son, but he felt that getting her away from Voskivy was enough of a start to help him understand what it was that they were doing. Any information he could get from Gene, at all, no matter how menial, would prove to be helpful. It would at very least be better than nothing.

It was also well within his realm of comprehension that Gene fell into the traitor category. It was only when considering her, Eleri, and Fyodor side by side that Ruben came to the conclusion that *he had directly contributed to all three of them turning their backs on him* - but he would never admit that. At least, not out loud. He knew that Gene had learned many things over her time spent on the other side and that she evidently saw purpose in their cause that outweighed what she believed upon joining the fight in the beginning. The selfish side of him, the powerful, the stubborn side, wanted to hear these reasons, to understand this purpose, in order to mock it. He wanted her to pour her heart and soul out to him, to tell him exactly what stupid humanitarian cause had helped her see the light of day so that he could belittle her and call her stupid. He wanted her to tell him how she felt so that he could explain how invalid it all was. A beautiful notion, really. How nice it would be.

But the rational side of him, the one that wasn't overcome with betrayal or frustration or confusion, the one that knew how a leader *should* behave, and how he only had a small chance to turn this disaster into a victory, wanted to get her to share her story so that he could pretend to care. He wanted to rebuild the relationship they had years ago - the one in which he actually *would* want to hear what she had to say - at very least on the surface so that her walls would slowly come down, and over the next hour or so, she would be able and willing to explain more than just the basics of what had happened. He knew that nothing was guaranteed, but being nice to her would certainly get him farther than bullying her would.

He had led her away from her building, inviting her silence, knowing that the less he spoke, the more inclined she would feel to fill the space. He knew that staying quiet gave her the impression that he was listening, which in this case he actually was, and that he would not have to prompt her for her responses. He would be much better off letting Gene work through her thoughts on her own, eventually landing on what she felt was appropriate enough to tell him.

Evginia, on the other hand, was overwhelmed. She noted two things about Ruben as they walked; the bruises around his eye were becoming rapidly darker, and he had become increasingly less talkative. It was a slow descent, but it was one that she could actively see. He seemed to have forgotten that for as much as he knew her, she knew him, too.

It was typical of him to think like he was the only one with any basic understanding of his surroundings. It was something undetectable unless explicitly outlined - Ruben would rarely talk down to people or make them feel inferior, but Evginia had watched him and worked with him, had fed his ideas and nurtured his habits, for long enough to understand that he would, for some reason, never think that anyone else knew as much as he did. This attitude got him far enough - it was the reason he had gained so much control - but he failed to understand, or even consider, that things were not the same now as they were when he began to further his career.

She knew this was going to be a painful time - his silence, hoping she would fill it, her doing so with nearly nothing of substance just to make him feel as though he was getting somewhere - ultimately leading to nothing.

Evginia wondered if he would kill her.

***

Eleri knew that Clover and Clarissa were waiting on them, but there was something more urgent pulling at her mind. She, still the planner and the strategist, knew that they had not yet reached the end of this mission. She knew that they would still have to successfully find and destroy the housing district. She knew that they didn't have the luxury of time, and she knew that the fight Claire and Clove were involved in was one that would end in time for them to be able to get over their third stop, to detonate, and to escape. There was no time. There was only this moment, and if Eleri was able to turn it into two, she had already won.

She and Fyodor had always worked away from larger groups. This was their forte. This was their specialty. Something needed to be done, and they were the only ones in a position to do it. So as Eleri changed direction, with Fyodor closely following behind her, she became thankful for the extra materials they'd collected from the basement of the military building.

"Are you planning on letting them know what's going on?" Fyodor asked, walking in stride with her, adjusting the strap of the bag across his back.

Eleri kicked a pile of snow to the side. "No. They'll find out once we're done."

"Think about it, though, from their perspective. Us going out on our own… doesn't it seem like we're lying about something?"

"They don't know what we're doing, and I think they may be too preoccupied to care."

Silence fell for a moment, and Fyodor spoke again. "It's going to start raining soon."

"Is it?"

He nodded. "Yeah. The clouds and the wind are -"

There was a pop, a loud bang, and before either of them had time to process, they were on the ground, crouching behind a bench, breathing erratic.

They waited for a moment, met with silence, and Eleri squeezed Fyodor's knee, rising to her feet. She held her rifle ready, pointed forwards, as her eyes darted from place to place, wondering where the shot had come from. They both knew it, there was no need for deliberation, but there was someone out there trying to kill them.

It was nothing new. It was just unexpected.

There was nobody as far as she could see, and crouching, she began to move. Her steps were slow and careful, as was her breath, as she found the trunk of a tree wide enough to hide her figure.

As she was about to beckon for Fyodor to come over, she heard something. She tensed, and Fyo saw it. He stayed put.

She craned her neck around the side of the tree, looking out at the space around her. If there was someone still there, they had to have been hiding somewhere. They would surely stand out against the snow. She just wanted to see the target.

Eleri was growing impatient. The wind had picked up and her fingers were freezing under her gloves. She adjusted her grip - once, twice, three times - a small pattern of movements that had helped her fingers regain feeling time and time again, only now, it wasn't helping. She huffed in frustration, her nose was running, and her lips were chapped, and she just wanted this stupid bitch to get their head out of their ass and -

There. It was a fleeting moment, a passing second in which had she blinked, she would have missed entirely. The top of a rifle barely peeking out from behind the house that was being used as a shield.

This guy had an entire building, and Eleri was granted a tree.

She whipped her head to the side, making eye contact with Fyo, cocking her eyebrow and shooting her gaze to the house. He understood.

She wanted, so badly, to use the Dellers, but the risk of being heard was not worth the trouble, and she wasn't even sure how well hers would work given its condition. If there was only one shooter, either Fyo or Eleri would survive without question, but the prospect of losing even one of them was too much. Beyond this, Eleri had learned that the safest way to go through things was by assuming that there were always ten times more people than she could see - if there was one man behind that house, nine more were behind him. That would land both herself and Fyodor killed. That was not a risk worth taking.

He flattened himself onto the ground - she saw him wince at the cold - as he looked from underneath the bench, trying to see anything that may have been of use.

The conversation he had heard his mother have only a short time ago was still stuck in his mind. He wanted answers, and he wouldn't get them. And then, the news that he had been a target by his own leaders. It all made sense now, at least, in that regard - why he was always on high alert for calling out issues that he had seen, why they always seemed to be keeping tabs on him. They had been planning to take him out again, and he had no idea.

Fyo sniffled, pulling his scarf over his nose, scanning the ground for any footprints or tracks that seemed to line up with the directions in which the space beside the house could've been reached.

He furrowed his brows. Eleri didn't have a scarf. He wondered if she wanted to use his.

As he reached for the scope he had strapped against him, the thought that violence and love were more similar than different crossed his mind. As far as he knew, love had only come from violence, and violence had only come from love. The two were almost interchangeable - their descriptions almost identical if not for any connotation associated with each. Their outcomes almost always led down the same path, as well - some sort of iridescence, for better or for worse. They charted the same course. They evoked the same response.

He scoffed, setting the scope onto his rifle. If everything could be stripped into two categories, they would be violence and love.

His finger moved before he focused back on the task at hand, the silhouette of a body hitting the ground as he finally clued into what had happened. He sat upright, abandoning his hiding place entirely, eyes wide. He had done this before, so why was he so uncomfortable? It had come so naturally for him, so much so that he had not realized that the trigger had been pulled, nor that he had shot the man right through his head. He blinked hard.

The chill that wrapped itself around his spine grew like vines through his ribcage and found its way through his throat was not one that was sparked by the elements. It came from something opening inside of him that he had tried to close time and time again. It was the last bit of hope he had for himself and for the future, finding its way into the air.

Whether it would fall or fly was to be determined.

Eleri stared for a moment at her friend, who looked as though he had seen the ghost of his father. He looked like he had jumped out of his own skin, leaving only the shell behind. Fyodor, by all accounts, looked horrified. It was a haunting, pained expression that she had never seen on his face before; a little boy who had grown up too fast, a good heart that had been made into a machine.

Eleri Roman spent four seconds looking at Fyodor Kacer in complete silence. In those four seconds, she felt as though she had explored every crevice of his mind.

She wouldn't talk to him about that, though. That wasn't their relationship. It more than likely never would be.

She did, however, make her way over to him. She eyed the body, only for a moment, as she moved, placing her bets selfishly on the idea that there was only one person behind the building, sliding down to meet Fyodor on the cold snow. "We have to go," she whispered to him gently, tugging on the back of his collar, ushering him to sit up straight. His eyes were forlorn, unmoving. There was no hope for either of them, not now, not like this. The truth that was so evident to her was so intangible to him. She could see in him the deaths of their friends. She could see the years of struggle. She could see the moral conflict… had she projected that onto him? Had he created his own?

"Fyodor," she said, sitting back on her heels, keeping her hand on him. "Come on,"

He closed his eyes, his lower lip trembling. Fyodor Kacer had known pain before but never like this.

He didn't know what it was that had set him off, and that was pulling him under even more than he could grasp. Fyo couldn't stop this from happening. He couldn't stop the world from spinning, and he couldn't keep people from fighting. He was one person, and he had one friend, and he had spent his whole life assuming that their power and strength could pull them through anything. He wished that Eleri could just see him as a weak link, that she would look at him and understand that he was holding her back. He wished she would put a bullet through his head. He would never take himself away from her, but he would be a liar if he said that he didn't think about finding a loophole for that.

Fyodor wished he was the body lying in the snow.

Eleri was anxious. They had to go. Being a sitting duck wouldn't help anyone, and being a sitting duck in front of a dead body was even more of an issue. But she wasn't going to *force* Fyo to do anything he didn't want to do. She wasn't going to drag him along with her. She wasn't going to bully him into standing. He had finished fighting until she had pulled him into this. He was done with this mess until she had the bright idea to take down the fabric of their society. Fyodor had begun to make peace - or at the very least, had begun to come to terms - with who he was and what he had done. He was only beginning the process of acknowledging everything he had seen and heard and lived through, and she ripped him away from all safety into an avoidable conflict. It was because she was impulsive. It was because she believed in vigilante justice. It was because she couldn't stand the thought of being used as a pawn.

It was because she was a monster.

Eleri turned her attention to the scar that ran down his face. She gently traced it, the ghost of her fingers leaving a featherlight trail of warmth around his least favorite feature, the tears in his eyes falling without a second thought. He was barely crying. Saying that he was would not do the situation justice. Fyodor was *cracking*. The two tears - falling from his eyes into the snow, never once touching the skin on his cheeks as he looked down - carried so much more fear and doubt than he would be able to express. Fyodor felt like he was disconnecting from the world. The cold seemed to subside, the pain disappearing into nothingness, the frustration falling off of his frame. He didn't know what to think. He couldn't think at all.

Eleri swallowed thickly before pulling his body to hers. She wrapped her arms around him, one hand on the back of his head, holding it against her neck, the other hand pressed into his back. She wanted him to remember that she was here. She didn't know what to say, and she probably never would, but she would always, *always* be right beside him.

He struggled to reciprocate the gesture, but when his arms finally found their way to her body, she exhaled. Fyodor was never built for this. She had known this from the first time they'd spoken. Fyodor Kacer was an artist and an empath, and he did not belong here. He was not a killer, and he was not a soldier, and he was not a monster.

If he made it through this, Eleri would ensure that he never even thought about a weapon again. She didn't know how she would do it, but she got what she wanted. And if she wanted his mind to be at peace, then she would find a way to make it happen.

He rose eventually. Eleri kept count in her head - two minutes and fourteen seconds - and as her hands left his body, he shuddered.

"We have work to do, yeah?" He said, smiling weakly.

She patted his cheek twice. "We do."

Nineteen.

Nothing is more worthless than life itself. We all die in the end, anyway. Who cares what we do? We can write ourselves into history, but the next person will just write us out.

- The Found Diary of Eleri Roman, p. 88

—

"And you're okay?"

Clarissa nodded. Clove had finished bandaging her girlfriend's hand; a bullet had ricocheted off of a wall and grazed the back of her palm, and though Clover *knew* it was not that threatening of an injury, she hated seeing Claire bleeding.

"I'm not made of glass, angel," Claire said sweetly. "You know that. I'm fine."

No, she didn't know that, but she wasn't going to make an argument at this time, either. They were busy. They didn't have the time.

Claire clenched and unclenched her fist, snapped it once, and rose to her feet. "Come on, let's go."

Clover smiled softly, watching her girlfriend pick up her weapon. The chaos outside seemed to have evaporated. They were in some garage, so close to everything yet so sheltered from it all. This moment, if anything, described them in ways words never could. Always so close. Never close enough.

"Do you ever feel like you're waiting for the world to end?"

Claire stopped, turning back to Clover. "What?"

"I - I don't know. I just feel like… what are we even doing, you know? Why are we doing all of this?"

Claire shrugged, frowning. "What's the other choice we have? We keep living in fear?"

"Do you really think the fear stops with a win here?"

Claire looked at her feet. No, she didn't believe it, but Clove was normally the voice of reason and of confidence, and Claire hated lying. "I don't know what I believe," she said, finally, "but I know that even if the fear doesn't stop, the anguish will."

A loud explosion was heard somewhere in the distance. They both flinched.

"Think about it," Clarissa continued, "we win here, we get to do whatever we want. Yeah, we'll have to rebuild, but with no restraints. With no rules. And we can grow and develop and change the way things work."

Clover took a deep breath. She was interested in international relations as a child. Maybe when this was over, they could find a way to put Voskivy back on the map in a way that made sense. Maybe they could become a force in the world again.

"I guess so." She smiled. It was small, but it was *something*.

There was a moment of silence as they stepped back out into the light. Clover could only think about how wrong this all felt - fighting, dying, for nothing. For something that wouldn't matter. For the notion of a better future - maybe - but not guaranteed. She wasn't selfish, and especially knowing the kids she had taken care of, all she could ever want was to give them something more than she had, but it seemed so feeble. It seemed like such a stupid idea. They were hanging onto this by a thread, and they knew it.

And then, the hypotheticals began. Voskivy succeeds, they regain freedom, they gain another territory, but how do they reintegrate? How do they once again become a part of the rest of the world, who evidently didn't care enough to help them stop this unsolicited attack? What were they going to do now that they had no leadership, anyways? Sure, Clover and Clarissa had taken over some sort of role, but was that sustainable at all? They had no idea how to conduct themselves internationally or how to run an area larger than their safe house. They, frankly, had no idea if anyone from

Voskivy was hiding out anywhere; they had no numbers, they had no sources, and they had no plan.

Eleri was surely somewhat knowledgeable on this. She had to have been, at least subconsciously, given all her time and work. But the thought of an actual partnership seemed surreal - for reasons both good and bad. First and foremost, as she had said before, Clover had, to an extent, admired Eleri and had modeled herself after the Reaper. She had always wished for the girl to be on *her* side instead of the enemy. The prospect of having her as an ally for the future seemed too good to be true. But then, again, came the doubt in her mind - Eleri had dedicated her life to Aloneia, and despite helping Clove and Voskivy, she couldn't help but think that maybe she had some ulterior motive. Clove could never be sure.

But the arrangement could at very least be discussed. There would be a time, maybe in the future, where they could be in a full partnership, where they were both striving for the *same* better.

Clover had put a lot of thought into the war, to the conflict, and if she removed the fact that there were people making these decisions who would never see the field, she could sympathize with those who fought for Aloneia. Most of them didn't know any better. Hell, Eleri, who was so deeply intertwined in every decision, didn't know any better until recently. These people, these soldiers, who would never reach the top, who would never have the outlets or the authority to uncover the truth, couldn't be held accountable for being forced into a fight they knew nothing about. Especially now that she had been made aware of their doctored history, of a story full of lies and of falsified claims, she couldn't help but feel sorry for them.

Especially the younger ones.

She tried to imagine one of the kids she had housed in this situation - knowing only a lie, knowing only that they needed to fight or they would die. She tried to picture them strapping into this amour and these suits and going off to kill people because they were told they had to. She couldn't picture ever sending them to their deaths, especially in that way. It was dishonorable, and it was scary. She knew that excluding the people who had been part of the decision to attack Voskivy, most people in Aloneia didn't understand what was happening. It was a sheep's mentality. They were being shepherded by selfish men in power, and they'd never know any better.

It was unfortunate. Truly.

She knew that regardless of what was to happen now, with the rest of this seemingly impossible fight, the real struggle wouldn't come until later. There was nothing she could do - nothing any of them could do - to stop it. She wondered how much worse things would get.

Clover was only sure of two things; the first being that she was glad that Eleri and Fyodor had taken out the Aloneian station and all of its occupants, because had they not, they'd have lost the fight by now.

The second being that despite everything, she was unsure how they'd possibly manage to get through this and get to the housing district in time.

Eleri and Fyodor, however, were nearly there.

Ignoring the cries and shouts and chaos from only a few blocks away, as they always had, they had managed to weave their way through Aloneia untouched. The housing district was in sight. It was painful.

They wanted, so badly, to take one last look at their rooms. They wanted to go in and collect small belongings. Fyodor thought of his record player and of all the things his family had passed down for generations. He assumed that if he had to get rid of it all, they would all be okay with it happening like this. In the name of righteousness. Of justice. Of undoing all the horror that he had caused.

It was symbolic, in a sense, he had concluded. He had spent all of these years destroying Voskivy, taking away the homes and the lives of these people he would never meet. It somehow only seemed to make sense that he would have to create the same fate for himself.

There was an old saying he had heard once or twice in his lifetime - *the ends justify the means* - and he wondered how applicable that was for this situation. Of course, it meant something for a small crime or a white lie, but for a large-scale war? Especially one that led to a second wave of deaths? He wasn't sure if he and Eleri could get away with it, morally.

How would they be referred to when they were gone?

Eleri, on the other hand, had somehow managed to contain all her thoughts. She had barricaded her mind, extremely conscious to ensure she didn't stray. She only wanted to think about the task at hand. She didn't want to think about Xavier, or Sevyn, or Kassander. She didn't want to have to consider the distant future, or the near past, or anything other than what was meant to be done in the moment. She worked best on the premise of a never-ending tragedy, on the notion that her entire life would be spent fighting through muddy waters. She worked efficiently while thinking that there was no end in sight. It was an incredibly backward philosophy, but it seemed to be the only way in which she could get things done.

She felt, though, that she was marching towards death.

It was overcast, but the snow had melted. There were puddles, but they were full of dirt. She couldn't see her own reflection. Not even skewed.

The housing district had been evacuated. She didn't hear it happen, nor did she have any proof, but the dead silence and the creaking doors were enough. She was glad. She didn't want to have kill more people than she already had. She didn't want that on her resume.

The rifle was hanging at her side, fingers barely gripping it enough to keep it from falling. She felt that there was no use, no need for it, but there was no way to be sure. From her peripheral, she could see Fyodor adjust the straps along his back. She knew that he, too, was preparing for worse than what they could see.

It seemed stupid, but it was habit.

"Yours or mine?" She said as they approached the buildings, not looking at her friend.

Fyodor smacked his lips together once. "Our respective ways?"

"Meet back here in, what, ten? Fifteen?"

"Yeah. Don't blow shit up without me."

There were tears in Eleri's eyes as she turned away. She would never let him see that. She thought that maybe, it was the cold, or she was getting sick. Of course, this wasn't the case, and deep down, she knew it. She knew that she was overwhelmed. She knew that this final task would take it all out of her.

Fyodor walked up the steps to his room. He had evidently left the door unlocked, not shocking, and he sighed as he stepped inside. Everything was just as he had left it, and though he knew he had no time to wade through it all, he couldn't help but appreciate all the little things he would never see again.

Critically thinking, he should not have been so attached to the place. He had only lived there for months and had barely created enough memories to make a lasting impact. He was more upset about what the building represented being taken from him. The peace and the freedom - all of it, evidently, an illusion - the knowledge that he had fought and suffered and would have to no more. There was a chip in the paint right by the front door from when Eleri had once swung it open too aggressively and the knob crashed into the wall. There was a drawing up on the wall in the kitchen - a haphazard sketch of the cityscape, one that he had done in a half-present mindset, but one that seemed to be a more accurate representation of the world around him than any true image could capture.

There was a certain desperation in his movements as he wandered further into his room. Was there anything salvageable? Was there anything *worth* saving?

Fyodor thought, for the first time, that leaving all of his belongings to be turned to dust would surely be his sendoff to a new start - but one that he did not want to endure. There was something comforting, he had realized in the midst of the war, about suffering. There was a certain warmth that came with being buried in the depths of no return - a familiarity in sorrow that could be found nowhere else. He had felt it for the first time when his father died, the next when the heartbreak of his brother's death and his seemingly never-ending connection to violence and destruction seemed to overtake him. When there was finally a surrender, when he and Eleri and many of the other long-standing senior officers were allowed to go back to a warm bed, Fyodor felt that a part of him had been destroyed. He couldn't grasp the idea of being *safe*. He had never had the space to consider a time where he would be able to sleep an entire night. He didn't know how he would do it - the concept of rest foreign to him - and he knew that he would have trouble adjusting. He was right. He couldn't sleep on his own, he couldn't breathe when it got dark, and he didn't know how to spend long hours without someone else to talk to. He felt that he had too much time and that he was wasting it all. There were no plans to be made. There were no coordinates to double check. There were no patrols, there were no rendezvous, there was nothing to serve as a distraction. He had no notes to take. He had no rifles to clean. He was alone, and he was unoccupied, and he was scared.

He was much more on edge in the comfort of his room than he had been at any point over the past five years.

It had taken him every waking second over the months spent in this apartment, adjusting to life without the war, to even begin to feel okay. It had taken long, strained efforts and restless weeks at a time for him to adjust in the slightest. He had been starting over, every day, for so long. He didn't want to do it again.

What choice, though, did he have? He knew, in the depths of his heart, that he was doing something far beyond himself. He knew, in the back of his mind, that any decision he was to make now would ultimately permanently impact those around him. His entire life - every waking moment he had spent fighting in this godforsaken war - had conditioned him to think selfishly. It was a premise that he was sure allowed their group to live for as long as they did; for Eleri to lead him out of the rubble for the two of them to survive the unthinkable. The selfishness that had embedded itself into his being, the pull in his chest that led him to make decisions for his own safety and not that of others, was strong, and it was tested. It was something that he knew would have him survive. But it was not what was needed now. And that was where Fyo struggled.

And suddenly, the apprehension turned to a bitter rage that he could feel in the sharp pain behind his eyes and taste in the blood that came from the inside of his cheeks. He could breathe, but he felt as though even that was limited. And as he made his way through the room, planting explosives, remembering moments, he wondered how much of this was worth it.

He lit himself a cigarette as he worked; letting the warmth and the stale taste of nicotine fill his lungs and his throat and his mind. *Ten. Nine. Eight.*

His room, just his luck, was situated right above key rigs in the building. The explosives destroying his space would bring down the rest of the structure as well. There was no point in exploring the stairwells or the other residences. He knew that even considering it was a waste of time. He knew that he was only stalling, desperately trying to find some sort of excuse. Surely, Eleri was near finished by now, and the ten to fifteen minutes they'd allotted themselves would be over soon. He hadn't kept track, stupidly, and in a moment of realization, he stepped onto his balcony.

Her windows were open, as always, and he could still make out the silhouette moving inside her apartment from across the street. He still had some time.

He finished setting the explosives, and against his better judgment, opened his closet. There was all the music, all the photographs, all of the parts of his history that his family had tried so hard to preserve.

Was there anything salvageable?

He removed the bag from his back, opening the pouch, eyeing the space. How much could he fit in the sleeve?

He knew that it was a bad idea to take the vinyls - they'd break, and he'd have wasted space - so he opted for a photo album and a folder that housed letters that had been sent to and fro over the years. With a final glance at all that he would never see again, he flung the bag over his shoulders and stepped out of the apartment.

Eleri was already on the street when he made it down, and she smiled at him gently. "Get anything good?"

He shrugged. "I only took a couple of things. No way I'd be able to grab it all."

She nodded once, understanding, and she opened her palm. "Found something of yours."

He looked down - he never forgot things at Eleri's, he was sure of it - and his eyes went wide. He could hear her small laugh as he reached for the lighter. It was old, and it had long since stopped working, but he had stolen it from one of their superiors *years ago* and had kept it as a prize. "Holy shit, I thought I'd lost this."

"Never you. Only misplaced it." and then, her smile faded. "Ready?"

He slipped the lighter into his pocket, his free hand holding the detonator. "I guess so." He shook his head. "This was not what I had in mind when I said I wanted to redecorate."

Eleri nudged his shoulder, a smile on her face, and she exhaled deeply.

"It is what it is - we can always do a huge reno later." She paused, looking up through his window once more. "On three?"

"Fyodor Kacer," the voice was shrill and loud from behind them. "You make one more move and I'll shoot your brains out."

The pair froze. They assumed that they were alone. They hadn't considered someone else here. They were sure that as they had arrived, they hadn't seen anyone.

Eleri turned first, finger resting gently over the button, wondering if it was too big of a risk to just press it and hope for the best. She thought, for a moment, that if she were to hit the detonator, and her building was to collapse, that though she, Fyo, and whoever had just arrived would all die, it would be worth it. But there was some childlike curiosity nestled in the pit of her stomach, and in a split second it took for her to turn to face the source of the voice, she decisively chose not to blow the whole place to bits.

Yet.

Evginia was standing, watching them, an arm outstretched as if to stop the two from continuing on their path. She looked desperate.

Fyodor didn't move towards her as she expected him to.

It didn't hurt her as much as it did irritate her - the kind of bitter annoyance that found its way onto her tongue and forced her to hide the cringe that she felt creeping into her skin. She knew, all too well, how her son behaved. He had certain traits as a child, and she saw them again now. She knew that he was angry at her by his entirely too calm demeanor, by the eyes that were looking at her but seeing nothing, by the way that he seemed so incredibly unbothered by the fact that she had returned to him.

Fyo didn't care. It was not fear, nor negligence, nor apathy that made him indifferent. It was not spite, nor pride, nor ego.

It was sadness.

Fyo didn't feel sadness in its entirety often. Usually, it was something else - grief, fear, disappointment - but rarely sadness itself. But this, what he was feeling now, looking at his mother, was undoubtedly just that. A deep, dark hole that had found itself beneath his ribs. It nestled itself between his lungs, spreading through his chest to his heart - a hand that rested just along the edges, waiting to squeeze. It blanketed him from the inside out, desperately clawing at his veins and his bones, preying on whatever it could find.

It was one emotion that, in theory, he never believed he could feel looking at his mother - this woman who had raised him and showed him more love than anyone else ever had, the person he looked up to most, someone he said he would do anything to get back - but as it unfolded, he understood. This woman, for all her love and light, was someone who had reached her end in terms of the impact she could have on him. He thoroughly believed that now, at this point, he had grown and learned so much without her that she had nothing else to teach him. She had exhausted her efforts. She had removed herself for so long that he could no longer maintain a relationship. He didn't owe her anything. He never would again.

Eleri could feel his tension from beside her. She stepped closer, resting a hand on his arm, looking up at him. Fyo usually waited for her to speak first. Eleri was normally the one to assess and take control of a conversation. She could read a room and manipulate it to her advantage without a second thought. But she, even now, felt a pressure in her heart. She knew that this was not her place to speak, and she knew that she had to communicate that to Fyodor as best she could without opening her mouth. In her eyes, all he saw was adoration. In her eyes, he saw support, and he saw love, and he saw the single thing she wanted him to know: that this was all up to him, now. That this was his conversation to have, not hers.

Fyodor resisted the urge to kiss her right there. He had spent a long, long time trying to comb through the feelings he had towards her, trying to organize them, to justify them, to understand if he loved her as a friend or as more, to truly get to the core of if he cared about her because of their shared trauma, or because he had fallen for her, to be able to wholeheartedly, confidently, trust what he was thinking.

Years of his life, and he didn't have a damn clue what it was he felt.

One look at her, in this moment, and things fell into place.

He turned his gaze back to his mother, raising the detonator so she could see it clearly, his thumb hovering over the button.

"What is your plan, *exactly*, mom? You raise the gun, I press the button, *we all die anyway.*"

Genie was thinking, hard. When she had talked this over with Ruben Yorke, they hadn't considered this defiance would be possible. She was so accustomed to her son being on her side - to Fyodor listening to her above all, to his undivided loyalty - that this was never in the question. She, of course, like an idiot, hadn't added Eleri to this equation. She hadn't thought about how much pull the Reaper had on her son, and she assumed that if it truly ever came down to it, he would choose his mother over his friend.

Genie cautiously began to walk towards the pair. "Just... please... let me talk to you."

"You're doing that," Fyo snapped, "right now."

Genie pursed her lips. She closed her eyes for a moment, collecting herself, weighing her choices. She didn't *want* to do this, but Ruben said if she did, her son's life would be spared, and she, frankly, didn't like the idea of all these houses being blown to bits.

The proposition Ruben had offered her went deeper, though. They always did, with him. It was strange, Genie thought, in a fleeting moment, how all this time had passed, and everybody was exactly as she remembered them.

Maybe people never changed.

Ruben had proposed more than her son's safety; he had offered her power. He knew that if this - whatever *this* was, anyways - concluded in the way that Eleri Roman and her newfound colleagues in the resistance had planned, there would be nothing left for him. But he was never one to lose hope - maybe a flaw of his, maybe the reason he had made it this far - and he was incredibly aware of the opportunities that laid ahead if he was able to stop it. So, with Genie on his side, he felt that he could. It was his only chance. People thought that he was dead. They'd never assume that Gene was conspiring against her son. And to have her by his side, leading an entirely new nation that they could build from the ground up... It seemed like a dream.

Gene agreed.

"You don't know what you're doing, Fyodor. You don't understand the impact -"

"Oh, for the love of God," Fyodor groaned, throwing his head back in pure irritation. Eleri watched him intently. Her eyes locked onto his finger. She knew exactly what he was doing. He didn't have to say it, and he knew that she would understand.

Eleri wondered if she would die a martyr.

Fyodor couldn't exactly pinpoint the root of the sudden anger, but it was an alluring change of pace. His evaluation of what was right and wrong, the outlook he had built for himself his entire life, was skewed entirely. He had always thought to ask for permission to prevent having to ask for forgiveness. There would be no need for recompense if the action was supported.

Eleri believed to ask for neither. "It isn't up to anyone else," she would say. "Learn that it is up to you and that you're allowed to think for yourself."

Her words played in his mind as he squeezed her free hand with his.

"Do you ever shut the fuck up?"

The buildings came down before the response could escape her.

I guess she does.

Twenty.

I've never tried to play God. Maybe I should.

- The Found Diary of Eleri Roman, p. 90

—

Delaney knew that something was wrong when she felt the ground shake. It wasn't like the usual unsteadiness, and it wasn't her own thoughts getting to her. No. None of that. It was something more. It was subtle. It was barely detectable in all the chaos.

She felt the shift.

She had to find out what it was.

Delaney wasn't sure where anybody was. She hadn't seen Clover or Claire in what felt like forever. She had never worked with Eleri or Fyodor - at least, not personally, and had not seen them at all. She didn't know what was going on, nor how to help, but she *did* know that if she was the only one who had felt it, then she was the only one who could explore it.

Delaney took a breath, moving away from the fight, knowing the odds of being scolded by Clarissa were high but not caring enough. She felt it. She knew she did.

She thought, hard, about what was next. Her spatial awareness and orientation were fine. Her ability to use herself as her own compass was fine. But she was painfully unaware of her surroundings. She had no idea where she was. She had never been to Aloneia before, and even if she had, she surely wouldn't have ventured to…

The housing district?

That was the third stop, right?

She shook her head. She knew it was. There was no room to doubt herself.

There was an air of caution as she moved through back roads and alleyways, careful to check around corners and in windows and underneath fixtures before walking through any section. She didn't know how this place worked, but she did know that she was never safe. She was a target. She had to understand this.

Part of the reason Delnaey didn't prefer this side of things was her constant need for comprehension. She didn't mind fighting at its core. She minded being in the middle of things. When you're in the middle, it is impossible to see the big picture, and when you can't see the big picture, you have a certain tunnel vision, whether you'll admit to it or not. This standard fact seemed to apply to everybody *except* for Eleri Roman - Delaney had thought about it multiple times, the way this girl was always in the mess when she did her best work - and she once again slotted her into the outliers category in her brain. She didn't get it, and what she did not understand, she did not trust.

She wanted to stop comparing everything to Eleri. She wanted to be able to start seeing things just for what they were without thinking about how they lined up with the Reaper. But the problem was that she was a researcher. She was someone who put things together. She collected all of the information and made sense of it. And this entire war, both sides of it, seemed to hinge on this one woman. Delany was aware that Eleri knew her worth. She was aware that Eleri understood the weight she pulled and that her decisions would forever leave a mark greater than herself. She just wasn't sure if Roman *truly* understood the magnitude of it all.

It would be hard to do so, she concluded finally, as she continued to walk towards a seemingly sudden cloud of smoke in the distance. She assumed that the reason she was able to understand this huge impact was because, as always, Delaney was on the outside looking in. She was able to see, measure, and process.

Eleri would never be able to do that for herself.

Delaney didn't blame her for it.

She moved with ease, but the strong sense of caution never left her. Delaney was not about to die on this walk, that was for sure.

She reached the space that she assumed *was at some point* the housing district. The rubble and the destruction and the smoke would say otherwise, but quickly she decided that this had been a group of apartments. Her mind reeled - *weren't we supposed to do this after the rest of this region was secure?* - eventually landing on the same name she'd spent every waking moment trying to find. Eleri Roman.

Delaney's first encounter with the Reaper occurred in the last way she would have ever pictured it. She had imagined it time and time again - maybe Eleri would attack their headquarters, maybe she'd invade their safehouse, maybe there would be a second invasion and the Reaper would only come face to face with Delaney to kill her - and in every event that crossed her mind, she felt the pull of fear. She knew that this was one dangerous person and that this person would more than likely be looking to end her life.

Stuck underneath a small pile of debris, eyes closed, was the woman she had looked at for so long. The first thing Delaney noticed was the blood coming from her temple and from her nose. There was a scar that ran from her lip, down her chin, to her neck. It looked old. It looked faded - a shade of white, resembling a strike of lighting.

She knelt down, hand hovering over the body. What was her place here? What was she supposed to do?

Delaney's decision didn't come until she heard a cough.

She was alive.

There was silence for a moment until she decided to start pulling the debris off of her, wincing at the sight of the tears in her clothes, inhaling sharply at the awkward position in which her wrist sat.

At this moment, this was not the Reaper. This was someone on her team who needed help.

"Shit," Delaney cursed under her breath, her hand reaching behind Eleri's head, lifting it off of the rock it had hit. She tried to ignore the blood on her hands.

Eleri's eyes opened slowly, taking a second to focus, before painfully lurching away. "Who the fuck are you?"

Delaney moved back. She was still scared. Her hands were up. "I'm not here to hurt you. My name's Delaney - Claire has me as a sniper -"

"Fuck," Eleri put her head in her hands. "Okay. Fuck." She stood, wincing, but beginning to walk anyways. "Where's Fyodor?"

Delaney shook her head rapidly. "I - I don't know. I just saw you and I -"

"So help me look then, yeah?"

Delaney could see Eleri limping. She could see her struggle, her immense pain, and the tears collecting in her eyes.

She said nothing.

Delaney did as she was told, digging through the rubble, looking for any sign of a body. She assumed that the two were close together when things went off. She assumed that he couldn't be far.

She found the body of an older woman first - and lurched back at the sight. Her face had caved in, bruises already forming, a piece of what she was *sure* was a skull pressing through the skin. She felt vomit in her throat. She choked it down as she called out.

"I found Genie!"

Eleri trudged over. She had forgotten, for a moment, that Delaney surely knew Evginia as well. It was a lot to process all at once. She was already tired, she was dizzy, she felt sick. She knew that *something* was wrong with her wrist - not that she cared, at least now, to find out - she felt the blood coming down the side of her head in waves, there seemed to be a haze around any light she looked at - which, in truth, was the worst part, given there was still some snow on the ground - and she had lost one of her knives. She didn't know where Fyodor was, and she didn't know what she would do if they didn't find him.

Finding Genie was a start, though.

Eleri hadn't considered living through this event. She hated that she had. She didn't want to die - not at this moment, anyways - but she didn't want to live through more. It was a tightrope on which she had walked for most of her life. It was something that was so painfully difficult to do. It was one of her innermost thoughts, one that almost never surfaced. It was part of the reason she refused to be truthfully, fully introspective. She could do it if she tried, she supposed, but it was not worth the trouble. She wanted clarity, but the muddy water she swam through every time she peeled her eyelids open was warm and inviting. She couldn't see the bottom of the lake, but she had learned to love the surface.

The surface. That was all that she needed.

She could drown, she had realized one night, years ago. She could drown because the gaping hole inside of her and the water surrounding her being could not possibly have been a good combination, and it was nearly inevitable that at some point, she would dip her head underneath and never come back up.

There were no lifelines, either. It was sink or swim, and she knew this.

So she ignored every sign of the water rising and she went along, as she always did, with her thoughts to herself. She didn't share with Fyodor. She didn't share with Kassander when he was around. She would close her mouth and keep to herself.

She was beginning to think she didn't know how to swim.

She thought about crying, letting some of the water go in a desperate attempt to create more breathing room, but she ultimately decided there was nothing to gain. That would take a lot of energy - which, especially now, she did not have - and it would do nothing to change her situation. She decided that she would accept whatever came her way. Whether the water rose or fell, she felt that whenever her last breath came, it would be in the name of *divine timing.*

She had thought she was on the brink of death many times. It was as if something was physically stopping her from letting go. She wasn't sure what it was, but she was sick and tired of it.

So she didn't want to die, but she wanted death to stop teasing her.

She was jealous of Genie, she decided, looking down at the woman's broken features. She knew it was twisted, but it was honest, and honesty was rare.

Eleri sighed deeply, brushing the woman's hair back, rising back to her feet. "Yeah, well, may she rest in peace."

She stepped back off the rocks, wandering back to the center of what was once the path, stopping in her tracks when she saw a familiar piece of fabric.

It was one of his straps. It was one of the straps on Fyo's bag.

"Fuck," She hissed in pain as she made her way over the pile, Delaney following close behind. She fell to her knees, ignoring the sharp stinging sensation, as she started to move rocks and concrete and wires out of the way. "Are you going to help me?"

Delaney, who was frozen, nodded aggressively, following Eleri's lead, pulling whatever she could away from the strap. She saw the body underneath. They both did. They worked faster.

Eleri reached through the rocks once there was enough space and pulled Fyodor's head onto her lap. She raked her fingers through his hair. She wiped the blood from his face, she ran her hand along the scar across his head, and she pressed her fingers into the side of his neck, closing her eyes, focusing on her trembling fingers, looking for a pulse.

She bit down on her lower lip, trying her hardest to prevent tears from spilling through her closed lids. She was not about to cry, especially not in front of some girl she had just met. She was not going to allow that vulnerability. Never.

But the weight of Fyo's cold skin in her hands, the feeling of his head on her lap, the knowledge that her fingers pressing against his neck would leave a bruise - it was too much to handle. She couldn't lose him. He was all that she had left. She vaguely took note of Delaney sitting on the other side of the rubble, watching intently. She didn't care.

"Fyo," she whispered, to him and to him only, her forehead pressed against his, her nose against the top of his head from where she sat. "Fyodor, please,"

She ran her hand down the side of his face, gently, as if trying to coax him back. She could've sworn she felt a pulse, but she had touched enough death to know that it meant almost nothing, that the body did what the body wanted to even in death. She wasn't holding out hope - not until he breathed, not until his eyes opened - and she knew that it had some value. She had her walls up all the way. She couldn't pull them down. Not now.

She had let him down. She had let him down every single day since meeting him. She had never appreciated him in the way that she should've. She had never allowed him to be the person he could. The anger that rose in her throat was one that was so *hot*, so full of pure, unbridled venom and fury that she wanted to scream right there.

But she couldn't. She wouldn't.

She pressed her lips to his forehead, then. The first time she had ever done such a thing with such love in her heart. They lingered, millimeters above his skin, as her fingers continued to dance along his cheeks. "I love you, Fyodor. Come on,"

She had things to do, and she knew it. She had a war to finish fighting. She had people to help. She had people to *kill*.

But she couldn't leave him. Not sweet, sweet Fyodor. Not like this.

Her fingers trembled as they reached for his hair again, gently brushing through it, for what she was sure would be the last time. He deserved a better ending than this. He deserved all of the good that the world had to offer.

There was not enough of it - the good. Nowhere near enough, and Fyo was one of its only sources.

She leaned back, taking a deep breath, looking at the now cloudless sky.

"El,"

The sound was so small, so rough. Had it been any quieter, she wouldn't have heard it at all. She was making it up. She had to be.

Then she felt a cold grip around her wrist.

She looked down. Fyodor - weakly - was holding onto her, breathing slowly, shallowly, eyes closed.

She wanted to cry. Again.

"Fuck," she breathed, "Fyo, shit, you're alive."

He nodded, barely moving his head, and continued to hold onto her wrist. "Can you open your eyes?" she asked gently - not condescending, nor rude - simply out of worry and concern.

He swallowed thickly. His eyes fluttered - once - before closing again.

"Okay, okay. Don't stress."

Delaney watched carefully. She never thought that a scene like this would be unfolding at all, let alone in front of her. She never assumed that this kind of action could be taken by the woman she had feared for years. She assumed - *no, she fully believed* - that Eleri Roman was the closest thing that a human being could be to a machine. She didn't think that this was possible. It was stupid, she knew, and it was definitely not the time or place to be analyzing her character, but Delaney had spent so long putting everything together only to be shamefully wrong. Maybe she was right about her violence or about her aggression. Maybe there were points that held up in her quick thinking and abundance of knowledge. But the one part she had never even considered was the first thing she was seeing upon meeting her.

"Does your Deller work?"

It took Delaney a moment to realize that Eleri was talking to her. When she did, she nodded. "It should."

"Mine's been broken for a while. I'm assuming his is, too." Eleri nodded towards Fyodor. "Can you try getting into contact with Clove or Claire?"

Delaney nodded, tapping twice on the side, beginning to speak. Eleri fully turned her attention back to Fyo.

"Your mom's dead," she said, rooting her hand in his hair. Ash-covered blond strands tangled around blood-stained fingers.

He gulped. "Yeah. She has been for a while, hasn't she, though?"

Eleri nodded gently. "Yeah. I guess so."

There was a comfortable silence. Delaney was talking somewhere in the distance - a sign, at the very least, that someone had been able to respond. Eleri looked down again, staring at Fyodor with deep intent.

She was so lucky.

He opened his eyes, slowly, carefully, almost timidly, immediately taking her in. His head was throbbing. She noticed that he had stopped bleeding - for now, at least - and she smiled. "Look at you," she whispered, "almost back to yourself already."

Fyodor laughed lightly, wincing at the pain it caused in his chest and back. "I don't know where my rifle is."

She brushed through his hair again. "I lost a knife. C'est la vie."

"You're French now, huh?"

She rolled her eyes. "Maybe."

"Well then, chérie," he smiled, weakly. "I'd love to hear more."

She snorted. "You're cute."

Then she paused. He caught it. "Yeah?"

She shrugged, playing it off as nothing. "Sure. Why not."

Fyodor was silent for a moment. If his heart had stopped beating at some point, it had surely started up again now.

"El?"

"Yeah?"

With all the strength he had, he reached up, holding the back of her neck. He wasn't sure if it would work, but he'd be damned if he didn't try. Not when he was given this second chance. Not when he was alive against all odds.

She allowed herself to melt into his touch, letting his weak hand guide her towards him. Rare vulnerability. Uncharacteristically timid.

He turned his head to the side, and before either of them had time to fully think about what it was that they were doing, their lips met.

It was gentle. It was desperate.

It made Eleri feel like she was going to burn up in a ball of flames. It made Fyodor calm down.

She pulled back, only slightly, eyeing his swollen lips. He smiled, falling back into her lap, allowing her to continue playing with his hair.

Nothing else was said. There was nothing to say. And as per Eleri - there was no point in asking for permission or recompense. Whatever happened, happened.

Que sera sera.

She was glad that she had taught him that initiative. She was even more glad that he'd taken it on himself and gone through with it.

All that needed to be said had been. They understood. They always would.

Love and violence, Fyodor thought, again, what is one without the other?

And then, as if on queue, Eleri spoke.

"Cigarette?"

Twenty-One.

As I write this, there is a soft rain outside the window. There is a light beat. There is a gentle reminder that the world continues on its own, that we are not everything. We are barely anything. I think that we lose that, sometimes - the knowledge... no, not knowledge... more so the awareness that we are a lot less important than we let ourselves believe. It's the one single thought that is able to ground me. Sometimes, and I won't lie, things get to my head in a bad way. Sometimes, knowing how much I, personally, have altered and changed things... makes me feel a lot more important than I should. But I have to remind myself. I have to remind myself that we are not as big as we want to be.

I could be God, but I haven't had the chance yet.

- The Found Diary of Eleri Roman, p. 91

—

Eleri was in the midst of fixing one of the buttons on the jacket - *Kassander's jacket* - when she saw someone in the distance. Delaney looked past her, eyeing the figure, raising her rifle. She was ready. It was only one body, in the broad daylight, and there would be no fight if they chose to attack.

Too far away to make a decision, Delaney began to walk. She had a good idea of who it was - it had to be either Clove or Claire - and though she had her weapon raised and loaded, she didn't anticipate having to use it. Eleri, who had managed to get Fyodor sitting up on his own, was watching carefully. Sure, she didn't have it in her to fight, but she did have it in her to throw a knife or shoot a gun, which she hoped she wouldn't have to do. Fyo was going through the contents of his backpack, gingerly assessing the damage, reluctantly putting aside the things that would no longer be of use to him.

Eleri wasn't sure what it was that had piqued her interest. Everything seemed tame, and normal, and inconspicuous. She didn't know if it was some sort of lingering paranoia from thinking she had lost Fyo, or if it was just her instinct and her subconscious telling her something important, but once the feeling came, it was impossible to shake.

Her hand fell down to her leg, gripping one of her knives.

"Everything okay?" Fyodor mumbled, rubbing his lip with his thumb, not turning his attention away from his task.

"I don't know," she said, standing, wincing as she did so.

Her eyes narrowed on the figure coming towards them, *towards Delaney, specifically*, and she froze.

"Are you kidding me?" she said, breathless, eyes widening. Fyodor looked up, looked past her, looked *at* her.

"What?"

"Shit," she breathed, then, loudly, "Delaney! Delaney, get back from there! He's gonna -"

It all happened in the blink of an eye.

The bullet left the man's rifle before Delaney had a chance to process what it was that Eleri was telling her. The knife left Eleri's grip before the man had a chance to move. Eleri, despite all the pain coursing through her body, was trying her best to run to the scene. She knelt down only briefly - taking Delaney's rifle as her own, whispering a quick 'it'll be okay' - before making her way to the man.

The knife had struck him in the upper thigh, a generally uncomfortable area to be hit at all, let alone to be impaled, and he was groaning and desperately trying to dislodge it without causing more damage.

Eleri took this as her opportunity. With her free hand, she reached towards him, pulling it out in one motion, eliciting a shriek from the back of his throat. Using the rifle, she pushed him down, holding it to his chest, staring him in the eyes.

"Change of plans, huh? You decided not to die?"

Ruben Yorke scoffed, occupied with the blood on his leg. "Maybe I had other plans to begin with. No change."

She narrowed her eyes at him. "How did you know we were here?"

"Kind of hard to miss an explosion like that." He said, a proud smirk gracing his features.

Eleri smacked him on the side of the head with the weapon. "You're not very funny."

He frowned. "Maybe ask the pretty boy's mother, huh?"

Eleri mirrored his expression. "She's dead, thanks for the concern, though - I'll be sure to pass the sentiment along." then, a pause. "You two knew each other?"

"I know *everyone*, Roman. You should know this by now. Keep up."

She scoffed. "Fine. You know everyone. What did she have to do with your glorious arrival, huh?"

Eleri hadn't moved the gun away from him. He noticed and stood incredibly still, despite trying to keep himself from bleeding out through his leg. "Well, she would've been able to tell you, if you hadn't -"

"I've killed you once, buddy. I'll do it again."

Wordlessly, he raised one hand to his ear, revealing a Deller. "I know more than you think I do."

Eleri's mind worked as fast as it could to connect the dots. She had apparently not killed Ruben, he had found Genie, who was still at the safe house, which meant that they had always known where the safe house was, which meant that there was someone sharing that information. It was Genie, evidently, which explained how he got there, how he didn't kill her, and how he managed to find her now.

She took a deep breath. "What are you thinking you're going to gain here?"

Ruben winked at her. "Shoot and find out."

The statement was big, but she had reason to believe that he was talking himself up again. This time, though, the difference was that in every sense outside of the specific situation in which she found herself, she had the lower hand. She was half-dead, she didn't know what was going on in terms of any actual fights and battles, and she had no idea who was alive and who wasn't. She, at this point, was so incredibly lost - something so rare for her - and she was sure that to some extent, Ruben knew it. He had to if he had managed to get Genie on his side and to this location. Hell, he wasn't supposed to be *alive*, and here he was. She had never underestimated Ruben Yorke, despite how their relationship had changed over the short span of time in which they'd known each other personally, but even for him, this seemed immense.

Ruben knew what he was doing. He knew that Eleri didn't have enough of a grip on the situation. He knew, after working above her for years, that her calculations could only be made quickly and confidently if she had been in control for enough time to understand the inner workings of what was around her. He knew that in a situation like this, whatever she chose would not be in full confidence, and when she didn't have full confidence, she was never able to choose the fastest option. She didn't mind dragging things on, and in this case, that would mean sparing Ruben's life, allotting him time and space to continue to plan out what he had to do. In truth, he had no plan. He had no option. He had no incentive for what was to come if he lived through this conversation. It was a fact - a sad one, one he hated to admit - but it was the truth, and he knew that as long as he didn't utter a word of the truth out loud, he would be fine. He could remain stoic, confident, and provocative.

Eleri swallowed. If she was any less hurt, she would've entertained his life a little longer. She would've taken the chance - taken the possible fight - on the grounds that he may have been honest. But now, though, with the pain she felt, with the way her blood felt like it was boiling, with the nausea she felt in her stomach, she knew she would never be able to rationalize it. She would never be able to outweigh the cons of having him around any longer. She had to remember that he already was never supposed to be here, anyways.

Without moving the rifle, she looked back to Delaney, who was slowly collecting herself, trying her best to move away from the altercation. She didn't blame her for it, and from what she could see, the bullet had probably hit her somewhere in the arm, so it wouldn't prove to be fatal. It was best for her to step back. Eleri understood.

She then turned her attention back to Ruben Yorke. "You have nothing else?"

"In what regard, my sweet, *sweet girl*?"

Eleri cringed. "You need a therapist, first of all," she cocked the gun, "second of all, if you have nothing else to say to me - to offer me - then I've made a decision."

Ruben felt his breath catch in his throat. He didn't think things would play out this way. "Can I see Gene?"

Eleri frowned. "You'd like to see her decaying body?"

Ruben didn't know how to respond to that. No, he didn't, but Eleri was going to put a bullet through his skull, and walking over to pay his respects would buy him another two minutes, in which he could *think of what the hell to do.*

"Yes," he said.

Eleri picked up on his hesitance, but she obliged, nodding. He stood and she waited for him to walk past her, ensuring she never had her back to him.

"There," she said, "the space to Fyodor's right,"

Ruben looked at Eleri for a moment before sighing and beginning to walk towards the space she had mentioned.

He fell to the ground before he was actually able to register the bullet in his back.

The vest didn't cover his shoulder blades or the surrounding area. Eleri must've learned from last time. Poor planning on his part.

His eyes went wide as he fell. He gasped, all breath escaping him, and opened his mouth to scream.

Nothing came out.

Eleri, long since unbothered by bodies and by death, kneeled beside him, flipping him so that he was on his back, facing her, wound against the hard ground. He let out a cry then - a short yelp, desperate - as she looked down at him. There was no pity in her face, no remorse in her features. He had, again, completely misjudged the situation. Somewhere in the back of his mind, he was scolding himself. He should have known better. He was given every single opportunity to better understand her, he had essentially been controlling her for years, and now, suddenly that things mattered, he thought he knew better. Her name, once again, seemed to mean nothing to him. It was as if she was only the Reaper to him when she wasn't in his presence. He had used her as a weapon for so long, yet it somehow never registered in his mind that she was deadly. He never learned. She had tried to kill him before, he didn't learn. She had a gun to his head now, he still didn't learn.

"Genie's head is caved in. Not sure you want to see that."

Eleri felt like she was going to pass out. She, at this point, was certain she'd broken a rib again - the familiar pain in her side was excruciating, and each breath felt like it was beating the life out of her. It had taken all of her energy to have this conversation, and she didn't have enough faith in herself to keep going much longer. She wished that Ruben would hurry up and die.

He coughed, blood trickling through his lips, cringing as his back once again hit the ground. "You are a bitch," he sputtered, with as much conviction as he could.

"So I've been told," Eleri said, trying her best to keep her eyes open.

"It's because you're a Kind Baby, huh?"

Eleri ignored the statement. She had only heard the term once before, and she ignored it then, too. The year she was born meant nothing. It should not set her apart.

She looked past the body lying in front of her. Delaney had made it safely to Fyo, who was now gently wrapping her arm with some sort of bandage he had found - whether it was in his bag or in one of her pockets, Eleri was not sure, but she knew that it was irrelevant - and the pair seemed to be working well enough given the circumstances. The sun was setting, the wind growing colder, and she shivered.

"You know," Eleri said, "We could've made a great team, I think,"

Ruben tried not to laugh. It would hurt too much. He did, however, manage a sarcastic smile. "Wow, thank you for your insight. I'll be sure to check in on that."

She was delirious, she had to be. She would never try to keep a conversation with Ruben Yorke light.

"Yeah, of course." Silence for a moment, then, "I feel like you did this to yourself."

He closed his eyes. "Mhm?"

"Yeah," she said, looking at him. "Too bad."

"The fucking Reaper," he exhaled, "who would've thought."

Eleri watched as his features almost hardened. She watched his chest still. The puddle of blood beneath him was still rapidly growing, but she didn't care to move him or herself. She was tired, and she felt like shit.

She didn't know why this hurt. Maybe it was the opportunity to guide him out of life into death. Maybe it was the fact that this had been a fully thought-out plan on both their parts. Maybe it was the knowledge that there was now so much that she would never know. Genie was a traitor both ways. Fyo's mother had a flair for the dramatic, it appeared. And Ruben potentially had more planned. She'd never be able to beat the answer out of either of them now.

Delaney appeared at her side. "You okay?"

Eleri nodded. "Of course. Just tired. Are you good? Do you know where Clove or Claire are? You spoke to them, right?"

Delaney nodded. "Yeah. I'm okay. Clove and Claire should find their way here eventually. We just have to wait."

Eleri sighed. "I hate waiting."

Twenty-Two.

I have such a hard time grasping time itself. I don't know how to reason with it. We were in a war for fifteen years, and in the span of a few months, we completely turned it over. Why did it ever take so long to begin with? How did we manage things so quickly on the counter?

I overheard Delaney talking once, saying that she believed that I was the reason it happened. Whatever side I was on seemed to find incredible success. The latter was true, but the former seemed incredibly far-fetched. There were always so many people involved. There was no way it could be dependent on one single thing, right?

On one person?

Of course not. That's impossible.

- The Found Diary of Eleri Roman, p. 94

There was no telling how long it had been. There was no way of measuring it. Days turned into weeks turned into months, as far as they were concerned. They'd stopped keeping track a long time ago, things piling together, grief blending into fear into hope into distress.

There was a slow descent into nothingness as they forged on. Clover had come to find Delaney, Fyodor, and Eleri two days after Ruben's death. She'd made it painfully clear that they did not have time to spare. There was still so much going on. There was still a job to complete.

Everything that Aloneians held close to their hearts had been destroyed. At this point, whatever fight they had left was only to preserve their own sense of importance. Eleri wasn't exactly in love with the idea of *wiping out an entire population*, especially not when that was the entire notion that had lit the flame, but they weren't surrendering. They weren't backing down. She and Clove had created an advantage for Voskivy that was nearly impossible to recover. The plan that was full of chaos and headstrong movement, one that in theory seemed too difficult to be true, was what had allowed them to get this far.

Most of the children in the region had long since fled, their parents staying behind to fight. Eleri wasn't sure where the Aloneian children would go - most of them were very sheltered - but she hoped that they were safe, wherever it was that they felt they were meant to go.

She was exhausted. This was, somehow, a million times more tiring than their entire time spent in the team of six before the war had ended. These months had been draining in every way possible. Eleri hadn't realized how different it was to take care of an entire population than what it meant to take care of an assigned team. She underestimated it. She had always respected Clover and the resistance, but the feeling of admiration she hid away seemed to be growing by the day.

The entire spectacle still, somehow, seemed surreal to Eleri. She measured the situation. She knew that she was in it, and that she had initiated it, and that she was one of the reasons it was unfolding successfully. She knew that she had directly contributed to the destruction of her home. She knew that it was her plan to throw everything into disarray. She knew that she had become the worst kind of *solider*, she had committed treason, for sure, and she had gone against everything she had originally sworn to protect. She knew that it was different - that things had changed, that she was ultimately her own person, and that everything she was doing was for the greater good - but she struggled, deeply, with the reality of the situation spanning back to her childhood. She wouldn't call herself an experiment, but it was evident that she was much more of a state-funded science project than she had initially believed. She still had trouble comprehending how involved Ruben Yorke had been in everything. She still couldn't wrap her mind around who Xavier Talon truly was. She had always been slightly suspicious of those in power - only because she wasn't able to see what they were doing, which only added to her stress - but had she known the severity and the magnitude of their influence, she'd have done something about it much sooner. Eleri always took pride in who she was. She always tried to be good for herself, to stand up to those who didn't care to hear from her, to make sure that she was seen, heard, and felt. She knew that she was an unorthodox walking disaster, and she knew that the trail of blood and bodies she left behind could be seen from everywhere. She knew that despite her lack of understanding and lack of personal communication with the world outside of Voskivy and Aloneia, there was a good chance of others being aware of her and *fearing her*. She understood, though she wished she didn't, that everything she had done in the name of self-righteousness or in the name of a fight that she never fully understood would add to her legacy. She knew that she was too young to be able to measure the weight of what she was being thrown into when it began, and she was angry at herself for it. To think that someone like her, who was so strong in her beliefs, who was so sure of herself, had been used as a prop for so long… it hurt her to an unfamiliar degree. And the worst of it was the inherent knowledge that there was absolutely *nothing* that could be done about it. She had considered stopping everything, pulling back from whatever it was that was happening at any given moment. She had thought about taking the group of six and running. She had thought about sabotaging assignments when she was an Intelligence Officer.

She had considered it all - but had always decided against it. There weren't many people she cared about, and she knew that it was painfully obvious that she *barely* cared about herself - the way she threw herself into suicide missions, how she seemed to be more than willing to take the full force of anything that could be thrown at her - and she was well aware of the fact that if she did step out of line, it would be taken out on those around her, not on her specifically.

She thought this as she wrapped Kassander's jacket further around her trembling body.

In retrospect, they'd done it anyway. She'd given them all she had, and they'd gone and done the thing that should've been reserved for malpractice.

She looked to her left, where Fyodor was staring into nothingness, arms wrapped across his chest, head resting against her shoulder. They were taking this single opportunity alone, this moment of peace and tranquility amongst everything going on around them, to breathe. It sounded so *stupid*. It sounded irrational. But they hadn't been able to do so in so long. They were given a quiet space, and they knew they would have to trade with Clover and Claire soon enough. They had to take every moment of grace, every second of being given the luxury of nothingness, and cherish it.

Fyodor was struggling himself. His cigarette dangled from his lips, but he wouldn't smoke it. He couldn't bring himself to move at all. He had lost some part of himself when he had lost his mother, and though time had passed, he couldn't forgive himself for it.

The feeling of joy he felt when he was young was something he knew he would never feel again. Not when he had consciously made the choice that he knew would kill her. Not when he had allowed the thought of her wear him to the bones. Not when he had waited so long to find her again, only to be destroyed by what he saw. Fyodor was exhausted. He was tired of fighting. He was tired of living for other people. He felt as though he was drifting away from the world, slowly but surely, and that one day he would be too far to come back. The surreal feeling that completely encapsulated his being was something out of a nightmare. He had a hard time distinguishing his memories and his dreams from reality. His mind was always somewhere else - he was so deeply broken, so tragically incapable of feeling anything that was happening in the moment. He had gone so long without ever fully becoming himself that he didn't know *who* that was. He had lost something that he could never regain. He had become something that he didn't recognize. He didn't know what to do. He hated it.

His hand slowly, subconsciously, made its way to the necklace - to the dog tags from centuries past, the destroyed metal pendant around his neck from someone he would never be - and he clutched it, feeling it against his palm, fixing the grooves in his skin with those of the piece. He closed his eyes. He tried to feel something. Anything. He wanted to feel what it was like to be *there*. He wanted to feel what it was like to *come home*.

That was the kicker. Coming home. He would never have that. There was nothing like that any longer.

He was missing a lot of things that he never even knew. He cursed his mother for teaching him about the past. He rarely felt jealousy - he thought it an emotion for those who were too dense to appreciate what they had in front of them - but he could not deny the fact that it rose within him when he thought of a time that was *not now*. He had read those letters from wars passed, and he had wondered how horrific it might've been to be a part of them. The first one he had ever read was when he was only ten years old, clutching a paper that had arrived for one of his great aunts from somewhere in Normandy, dated from some autumn night in 1944, detailing death and chaos and destruction, detailing the movements, detailing all that could be described with pen on paper. It was so long ago. It was so *long ago*. And yet, things were exactly the same.

Even from the basement in which they hid, they could hear the rain. Fyodor had noticed it long ago - the rolling thunder, the soft patter - it was so different from the snow they'd grown accustomed to. It was light, droplets against a structure that housed two people who could destroy the world. The rain outside, the natural cycle, a breath of life into a world long since demolished.

And the two of them, inside, chaos following their every move.

The thoughts in Fyodor's mind seemed to echo - as if he was in a large ballroom, as if he were trying to scream them to the world and nobody was there to listen. It had been a while since he had felt this way, not since right after returning to his apartment months ago, and he hadn't realized at the time how horrid it truly was.

He knew that he was not alone. He was resting against Eleri. Her breath matched his. Her body was warm. She was his anchor against the rain outside and the flood within him.

But he didn't feel like it was true. He couldn't see it. He couldn't grasp it.

There was something incredibly helpless about the way his eyes opened, staring at the yellowing ceiling lights, watching as they flickered down onto the small puddles against the concrete floor, watercolor that had been left out too long, something so mundane that had been overlooked for as long as it had existed. There was art in everything. He knew this. His mother had taught him this. It was part of her optimism - finding beauty in tragedy.

Fyodor's opinions differed, but he always listened. He thought about that notion often. He assumed that her thought process was nothing more than faith placed in a flawed idea of what human beings were and were not capable of.

He always listened, but he gave her no opportunity to speak at the end. He always listened, but he took her voice and her life without a second thought.

Never ask for permission. Never ask for forgiveness.

He had half a mind to blame Eleri for his decision, but he knew better. He knew that she would, as always, explain that she had no part in it. He didn't have to do anything she told him to - she never did. And she would be right in saying that. But he felt alone, and he felt the guilt eating away at him. He wanted someone to blame.

He watched the lights flicker again. He leaned his head against the wall. He wanted everything to be over.

Eleri noticed that he was struggling with something, but she, as always, was never one for words. She had been there for him time and time again, but in every instance, she knew what his problem was. She knew the before, the during, and she was usually able to figure out the after. This was different - that much, she knew. What she didn't know - what she was sorely unequipped for - was how to deal with it.

She pondered for a moment, eyes trained on his face, looking at the scar. She gently took the cigarette from his lips, putting it between her own, taking a drag.

He turned to look at her, piercing blue eyes full of worry and of rage.

"You okay?" She asked gently, placing her hand on his cheek tenderly, as if he would pull away from her at a moment's notice.

He pursed his lips, gently leaning into her touch, letting his eyes flutter closed for only a moment before looking at her again. She raised the cigarette to his lips, and he pulled, letting the smoke sit in the back of his throat for a moment before pushing it to his lungs.

He shook his head. *No.*

Eleri frowned. She felt a weight in her chest; a genuine sadness and compassion that she rarely ever felt. She didn't love many people, but she was more than happy that Fyodor was one of them.

She tilted her head to the side slightly, looking at him, studying him.

She hadn't previously realized how crystalline his eyes were - she could see herself in the blue… she could see *everything* in it. Pandora's box. Secrets that could never be spoken. His eyes held everything but his immediate source of distress.

She couldn't make out if his eyes were windows or mirrors.

She wondered if he knew he was doing it.

She pulled the cigarette from her mouth and pressed her lips gently against his forehead, right where his hair met his skin, just beside that jagged scar that she loved so much. She had nothing to say. She never knew what would help, anyway, and she didn't want to accidentally make things worse. She would hate to know that she was the cause of further distress.

She was always scared of falling in love. Maybe that's why she was so hesitant with it now.

Eleri was careful with the word love, and she had only ever said it to Fyodor once; when she thought that he had *died*. She hadn't said it to him in the wake of their friends being taken. She hadn't said it to him when he had saved her life, or when he had disposed of Milton Haas, or when he had given her his jacket, or when he had come over because she was having an issue, or when he had put everything down to help her. Maybe, all those times, she hadn't realized it. Maybe she had taken too long to process it. Maybe losing him was what had sparked it all. She would never know.

His hands came up to hers, covering them on the sides of his temples, breathing her in. Fyodor was sure that if she was not by his side every waking second, he would have killed himself. Plain and simple. He had been wallowing in whatever it was that he felt for far too long, and he knew that the only way to make it all go away permanently was to take away any opportunity of feeling something more.

They were both bad with their emotions but in different ways.

"I miss my mom," he said finally, "but I think I just miss who I used to think she was. I don't think I miss who she became."

Eleri nodded, listening with intent. She knew that if a conversation was started, and she was quiet, the other person would fill that space. She needed Fyodor to keep going - not only for her to understand what it was that was bothering him but also for him to work through it himself.

"I guess I'm just so… disappointed… in myself and in her. I don't know. I shouldn't have expected anything more."

The rain outside seemed to be getting louder. Neither of them was sure if it was their imagination or not.

"You've got no reason to be disappointed in yourself," she said finally, quietly, picking and choosing each word carefully. "None at all. You're so *good*."

He shook his head slowly, kissing her palm. "Not now. Not when I've just…" he sighed, the melancholy swimming through his bones. "I just don't know how to keep going."

She bit the inside of her cheek. "Want to know a secret? Neither do I."

He laughed. It was small, and it lasted only a split second, but it was more than he had done all day, and she would take what she could get.

"So we're both just figuring it all out as we go," she said gently. "And I know that it's complicated, and I know that it's scary, but we've got each other, okay? We always will."

Her hands dropped to his chest, placing the cigarette back between her teeth, eyes following his movements.

There was a loud bang, and they pulled away from each other, instantly. Eleri rose to her feet in record time, her knives in hand, readying herself for a throw.

"Hey!"

The voice was familiar. The sound of boots slamming against metal steps echoed through the room.

"Clover?"

Clove burst into the room, blood coming from her nose, hair drenched from the rain, clothes tattered. She was holding her rifle in her hand, fingers desperately gripping it, her eyes wide and frantic.

"Hey, hey, hey," Eleri said, walking over to her, putting her knife back into its sheath. "What's going on?"

"You need to come with me."

Fyo had found his way behind Eleri, watching the situation unfold.

"Why? What's happening?"

For the first time, Clover's unreadable expression broke into a wide smile. She laughed - the sound of pure joy drowning out any misery felt - and she hugged Eleri.

"El," she said, "they're surrendering."

Twenty-Three.

Years ago, before I had any sense of how the world worked, my dad tried to teach me about God. A few weeks later, he tried to talk to me about Hell. I couldn't quite wrap my head around it. If this being loved us unconditionally, and he sent his only son down here to die for us so that we could live in peace forever, why would he create somewhere where we would go to be punished eternally?

I brought the question up to my dad, and I was met with a backhand. I just wanted the answer.

I suppose, though, that this mentality applies to a lot of people in power. Not everyone - at least, maybe not everyone consciously - does it, but I guess a lot of people do. The notion of altering things to apply what fits. The idea that you can create and destroy reality as you please if you have the means to do so. Milton and all of his friends tried that, didn't they? With the history textbooks, right?

I wonder how we are going to teach future generations the truth if none of us have a full grasp on it ourselves. I wonder who we're meant to turn to, and even then, how can we be sure that they're being honest?

How are we ever supposed to know what's real anymore?

- The Found Diary of Eleri Roman, p. 97

—

Clover, Eleri, and Fyodor stood before three Aloneian men, one of which Eleri recognized vaguely, a distant memory of something she no longer needed to know. She saw the labels on all of their chests - small, golden pins, marking them as Commanding Officers - and she smiled to herself.

The man in the middle spoke first, looking at her as he did so. She hadn't met him before, she was sure, but he seemed to know who she was very well. This happened often, and would continue to happen as long as she was alive, she concluded. She would have to learn to accept it.

"Miss Roman," he said, his voice gruff, "Mister Kacer," he said, turning his head to Fyodor, "I first and foremost would like to express my utmost disappointment in the two of you."

Eleri laughed, covering her hand with her mouth. "It's mutual. Move on."

He scowled, and the man that Eleri felt that she recognized placed his hand on his shoulder. "We have too many casualties. We have lost too many resources. We would like to propose a conditional surrender."

Clover raised an eyebrow. "*Conditional?* You're either going to keep fighting, and you're going to die doing it, or you're not. No conditions."

"There is only *one* thing we ask for." he said, continuing to keep his eyes on Eleri. "We put our guns down, we say you win. You do not kill or convict anyone in this army."

Eleri narrowed her eyes at him. Clover laughed. "Why would you ask that? Considering everything you guys have done over the years..."

Eleri's brows furrowed. Why would he say *that?* Wouldn't it be a given that the people who had done bad things would be somewhat punished for them? She didn't like the idea of making them laborers - that walked a dangerous line- but she didn't fully enjoy the prospect of throwing people in jail, either. In all honesty, the notion was not bad. The conditions were not hard to meet. But they seemed too easy... what was it that was so tempting for them?

Fyodor grabbed her arm. He looked at her. His hand motioned to the pendant around his neck, the one he had always worn.

Her eyes went wide. He was right. History could not continue to repeat itself.

"You won't be arrested or killed," she said, turning back to the man, interjecting. "Fine. But that means we are writing up a contract, and there are regulations that you and all of your little followers will have to abide by."

Clover looked at Eleri with an expression that read as nothing other than *what are you talking about, you idiot?* Eleri widened her eyes at her, *stop it*, and thankfully, she backed down. Eleri would explain later. She was glad that over the years, she had listened to Fyodor talk about the world before them.

The man frowned. He didn't respond, looking at his comrades for support.

Eleri spoke again.

"Or you can just die," she said, "that works too."

The man sighed deeply, her phrase catching his attention. He knew that the Reaper did not take death lightly. "Conditional surrender accepted, on the grounds that the document is written and presented once, and only once."

"Easy enough, right?"

He outstretched his hand to Eleri. She shook her head. "Not me. You shake hands with her on this one."

Clover raised an eyebrow, smiling at Eleri, before turning back to the man expectantly. She stretched her hand out, holding it steady, saying nothing, waiting for the gesture to be returned. The man was struggling - Eleri wasn't sure if it was some personal thing he had against Clover or if the mere thought of shaking hands from Voskivy was enough to throw him off - but she found it laughable.

She couldn't help but wonder, though, if she would have been the same way in this situation had Fyo not found those documents.

Eventually, he gave in, shaking her hand quickly, tucking his hands away back into his pockets the moment their connection ended.

Clover smiled. This was something she never imagined she would feel.

***

Claire and Delaney were trying to make sense of whatever documents they had salvaged when the door opened.

They both became alert, reaching for their closest weapons, eyeing the space.

"Clove?" Claire spoke, raising her gun, expecting it to be someone else.

"Yeah," her girlfriend responded, closing the door behind her. Eleri walked further into the house they'd found and set up camp in.

"Gather around. We have a meeting,"

Delaney shook her head. "We do?"

"We do now that we have terms for a conditional surrender, yes."

Her jaw dropped. "No way."

Eleri nodded, smiling widely. "Yes way, my dear. We have terms and conditions to discuss."

"Why did you say that to him?" Clover said, taking her seat between Eleri and Claire. "That they wouldn't be put in jail. What was the point?"

Claire turned her attention to Eleri. "What?"

Eleri sighed. "They said they'd surrender on the condition that we don't kill them and we don't jail them. I said fine, but we're going to have to make a binding contract - some sort of rules that they'll all have to follow. It makes sense."

"It doesn't, though." Clove said, sucking her teeth. "If they're out there, there's no way we can control them, regardless of what they sign."

Eleri nodded. "See, I'm inclined to agree with you. But... think about it. Their one request is to not be jailed or killed, fine, we agree, they surrender. If we make a binding piece... a contract, or a treaty, or something... they can have that. They can have their 'freedom' but with restrictions, at least for a while. We can regulate them. We can make sure there aren't loopholes." Eleri said, sighing, "Clove, I know what you're getting at. I know you want to get even because of what they did... what *we did*... I get it. I do. But I've been on both sides - granted, not to the same extent - and while I understand your perspective, there genuinely are a few other things we have to consider. For one thing, we have to remember there are still a lot of kids in hiding whose parents are fighting right now. It definitely isn't going to be in our best interest to raise them ourselves or to create, like, foster homes or something. We can't waste resources like that. We've already lost *everything,* right? And then, we have these people who, if they were all in jail together, could congregate and plan, and if we killed them all, then we just essentially did something worse than they did. We don't have to follow that path"

There was a moment of silence that passed as Fyodor spoke up. "Look, I don't know what you all know about history…" he trailed off, looking around the room.

"Most of us who grew up here know about the past century or so pretty well," Claire said, looking at Delaney and Clove for a quick confirmation, "but beyond that, it's all pretty hazy."

"When the First World War came to a close," Fyo began, "they created this treaty, to make sure that the perpetrators didn't have the same amount of power as they did before… you know, to try and prevent another war. There were a whole bunch of things that they had to do like reparations, in a sense, and there was so much that they were banned from, as well. Ultimately, the whole thing fell apart. No one really maintained what had to happen, and from the start, no one could really agree on how to do things… what rules to lay out for them to follow. It was flawed in its inception and in its execution, and it indirectly led to the Second World War. We… we, all of us here, we worked so well together, right? We all want the same things, we have the same ideas, and we know what needs to be done - for the most part - to get there. We aren't a whole bunch of countries looking to see what we can gain by restricting one side… we're just a bunch of people who are looking to make things make sense again. That's why Eleri stopped you, Clove, from entertaining that conversation, you know? We have an opportunity to create some sort of document and make sure it holds up. If they don't listen to it, and if they compromise it or breach it, we still have the power here. Then we get to jailing and whatever else you want. But we can't start there. That isn't right."

Clover sighed, closing her eyes. She put her hands over her face - Claire slung her arm around her shoulders - and she spoke. "But it isn't fair."

Delaney, quietly, from across the table, looked up at her. "I agree, it isn't *fair*, but it's *right*. I think... uh, well frankly, I think that's what's more important."

There was a silence that followed, and Delaney was worried that she had overstepped. Sure, she had spent a substantial amount of time with these people, and she had always been respectful and respected, but she wasn't sure exactly how much ground she had to work with. She was not a leader here, and though she had worked through seemingly every document, she had never truly *done* anything with them.

Eleri smiled at her from across the table, a silent thank you, before turning her attention to Clove and Claire.

Fyodor picked at his hands underneath the table, a habit he had when he was nervous, as he watched the seemingly silent communication between the two. He knew that he and Eleri had a point, and he could only hope that they had communicated it well enough to merit more of a conversation. There was no other option here, really. They all knew, to some extent, that they wanted to reintegrate properly with the rest of the world, and in this, they knew that the rest of the world knew - at least a little bit - of what had been transpiring over the past two decades. He knew that nothing would be kept secret, even if they tried it. Everything would come to light eventually. It was a fact. And he knew, deep down, that Clove knew this as well. He knew that she was displaying a rare lapse of judgment, the emotions of all that had happened getting the best of her, and he didn't fault her for it. He just hoped that she would come around. She had to come around.

"You know," Claire said, finally, realizing Clove wasn't going to respond, "it isn't a bad idea. We would have to draft it out and make sure everything was right, and we would definitely have to give it time... it wouldn't be done tomorrow if that's what you're looking for... but from what Delaney and I could gather, we still have enough preserved documents to make compelling arguments... we obviously have testimonials..."

"I don't think we have to prove any of our decisions to anyone. We don't have to justify it, you know? This is our fight, not the whole world's. If we feel that something should be done, we should be able to do it. No one else helped us, right? So let us choose to deal with this how we want to. And, if anything, us doing this is much more... diplomatic... than the other option." Delaney said with newfound confidence. She was sure of herself now, and it caught Clove's attention.

"Do you really think so?" She asked. It wasn't condescending; Clover spoke in a hopeful, almost child-like tone, trying to see things from a different perspective.

In reality, Clover was just tired of making all the decisions. She was honored to do it, but it had taken a toll on her. Claire knew this, but she wouldn't share. That was Clove's choice. She would, though, let her hand fall onto Clove's thigh and squeeze it reassuringly, leaving it palm up, letting Clove find her way into holding it.

Delaney wasn't trying to become a leader, but she did want to make her opinion heard. She had relied too heavily on luck in the past, and though she had been noticed, she didn't want to wait for opportunities to come to her anymore. If she had something to say, she would say it.

"I think so, yeah." Delaney said. "Think about it. Nobody knows this thing as well as we do. Claire and I have seen every paper ever. Clove, you literally led armies and created safehouses. Eleri and Fyodor came from the other side - they've seen and lived and planned it all. We are probably the most qualified people to make a decision like this, right? We're normal people. We weren't elected or sworn into positions of power, so we don't have that bias, yet here we are, leading and creating and making sure shit works out. You know what I mean? I don't think anyone can tell us anything about what we choose to do. If they have a problem with it, they're going to have to keep it to themselves."

Clover sighed, pulling her face out of her hands entirely. "Okay. Fine. We'll create a treaty."

Fyodor's face lit up. "Really?"

She nodded, smiling down at the table. "Yeah. I see your point. I would love to brutally murder every last one of them… but I get what you're saying. I do. And I know that you two are maybe some of the only people who have realized you were lied to, and I know that it isn't necessarily fair to take everything out on people who don't know any better. Educate them, right? Don't belittle them."

"Exactly," Claire said, smiling. "So are we all co-writing it, then? What's the plan here?"

"We can all write up what we think is important, and we can come together and make sense of it all, put it all into some nice document, make it look all professional… they'll love it." Eleri giggled, pulling her knees to her chest, wrapping herself further in the jacket.

Then, remembering it suddenly, she reached into her pocket. "I have this, too, for your document pile of evidence - we need to get a better name for that, by the way, Claire - uh… here," she pulled the papers she had found upon finding the jacket out, handing them over to Delaney, who looked them over, brows furrowed.

"What's this?"

"That, Del, is the paperwork detailing how our own leaders were trying to kill us."

Delaney pulled a face that could be described in no other word than disgust. "What?"

"Long story, much of which I'm sure you already know, but just add it to the pile. If I need to go in-depth later, I will."

"They wanted to kill you two... after you were directly responsible for their biggest advances?"

"It makes no more sense to me than it does to you - trust me." Eleri shook her head, leaning back in her chair. "As we can clearly see now, I don't think they had the best thought processes."

Delaney laughed to herself, looking over the papers once more, before rising to go put it away with the rest of the documents.

"What do we do next, then?" Fyo said, looking over to Clover and Claire. "Do we just... start?"

"We can, and we should," Clove said, "but something tells me there's a bunch of kids in a bunker somewhere in Voskivy that we have to go collect."

Eleri sat upright. "There are kids in a bunker?"

"Well, you said that Genie is dead, right? She was watching the kids, and I'm assuming that they're all either dead now or hiding in the bunker."

Eleri blinked slowly. "Someone's about to go on a walk then, right?"

"Would you like to come with me?"

"Why not," Eleri said, standing, gripping Fyodor's shoulder in the process. "It'll be a fun little excursion."

Clove smiled, pulling her rifle over her shoulder, kissing Claire on the cheek, and waiting for Eleri by the door.

"You three," El said as she stepped beside Clove, "start working. And if any big men with big statements come to the door, tell them to fuck off."

Fyodor smiled. "Verbatim?"

"Take creative liberties."

Fyodor winked at her before standing, making his way over to Delaney, helping her sort through papers.

"Be quick, you two," Claire called out as the pair stepped outside, "don't do anything you normally would."

Clove flipped her off as they walked out, laughing as she did so.

Eleri couldn't help but notice how much the entire dynamic had shifted - how what was once a cold, tense relationship between herself and Fyo, and Clove and Claire, was now a light, easy friendship. They had grown to realize how much more similar they were than they'd ever have given each other credit for otherwise.

It was beautiful, somehow.

It had gotten dark now, the sun having just set, the moon coming out. The night was clear, and warm, and inviting. It was quiet. Despite the soft wind, the rain had stopped some time ago, and the puddles weren't too deep. If it weren't for the bloodstained walls, and the bodies scattered across the pavement, and the bullet casings littered in every corner, it would almost feel like a normal walk.

"Do you see all this shit we're going to have to clean up?" Clove scoffed, kicking a broken rifle off of the side of the road. "Insane."

"All of it is," Eleri mumbled, looking down at the faces of the deceased, remembering what Kassander had told her all those years ago. "Do you ever think about these people... beyond this? Do you ever think about what kind of lives they had?"

Clove was silent. They continued walking.

"Once," Clove said finally, looking straight ahead, "a long time ago, when this whole shitshow started, Clarissa and I were hiding out. I can't remember exactly what the context was, I think that there was an airstrike or something, or at least some sort of big bombing, and we had to go somewhere. We'd found this bungalow - I don't even remember what part of the region it was in - but it was this tiny, quaint house. We ran in, not thinking much of it, and we went right down to the basement, you know, the safest place, and all. There was a kid and her parents. They were so scared. We weren't going to kill them, and we tried to explain that because that's a crime and because we are decent human beings. The mother - she was crying, but she was trying her best - said that the last soldiers who had run through killed their youngest daughter as some sort of threat and had taken her body out with them. She told us that she had no idea what happened, and they would never be able to find their little girl and give her a proper burial, or anything. I had never thought about anyone like that before. I

359

had never considered that these people had lives and families… I knew that they did, I guess, but I didn't think about it. But since then… I haven't even told Claire this… but since that moment, I try not to look at their faces because when I do, all I see is that family. All I feel is all that they may have been before and all that they'll never live now. It's not fair, but it has to be done, and I just try to separate the two as best as I can, I guess. It is what it is, but even now, looking down at these people… it's tough. I think a lot about these people. I think a lot about if that family made it out alive. I hope they did. They seemed nice."

Eleri pulled her lower lip between her teeth in thought. She adjusted the rifle in her hands. She knew that some passing comment like sorry would never help this situation - whether or not it actually needed to be helped was another question - and she wanted to add something of substance to the conversation.

"I never used to care, either," she said finally, "one of my friends pointed out pictures and clothes and photo albums and stuff, once, and from that point… I paid a lot more attention to it all."

Clove nodded. "And seeing all these dead people made you want to switch sides?"

Eleri laughed. "Absolutely not - there are dead bodies on both sides."

Clover cracked her neck, huffing. "So what was it then, El? I'm not complaining, don't get me wrong, but my God, you've really mastered the art of becoming a traitor."

"I thought, you know, that I was doing what was right. I found out I wasn't, and I decided to change it."

"El," Clover said, stopping abruptly, "I know that it's easy for you to say that, but *come on*. I'm no sympathizer with, you know, your.... people.... But no way anyone would just give up their entire life's work like that. I mean, as messed up as it is, I looked up to you, man. It seems like it runs deeper like that."

Eleri smiled. "You looked up to me?"

Clover scoffed, bumping her shoulder against Eleri's. "Shut up. Answer the real question."

The pair started walking again. Clove didn't push. Eleri thought of how to articulate herself properly.

"I was fifteen when I started this, and I had been taught that it was the only aspiration I should have. They had me wrapped around their fingers long before I could even fathom getting into this mess... and they find me, and they bring me in, and they start telling me how special I am because every Kind year there are prodigies, and they thought that..." she sighed. She didn't say this stuff out loud. "My parents hated me, whatever, and I was thrown into this organization that was so prestigious and so sought after, and they treated me like gold, and they made sure that I knew how important and special and gifted I was. It was the closest thing I'd ever known to home, and all of a sudden, it came crashing down. To be honest with you, Clove, I don't have one big reason for doing this. I guess... I don't know. I guess I had to prove to myself that I was my own person, away from all of it. That I could actually do what was right because I wanted to, not because I felt that I had to. When I heard about the history books and about how they were picking you guys off... that wasn't right. I've done a lot of really, really unforgivable things over the past few years, but I could never stand by and let that happen. Not as long as I knew about it. It's... Aloneia is built on lies. I wanted to stop that."

Silence for a notable moment.

"You know," Clove said, finally, "I'm glad that of all people, you were the one I chose to look up to. I mean, it started with how you conducted yourself and how quick you were on your feet... but it's your *integrity* that I've really grown to admire. We've all done fucked up things - I'm sure you've done a lot worse than most - but you have a good heart. And I can see that. We all can. I don't think you were ever a monster. I think you were just a kid, and you needed answers. And I know you don't need my validation, but... it's okay. We forgive you."

Twenty-Four.

Peace never truly exists, I think, because conflict is the essence of who we are. We are at war with ourselves. We are at war with each other. We're at war with things we cannot see or feel. It doesn't matter if it is organized or if it is a spur-of-the-moment fight - conflict will always surround us. Violence begets violence, and we have actively been feeding the cycle for centuries. We have become dependent on it. We have become partisans of war, whether we will admit it to ourselves. And if war and conflict are eliminated - in the sense of what we have come to know them as, the norm will just change. There is no avoiding it. There is no holding it off, or abolishing it, or running from it. Conflict will always come. It will always rise. There will always be someone who wants more power. There will always be someone who wants more freedom. There will always be disagreement.

Peace never truly exits, but we get damn close sometimes, and when it's close enough to brush your fingers against it, and let it go... those are the moments where you truly feel lucky to be alive.

- The Found Diary of Eleri Roman, p. 100

—

Fyodor Kacer and Eleri Vera Roman sat on top of the roof of one of the few buildings that remained standing, the sun setting over the horizon, the night falling over the empty downtown space. Fyo, without thinking, lit a cigarette. He took a drag, wordlessly extending his arm to her, the stick resting gently between his pointer and middle fingers. Eleri, without turning her head, took it between her forefinger and her thumb, lifting it to her lips, allowing herself to melt into it. Fyo took a second from his pack, lighting it for himself, closing his eyes momentarily as he breathed.

His attention, as per usual, was fixed on the sky.

He would paint it if he could; the sunset before them was unlike any other he'd ever seen, full of purples and pinks and oranges and reds that seemed to be too intense to fit together, but that blended perfectly. He wanted to remember it for the rest of his life. This moment, here, legs dangling off of the side of a rooftop beside someone who meant the world to him.

He noticed Eleri's free hand still resting above her knives. He wondered if she would ever grow out of that habit - the feeling of being on edge, the constant high alert. He wondered if she would ever go outside without a knife, if she would ever be able to live properly again. He presumed that had this not happened - had the two been living in their apartments, doing their jobs - she would've eventually become comfortable with the idea. Now, though, after all that had transpired, he was nearly certain that was too much to ask for.

Fyodor's eyes would not see death, or violence, or chaos - he would only watch the hues in the sky change until they were replaced by the stars.

For a moment, he was okay.

Eleri and Clover had found nineteen kids in the bunker. Three apparently had died sometime between their move and their rescue. It was not ideal, but it was much better than what either of them had expected to find. It was a blessing in itself that these kids would be able to live freely.

Eleri felt a deep sense of guilt, and she knew that she would struggle with it for the indefinite future. These kids would live freely, but they were not hers. She was the reason that they were walking the tightrope - it was because of her actions and her blind faith that these kids had ever known suffering. She had freed them, but she had only freed what she had caged. She knew that she could never articulate this properly, much less have the conversation with anyone. Fyo would tell her that it was fine. He would offer an ear, but not a solution. Clove and Claire would both maintain their position - that it wasn't her fault, that her choice to help them was her true character, and that everyone had a past. She considered talking to Delaney, but they were nowhere near close enough to have a good conversation about such subject matter, especially considering how Delaney had been studying her for years. There was no way that Eleri would give her another section in her file folder.

She had grown to trust more people, but she was not planning on expanding the roster.

She reached to her side, taking the binder in her hand - the same binder that had held the contents of the proposed history curriculum - and opened it in her lap.

The plastic shell was the same, but the contents on the inside were incredibly different. The document - the *treaty* - was twenty-seven pages long, full of sections and specificities and clauses. They had taken their time to write it, but it was done, and she was holding the copy that would be handed to the Aloneians. She was holding the start of a new world entirely.

Fyodor looked at it, sighing, head resting on her shoulder. "Ma'am?" He asked suddenly.

Eleri felt her heart swell. She closed the binder. "Yes, soldier?"

He smiled, kissing her shoulder gently.

Kassander's jacket was tied around her waist.

"What do we do now?"

She knew that the implications of the question were much heavier than what could be conveyed through any given phrase. What do we do now? They had a lot to work through, personally, between each other, between the world. Eleri had already managed to get in contact with some world leaders. She knew that this was a huge step, both for her, personally, and for everyone around her. She knew that the moment she had a formal phone call with any of these people, she was going to be broadcasted to the world. She had to prepare for it. Even before this, she had to prepare for presenting the treaty. She would have to lay it out to communicate all of its nuances and technicalities in a way that made sense to everybody. She was going to have to make sense of this mess in front of her - the physical destruction that had been left in their wake. They had to decide what form of government was going to be used, if any, at all. She was young, and so was everyone she was working with. They were in way over their heads, and it was obvious to anyone with half a mind to look at the situation. It couldn't be stopped, though, and that was something she had learned years ago. Things would always be coming at her, and she would have to take them. There was no compromise. If this was the next step, then she'd have to go.

Eleri turned to look at Fyo. The flame that had burned behind his eyes when they had first met years ago had long since been diminished. The passion he had for life, the excitement he had for the world... it had gone, too. He was a fraction of who he had been when the pair had first been acquainted and a shell of who he was before that. He was someone entirely different, clinging to the only sense of safety he had ever known, hoping that by some miracle, he would once again become that child again.

He would spend his entire life searching, and he would never find it. This was something that he would have to come to terms with on his own.

This had destroyed them both. There was absolutely nothing left.

"I don't know," she said finally, her voice barely above a whisper.

Fyodor nodded and turned his attention back to the sky. It was darker now, and some of the few remaining functioning streetlamps had begun to turn on beneath them. He scratched at his neck, fingers catching on the multiple necklace clasps that rested against his nape.

"Do you think they'll turn on us?"

Eleri had pondered this previously but put thought to it again. It would be easy to get rid of them. She and Fyo could be exterminated in minutes if anyone decided they wanted to do it. They were still strangers. They were, to many people, still the enemy, regardless of what had happened and what had been done. Eleri understood it. She knew that she had done it to herself. She was the shadow that so many people saw in their nightmares. She was the face people saw before they died. She was the demon that haunted them in the darkness.

A monster.

Many in Voskivy had grown to love her, while many had begun to hate her more. The same notion was true for Fyodor, though not as polarizing, and she knew that at this point, if anyone was disposable, it was her, without a doubt. She had done her job, and she was no longer of use to them, except to be a name and a face. She had already seen this become her reality with Aloneia, and she was sure there was a chance for it to happen again. Clover was working in the same realm as she was now, anyways - both of them working together in the pursuit of publicity, in the name of truth and of honesty, and as some sort of representation of people being able to come together regardless of what had happened.

Something deep within her, though, told her that it was not something that they would have to worry about. She knew that their relationship with the Resistance, as a whole, would forever be complicated; Fyo and herself had caused the uprising that reinstated freedom, but they were also the reason that an uprising was necessary. And she knew that, if this entire movement to reconnect with the outside world was successful, she'd be questioned and scrutinized from all angles, especially from this one. She would be deemed crazy; she would be seen as someone who instigated both sides of this conflict for some personal motive.

Had she been any stupider, this entire thing would stress her out to no end. But she had thought it through, and the reality was that regardless of what people said about her, she had the upper hand. They had no concrete evidence, and all of their claims would be just that: claims. Nobody knew anything about the situation or the sequence of events, and anything they would learn would come directly from herself or Clover. There were no real sources, and that meant that most of her past was safe.

"No," She said finally, "no, I don't think that they will."

"And if they do?"

Eleri took another drag of her cigarette. She had tied her thick, dark hair up behind her head. Her eyes were dry. She wished she could cry and fix that. The sky was turning purple to blue.

"If they do, then you and I suffer through that together, just as we have everything else."

His hand found hers. "Sounds horrible,"

She laughed. "It does, doesn't it?"

He looked deep into her eyes. Oil and water.

He rested his forehead against hers, exhaling lightly, moving his hand to the back of her head, holding her in place. He was full of so much emotion - despite the abundance of it, he didn't know what word to use for it. Eleri brushed his scar gently, leaving her hand against his skin.

"Hey," she whispered gently, her heart aching for the poor, broken soul in front of her. "Fyo, we lived. That's all any of us can ever ask for, right?"

He laughed lightly, pushing himself further against her. "Shit, El." he sighed, his lips lingering just above hers. "We fucking lived."

Epilogue.

INTERNATIONAL SUMMIT: PARIS, FRANCE
July 9th, 2255

"Do I look fine? Is this fine?"

"You look great, babe. I promise."

Clover O'Caine pressed a quick kiss to her wife's lips, smiling as she blushed. All these years and Clarissa still couldn't suppress the rush of blood to her face when she was shown this affection.

The deep green dress fell beautifully against her body, the gold jewelry and perfect makeup only elevating her appearance. Clove was never a fan of luxurious aesthetics, but her dark stilettos and bright makeup were a welcome change, only for the night. She squeezed Claire's hand once before turning, walking down the marble hall, knocking gently on the third door.

Eleri Roman opened it only moments later, the black gown and black heels complimenting the green on Clove perfectly, the two of them harboring a beauty and a power that was unmatched.

Eleri made sure that the single knife against her thigh was undetectable. She figured she wouldn't have to use it, but she could never be sure.

Reivan - the region now containing what was once Aloneia and Voskivy split - had been officially recognized as a country by the international community only seven months prior to the summit, and their invitation was one that was unexpected. They were by no means big, and though their constant media presence was impossible to ignore, they hadn't thought that something like this would happen. They had no idea what they were meant to be doing there - what the world possibly wanted to talk to them about - but they understood that it was their one opportunity and that they would never pass it up.

Eleri and Clover had decided to run the country together, both as leaders, both with equal weight and ability. They had left it to the public - to the Reivian citizens - to decide if they wanted to have an election and on what grounds. They left it to the public to decide if they wanted any form of government at all.

The choice to keep Eleri and Clover in charge for the foreseeable future was nearly unanimous.

"Ready?" Clove asked, smiling, reaching her hand out to Eleri. She caught a glimpse of Fyodor further in the room, and she smiled at him. "And are you planning on joining us, or are you going to sit in here the whole time?"

Fyo rose to his feet. "My bad," he winked, pushing his hands into the pocket of his suit pants.

"Go find Clarissa," Clove said, watching as Fyodor pressed a quick kiss to Eleri's temple, "she knows where you two are sitting. She'll take you. And to you, Madam Prime Minister Roman, you look stunning. I hope you have the speech to match."

Eleri smiled, tugging Clove along down the hall, towards the entrance to the speaker's room - one that would serve as the common space for all world leaders, one that was surely going to go silent once they walked in.

"Well, Madam Prime Minister O'Caine, I surely hope it reaches your standards, considering we wrote it together."

Clove giggled, reaching the doors, watching as two men pulled them open. She had been right about many things over the years, and just the same, she was painfully correct about the blanket of silence that would fall as the pair entered. All eyes were on them immediately; they had grown used to it, and without a second thought, they smiled warmly, greeting those around them, forcing the conversations to continue. Their speeches would come soon. Their arguments would come soon. Their voice on the world stage would come soon.

For now, they needed to live it. Properly.

They had spoken to most of these people individually but had never begun to consider the possibility of having to face them all at once. It was an exhausting activity, but both of them managed to keep up and ensure that they were the best representation of Reivan possible, despite all that had transpired.

When the time finally came to speak, Eleri marched to the podium with pride. She and Clove had gone back and forth for a long time about who it would be giving the address, each insisting the other was better prepared and more worthy, but the decision ultimately landed on Eleri for reasons she didn't even fully grasp. She took it, though, as she did everything, and decided that if this was being thrust upon her, she would do it in the best way possible.

Eleri brought papers with her to the stand. She knew that she wouldn't need them, but Clove had made her promise to take them just in case. She patted them together, dropped them onto the glass podium, and looked directly at Clover.

Clove smiled brightly, clasping her hands together.

She looked onto one of the balconies, eyes locking on Fyo and Claire, both who waved, blew kisses, and clapped.

She smiled.

She took a deep breath.

Speaking on behalf of Reivan, we humbly introduce Madam Prime Minister Eleri Vera Roman.

Eleri waited for the voice to die down before she looked at her papers once more, then directly into the camera, which would be showcasing this summit to every single country in the world. She knew the magnitude of her outreach this time.

She understood how many people would be impacted by her this time. It was surreal—all of it.

Eleri Roman took a deep breath.

"Thank you, Madam Speaker." A smile. A pause.

"As many of you are well aware, I am a traitor."

Fin.

THANK YOU FOR READING THIS BOOK.

IF YOU ENJOYED IT, PLEASE REVIEW IT ONLINE.

GO TO
5310PUBLISHING.COM
FOR MORE GREAT BOOKS!

You might also like...

BEING A HERO IS HARD

HONEY BEAUMONT

SARA BUSHWAY

In a land destroyed by war, at a time that mirrored the excitements and dangers of the Old West, at a place where both magic and machine collide... a hero will rise from the darkest depths to the glory of freedom and honour.

This hero is Honey Beaumont.

The Adventurer's Guild stands for justice and serves the common man, provided they can pay.

With newfound skills and friends in tow, only one hero can find the strength and courage to return to the man who tried to destroy him and make things right for his people.

Embarking on a journey of a lifetime, being a hero is harder than he could have ever imagined, but at least he has his friends by his side to help him save the day.

"**An exciting tale in a unique world** featuring Honey Beaumont's magical journey from who he was when he was born to the hero he was meant to be. **A fast and exciting read. I couldn't put it down!**" — Starred Review 5/5

"Intriguing and messily realistic..." – Kirkus Reviews

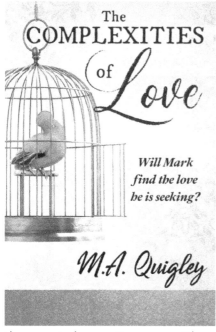

The COMPLEXITIES (of Love

Will Mark find the love he is seeking?

M.A. Quigley

An Australian teen learns about life, hidden love, and family secrets. Mark Cooney grows up aware that there is something different about him and hopes that his parents will never find out.

Mark's best friend Dave disappeared when he was thirteen and returned ten years later. Mark became more and more vulnerable as they got closer. It came with a price.

Tormented by his inner demons and refusing to be controlled by anyone, Dave reveals a secret that he has kept since childhood, which leads to grave consequences for Mark and his family.

The Complexities of Love is a coming-of-age story about Mark as he confronts the truth about his family and his identity.

All he yearns for is for Dave to return his love, but will that happen, or will he find someone else?

"**Heartbreaking**... I found myself rooting for Mark to accept himself... and ultimately find true love. — **such a profound novel**." – Mario Dell'Olio, author of Forbidden Rome

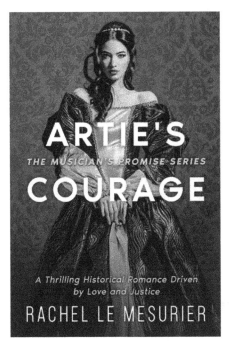

ARTIE'S
THE MUSICIAN'S PROMISE SERIES
COURAGE

A Thrilling Historical Romance Driven
by Love and Justice

RACHEL LE MESURIER

A courageous farm girl's life is changed forever when she falls in love with a charming street musician, opening her eyes to the cruel mistreatment of Mexico's mine workers and compelling her to stand with them against their oppressor — the man she is marrying.

Esperanza lives a charmed life. The daughter of a wealthy landowner, her family is thrilled when she attracts the attentions of the handsome and mysterious Don Raúl, opening the door to a glittering life of opulence for them.

However, a chance encounter with a charming street musician forces Esperanza to open her eyes to the cruel underworld of Mexico's mistreated working classes, and she begins to doubt everything she ever thought she wanted.

As the people begin to rise up in a bloodthirsty revolution against their oppressors, Esperanza is forced to make choices that she hoped never to face. Esperanza's decisions threaten to tear apart her family, her heart, and the country she loves.

In this brutal world where a few careless words can cost lives, will the price of freedom prove to be more than what she is willing to pay?

Led by strong female characters, *ARTIE'S COURAGE* turns the common damsel in distress trope on its head. Based on real historical events, this thrilling page-turner story of love and courage in the face of adversity follows characters on an emotional journey through laughter, tears, passion, and heartbreak.

HARISSON SHAWS

THE
LONESOME ROAD

Looking for the last remains of human life, a lonesome wanderer must find his identity and the reason for his journey.

The fallen Earth holds secrets, an ancient war that will show him he is not alone. With old forgotten feelings of mistrust and sorrow, **the Wanderer will have to navigate his path and remember his past.**

The journey is long, filled with thorns and friendly people with hidden agendas. And unfortunately, not all have his best interest at heart. **The Wanderer will have to stay neutral and true to his path if he wants to uncover the truth. But all things come with a price, and the cost might be his soul.**

Life as we know is gone. The once vivid city now stands abandoned. **Earth became a wasteland, stripped of all life.** Broken, confused, and in a desperate search for answers, **one person still roams its desolate remains.**

The Wanderer has no memories, no recollection of the events that led to the end of the world. All he sees are deserted buildings and the smoke that covers the sun.

While taking shelter in an abandoned house one night, the last man on Earth gets a knock on his door. He finds an unexpected guide in a woman who feels familiar.

Will he choose to keep traversing these lands, lost as before, or will he take her guidance to find the answers his heart so deeply desires?

You might also like...

A Kiss to Wake Me is a modern-day love story between Jamie and Cara. When the two first lock eyes in the high school cafeteria, "love at first sight" is no longer a cliché to either of them.

Their romance takes off at record speed but just as quickly crashes into a wall of disbelief when a figurative bomb is dropped into their lives, upending the world as they knew it: Cara is pregnant, even though she believed she was a virgin.

When these unforeseen circumstances threaten the couple's future together, everything comes into question. Is Jamie the father of her baby? Will he still love her and the baby if he's not? How did Cara even get pregnant? How could she possibly cope without him and his family, whom she has grown to love and depend on?

Will Jamie and Cara's love endure the hardships thrust so harshly upon them? Fans of romantic first love and those who desire to see first love withstand seemingly insurmountable obstacles will enjoy this sweet yet intense novel.

You might also like...

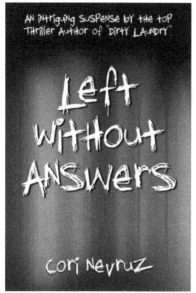

After the suicide of her only child, Alice is committed to finding out why her son took his own life.

With no warning signs or even a letter, Alice searches for answers regarding her son Hank's death. She turns to Hank's best and only friend, Arnold, for answers.

Arnold, like Alice's husband, has moved on from the tragedy and pleads her to do the same. **Arnold is confident that revealing Hank's big secret will help Alice grieve.**

But when Alice starts finding sticky notes that could only be from her dead son, her desire for revenge intensifies along with her desperate search for the truth. Alice becomes more detached from her friends, husband, and reality after each note. Eventually, a letter from Arnold provides her with insight and a target: Hank's ruthless bully.

Can Hank's notes provide the answers Alice is seeking before she completely unravels? When she is left with no one and nothing except sticky notes from her dead son, will Alice accept the truth, or will her need for closure endanger the life of yet another child?

Hank, Alice's only child, is dead. Unbeknownst to her, Hank had been bullied for years. Alice is on a mission to find the person responsible for driving Hank to take his own life. Certainly, someone was to blame. Be it one of the bullies who tortured Hank day in and day out, or was it his overshadowed best friend, Arnold, who must have seen more than he lets on.

As Alice searches for answers and closure, the more she learns about Hank's secret life, the more she feels *Left Without Answers.*

Bonus! - Exclusive interview with the author

Tell us about yourself and how many books you have written.
Andrea: I'm a huge fan of film, sports, and music. I want to be able to make huge, blockbuster films as well as have opportunities to create documentaries based on teams or leagues for various different sports. I've written one novel, and am always working on more - both for books, and screenplays.

What authors, or books have influenced you?
Andrea: I'd say all of the dystopian fiction that came out in the late 2000s and early 2010s influenced me greatly. I grew up reading those books so from the age of 9/10 years old, I knew what genres I liked the most, and what kind of storytelling I found impactful.

What is the name of your latest book and what inspired it?
Andrea: My latest book is called *The Art of Becoming a Traitor*. I often think of titles before I've finished writing, so it wasn't necessarily inspired by anything. I just thought it was a cool title.

Do you have any unusual writing habits?
Andrea: Every writing habit is unusual :)

What are you working on now?
Andrea: Short films, mostly, but I've got some other ideas for novels.

What is your best method or website when it comes to promoting your books?

Andrea: Twitter and Instagram are where I get the most interaction.

Do you have any advice for new authors?

Andrea: The idea of writing is a lot more intimidating than the writing itself! If you have an idea, try it out.

What is the best advice you have ever heard?

Andrea: Something along the lines of, 'learn something about everything and everything about something'.

What are you reading now?

Andrea: I just finished reading Where The Crawdads Sing by Delia Owens.

What's next for you as a writer?

Andrea: Lots, hopefully. More novels. Big budget films. Documentaries. Exposés. Limitless possibilities, countless options.

If you were going to be stranded on a desert island and allowed to take 3 or 4 books with you, what books would you bring?

Andrea: An empty notebook, a colour by numbers book, and something I've never read before. I don't know what that one would be, yet.

Where did you grow up, and how did this influence your writing?
Andrea: I grew up in Toronto. I spent a lot of time in Markham, Ontario, and have been to Ottawa and Montréal many times. English is my second language, and I learned a third when I was eight years old. All of these things influenced my writing - I love being in a city, I love learning things about new cultures and I love moving around. Some people I know who aren't from the city have said that they feel overwhelmed by it. The general consensus is that for those who haven't grown up in it, a busy city can feel a bit tiring. Oversaturated. Too much going on all of the time. To me, it is a preference to be within the noise and the chaos. I feel like all of these things are reflected in my writing. There is always a lot going on. There is never any room to breathe.

What's your biggest weakness?
Andrea: I'm never sitting still. I'm always doing too much.

When you're not writing, how do you like to spend your time?
Andrea: I'm in University at the moment, so there's no real free time between writing and school. I've also got a job, so there's that to take up free time, as well. Beyond that, and beyond going out with my friends, I watch more sports than anyone I know, and I'm always looking for films that'll inspire me, as well.

If you could share one thing with your fans, what would that be?
Andrea: I promise I'm not as intimidating as people seem to think I am.

Do you remember the first story you ever read, and the impact it had on you?

Andrea: Generally, no, but I do remember that the first novel I read that had an impact on me was The Gravesavers by Sheree Fitch. I read it when I was in third grade and I have a copy of it now. It was the first story I ever truly felt drawn to, and the first book I read where I felt like I actually wanted to know what was going to happen. There's this part in the book where the protagonist's father is crying, and he's ripping a tissue paper into shreds, and she says, 'Until that moment, I never really thought about how *tears* and *tears* were spelled the same'. I was eight years old when I read that sentence, and it blew my mind.

What has inspired you and your writing style?

Andrea: I don't know. I've inspired myself, mostly. I guess the world around me, and the way I perceive things, has turned my writing into what it is.

How well do you work under pressure?

Andrea: I have always worked well under pressure. I was an athlete before I was really a writer, and I find that from those big game moments and high leverage situations, I can work better with pressure than without it.

How do you decide what tone to use with a particular piece of writing?

Andrea: There's never an active decision for me. I don't try to overthink anything, at all. Whatever tone feels right when I'm writing is what I'll use. If I'm further in and suddenly feel it isn't great, I'll change it.